Eternally Damned

JANUARY RAYNE

COPYRIGHT © 2022 JANUARY RAYNE

ALL RIGHTS RESERVED. THIS BOOK OR ANY PORTION THEREOF MAY NOT BE REPRODUCED OR USED IN ANY MANNER WHATSEVER WITHOUT THE EXPRESS WRITTEN PERMISSION OF THE PUBLISHER EXCEPT FOR THE USE OF BRIEF QUOTATIONS IN A BOOK REVIEW.

PRINTED BY RAINING ROMANCE, LLC IN THE UNITED STATES OF AMERICA.

GRAPHIC: ADOBE STOCK

GRAPHIC DESIGNER: DALLAS ANN DESIGNS

WWW.AUTHORJANUARYRAYNE.COM

——————— M ———————

THIS IS A WORK OF FICTION. SHALLOW COVE DIMENSIONS IS A WORLD I HAVE CREATED. MY IMAGINATION RAN WILD AND WILL RUN UNTAMED WITH NO REINS. ONLY WHIPS AND SPANKINGS WHEN ASKED FOR. UNLESS OTHERWISE INDICATED, ALL THE NAMES, CHARACTERS, BUSINESSES, PLACES, EVENTS, AND INCIDENTS IN THE BOOK ARE EITHER THE PRODUCT OF THE AUTHOR'S IMAGINATION OR USED IN A FICTION MANNER. ANY RESEMBLANCE TO ACTUAL PERSONS, LIVING OR DEAD, OR ACTUAL EVENTS IS PURELY COINCIDENTAL.
FANG v---v BANG ON FANGBANGERS.

DEDICATION

To those who think love is too far away. It's there. It might be out of reach, but one day, you'll grab it and it will be yours.

And to Bailey. One of the best dogs who ever dogged. You're forever loved and deserve all the treats.

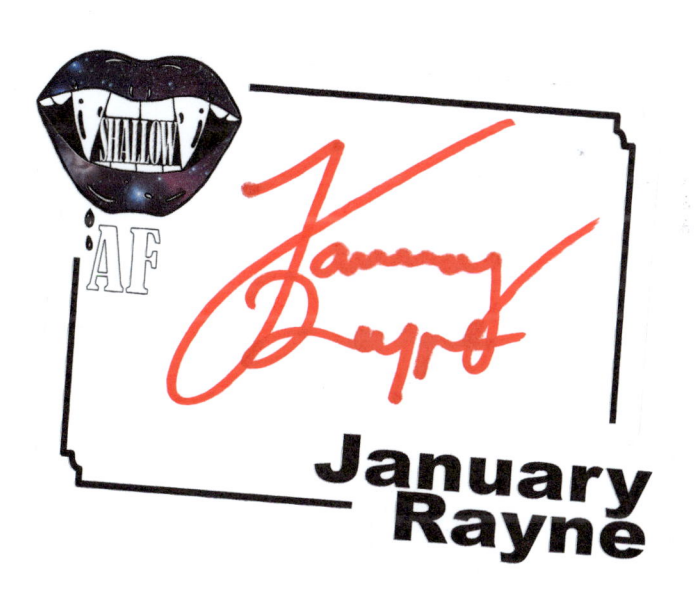

January Rayne

AUTHOR'S NOTE

There are no warnings you need to be aware of unless you need to be warned about vampire dick and blood. If so, turn around now because this is not the book for you. If you like being fangbanged, then read on....

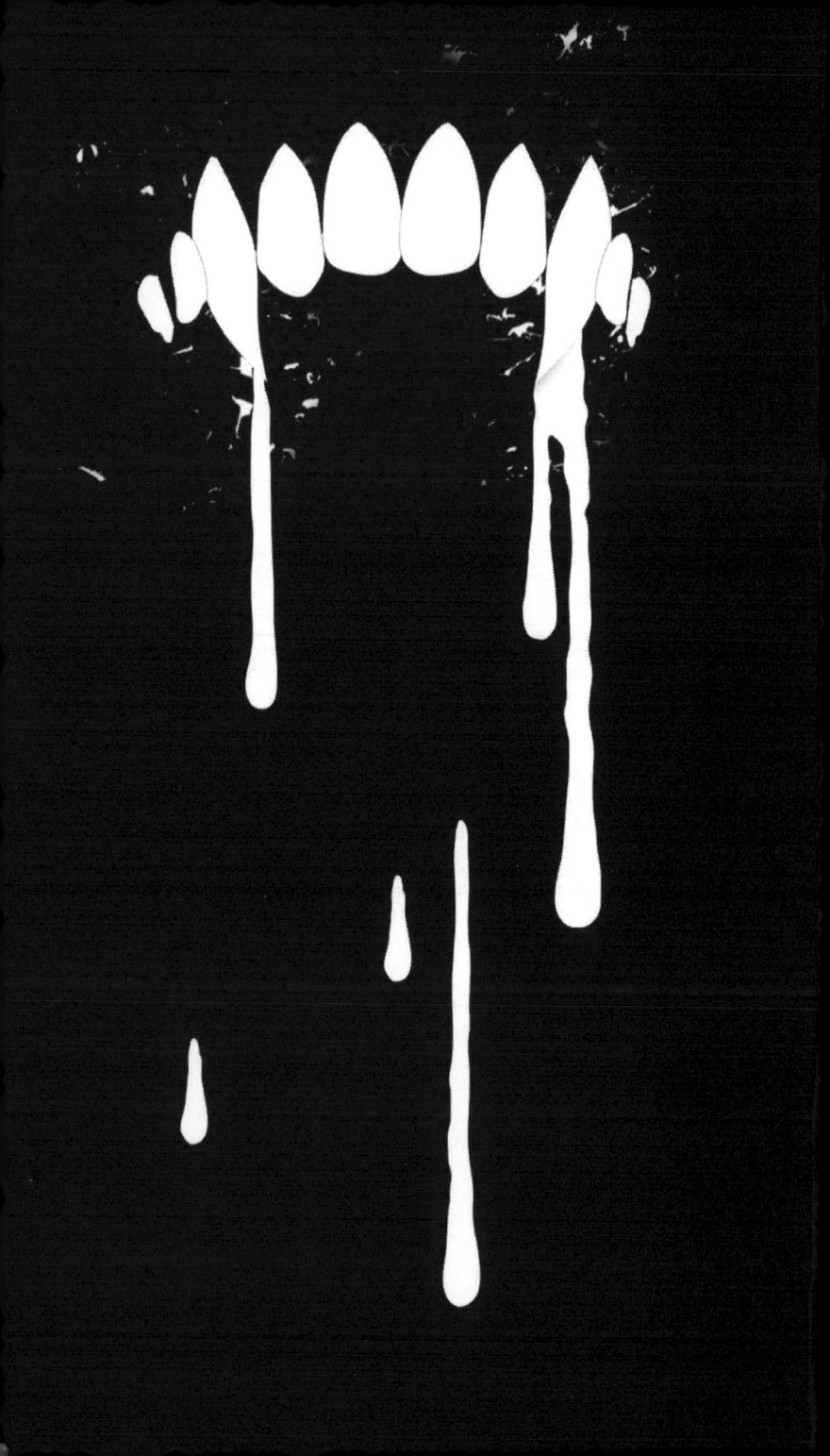

Prologue

ALEXANDER

Year 1900

A vampire can live for an eternity, but eternity comes at a price. A vampire can only live forever if they meet their beloved, the other half of their soul, their blood mate.

I have heard many stories of vampires meeting their one true love. Stories that were told while I was a baby, stories told on the hunt for blood, novelties I never be-lieved because every year I became older, the older the fairytale became. I'm seventy years of age, still a teenager in vampire years, but old in human, and still I have yet to meet a vampire that has met their other half.

Not even my own parents are fated.

It's been said that it's been well over two thousand years since a vampire has met their beloved and the only reason we have continued to survive is because we are able to change humans and mate our own kind. There are not many blood borns anymore, like me.

Our numbers dwindle by the decade, and it doesn't help that there has been underlying tension between wolves and vampires. We say we are at peace, but it's a lie. They are attacking us right now and they have partnered with humans. Werewolves have become the humans' pets, and together they have become a force that's hard for us to beat.

I don't know how or why, but I'm running for my life. I got lost in the havoc and strife trying to survive and dodge every wolf attack when I decided to go after my brother. It's so fucking typical for Atreyu to act first and think later.

And father knew I wouldn't be able to stay behind while my twin was on his own fighting our enemy.

I'll never forget the fear in my father's eyes. He looked at me as if it were the last time he'd ever see me. I think of Greyson and Uncle Luca, Atreyu, Mother, and Rarity, my newborn baby sister. Emotion hitches my chest. Nothing can happen to them. They are my family.

The ring my father gave me glistens in blood that isn't mine as I try to find a way to survive. Thinking about what that particular responsibility means has my legs giving out from under me.

"He's slowing," a hunter shouts with glee and his werewolf bitch howls in agreement, commenting on how much speed I'm losing by the second.

An arrow whizzes by my head as I attempt to run full speed, zipping through the two-hundred acres of thick forest that's been in the Monreaux Coven for thousands of years.

I have to get back to the estate, but the chaos erupting in the woods makes the task seem that much more difficult. Too many hunters, too many werewolves.

We are outnumbered.

I've killed my fair share of beasts but not nearly enough.

And that is not where my issues even begin.

I glance down at my side, wincing when I see the rips in my shirt and the blood turning darker by the second. I was able to kill the werewolf that latched onto me, but not before his sharp teeth tore into my side.

The warnings my father told me over the years ring through my mind.

Whatever you do, Alexander, never get bitten by a werewolf.

If you get bitten, you get to the catacombs immediately.

If you see a wolf, run the other way. Confronting a wolf isn't worth the risk of getting bit.

Not many things can kill a vampire, we are pretty resilient. Like every living thing, we have a weakness, and ours is a werewolf bite. Something in their saliva poisons us, but what's worse is that it doesn't kill us right away.

It takes a few hours to set in.

At first, it hits our lungs, the venom making it harder to breathe by the second. It wouldn't be so bad if I wasn't running. Using the little energy I have left is making the venom spread expeditiously.

Next, the cursed toxin hits our nervous systems, something I'm beginning to feel because my legs are becoming harder to move.

Then, it will be my vision.

And finally, my heart will slow to a dangerous rate, sending me into a deep coma that only my beloved can wake me up from before it's too late.

My life, as far as I know, is over.

I'm doomed. It's why I need to get back to the estate. If I can make it, I can go into the basement and underground where my father stores a few coffins that haven't been used in a few centuries.

We don't sleep in coffins, but father kept them around in case of emergencies because they are enchanted with Sarah Wildes magic that will protect us.

If I can get to the coffin, at least, I'll be able to fall into a coma safely.

"Fuck!" I roar to the sunsetting sky as a sharp pain ignites in my left leg.

I stumble over my feet, tripping over a tree root that finally sends me tumbling down to the wet, soggy leaves kindling the floor.

My talons elongate, digging into the soil as an agonizing blaze paralyzes me.

Laying on my stomach, my legs tingle and my breathing becomes ragged.

My vision spins and I rest my forehead against the moss-covered dirt, the strong earthy scent tingling my nostrils. I can smell yesterday's rain. There's a caterpillar crawling somewhere in the distance, it's body scratching along the ground.

Memories are next, they always accompany scents.

I close my eyes and see a young couple, girl and boy, teenagers, sneaking their first kiss next to this tree. She's wearing a full skirt and his shoes shine so much against the light, the moon is jealous.

I inhale again, the scent of rain drifting and morphing to a hot summer's day.

It's me and Atreyu around five years old, racing one another through the dandelions that had just bloomed. We wanted to see who had the fastest vampire speed.

He'd never admit it, but I won by a talon.

Breathing in, the vibrations of heavy paws have my eyes snapping open. Sweat begins to form along my brows as I drag myself to a nearby tree to rest.

I can't get up.
Everything hurts.
Everything burns.
My bones ache.
My fangs throb.
And my heartbeat is slowing as the venom takes over.

I clutch my leg, inhaling sharply while I stare up at the sky through the canopy of the trees. The branches spreading against the quickly darkening atmosphere, the stars bright above the leaves.

A scratch forms in the back of my throat and I try to swallow to coat it with spit, but not even that helps. Sighing, I tilt my head down to stare at what is causing the pain in my leg.

I chuckle when I see it, then curse, "Son of a bitch."

A pure silver arrow pierces the meat on my bones, the tip dripping with what little blood I have left. I hold a hand to my side and grunt, swaying in place as a round of dizziness hits.

Goddamn were-fangs are sharp.

Reaching for the arrow, my hand goes to grab the tail end of it, but I miss.

Huh.

Suddenly, there are two arrows.

I squeeze my eyes shut and open them again, my sight returning to normal long enough for me to realize there's just one arrow.

Not good.

I don't have much time left.

My hand falls to my side, grazing over the clover and moss. I'm not sure I have enough strength to yank the arrow out of my leg, anyway.

Reality hits me hard.

I'm going to die.

And I'm going to die hearing the screams of my coven, the howls of the murderers, and the cackles of the sordid humans.

"I smell his blood," I hear the deep voice of a werewolf about a half mile away.

"Good. I want his fangs. I don't care what you do with the rest of him," a human replies, my advanced hearing picks up his every step and every time one of my kind fall.

My fangs.

Idiots.

That's always been the commodity when humans or werewolves hunt us. Our fangs are linked to the longevity of life, healing, and sometimes pleasure. There's a rumor these hunters believe— that our teeth will give their pathetic love lives a boost by inducing intense orgasms. The pleasure accompanied by a vampire bite is only with mates or a beloved, anyone outside of that, if we sink our fangs into you, it's going to fucking hurt.

It's our tears they really want though. Our tears have abilities beyond human comprehension and understanding, but it's such a well-guarded secret, no one knows. The ones who haunt us think the answers are in our fangs.

Let them.

Our fangs can grow back.

But our tears? Those are sacred.

You're going to wish you were dead if we bite you. The pain boils the blood, which makes it deliciously warm as we drink it down.

The thought of a nice hot neck has my mouth watering. That sounds divine right about now.

"What the fuck, Alexander?"

I turn my head to see my twin fall to his knees at my side, the leaves cracking under his weight.

"Get the hell up, Lexy."

I curl my lip at the nickname. He knows how much I hate it, but I don't have the strength to fight him right now.

Plus, my anger diminishes quickly when I see the claw marks on the side of his face. Five thick gashes travel from his forehead, through his left brow, down his cheek, eye, and neck.

He's blind in that eye now, no doubt.

"Atreyu..." I say breathless, reaching for his face but he pulls away. "If you wouldn't have ran off when you heard—"

He cuts me off, "Don't." He stares at my leg and debates how to take the arrow out, then analyzes the rest of me, his sights setting on my side. "No! Lexy, your side." He rips my shirt in half to see the teeth indentations along my ribs. "Damn it, Lex." Atreyu isn't the emotional type, but I swear I see his good eye fill with tears.

"I could say the same for you," I rasp, the howling around us closing in.

Werewolf scratches are different from bites, while I'll fall into a deep coma, Atreyu will have scars forever. We can't heal from werewolf marks. We either live with the burden they leave us or die a slow death that lasts two hundred years.

Blood drips from the wide wine-colored gashes in his face. "We'll be okay," he somehow manages to remain positive.

A weak laugh escapes me. "Just leave me, Atreyu. You still have time to get to the estate."

"No, you stubborn asshole. Get up right now. You can't leave me. We're in this until the end." He yanks the arrow from where it was lodged in the bone, his palm sizzling from the reaction to the silver. He tosses it to the side and his skin heals from the burn quickly.

Me on the other hand, I scream in pain as the tissue, muscle, tendons, and flesh try to stitch themselves back together, but they can't.

I'm too weak.

"Come on, let's go home." He throws an arm around me to lift me to my feet, freezing in the next step. He sniffs the air, eyes flickering from blue to pools of silver.

A ferocious growl trembles his throat and he bends down to pick up the silver arrow. Launching his arm back, he flings it using his vampire strength. It's a blur through the air and a second later, a yelp reverberates nearby.

"Good. Fucking dog," Atreyu sneers and helps me to my feet once more. His hot breath fogs the cool night while mine merely makes a cloud. "Don't give up on me. I need you. They are closing in and the estate is just up ahead."

The thought of walking any further makes my bones hurt, but I nod numbly, not wanting to disappoint my brother. The bite on my side burns with more intensity as we walk and the feeling of despair falls over me.

I don't want to die. I've barely lived. And there is a part of me that had hoped I'd be the rare one of our kind to meet his beloved.

Atreyu always said I was the dreamer while he was the realist, but there are no dreams anymore.

Reality has set its teeth in just as deep as the werewolf did.

"Your side..." Atreyu lifts his hand to reveal black blood, similar to the consistency of oil.

Time is no longer on my side.

I snort, finding it funny he is mentioning it. "Your face."

"Fuck you."

"We're both fucked, I'm afraid." My feet begin to drag, the tips of my shoes stained dark red as we hurry through the woods. "Did mother make it? Sister? Father, Greyson, Uncle Luca?" I ask about our family, hoping we will see them at the end of this.

His lips press into a firm line. He says nothing and gives the slightest shake of his head. "I've ran all over, Lexy. There's no one left. I've been looking for you. Don't you feel it? Everyone is gone."

No. That can't be. It can't.

I close my eyes and a choked sob leaves me. My sister was only a day old. One day.

"I know. I know. Look at me."

I don't.

I *can't*.

"I said fucking look at me." He spins me around and his fingers dig into my shoulders, shaking me. "I know it's too much to process right now and we can't. Focus on surviving. Everything else can come later."

I nod, the pain of losing them an additional wound to by body.

If I had enough energy, I'd cry and go on a rampage of a hunt to avenge their deaths. There's no time to process though when my life and Atreyu's is on the line.

"The rest of the coven?" I question in a slur, desperate for the fickle bitch of hope to appear in this fucked up nightmare.

"I don't know. I haven't seen anyone, but it doesn't mean anything. I've been looking for—," his sentence is interrupted as a werewolf tackles him from the left, knocking the air out of his lungs with a grunt.

We should have smelled the wolf or at least heard him coming. Our wounds being infected with werewolf venom is affecting our ability to protect ourselves.

"Atreyu!" I scream, his name ripping from my throat, leaving a bloody taste against my tongue.

Right as I take a step forward, the wolf knocks me away with his massive paw and I fly through the air, watching the green plants blur together below me.

Somehow, I land on my feet, the buoyancy in my body still making it impossible to stand straight. Through the agony firing through my nerves, I inhale as deep as possible, grinning when I smell the weakness of my enemy.

Human.

His bitch of a wolf left him alone to fight my brother.

All by himself... with no one to save him.

And the dumbass didn't even take silver supplements to taint his blood.

With as much smugness I can muster, I turn around and smirk at the man. He must be in his fifties with gray hair and a matching mustache. He has wrinkles around his eyes as if he has lived a thousand lives, but he'll never have that opportunity. This life will be his only and I'm about to take it from him.

He slices a wide, long silver blade right in front of me. He's confident. The human sucks his tongue across his teeth as he gives me a hysterical cackle jabbing the knife toward my head. I dive to the right, dodging the sharp point by centimeters. My palm slaps against his neck and my black talons lengthen, pressing against his jugular. I can hear the beautiful flood of his life-giving elixir coursing through him, the vein in his neck pulsating with every excited, adrenaline-filled beat of his heart.

"Ah, there it is," I whisper into his ear. "You know what I love about humans?" I trail my nose across his cheek, breathing in the luscious scent. "You always give away when you're scared." I tighten my grip, my nails sinking further into his aged skin. "Your heartbeat changed. You're not so big and bad when you don't have a dog by your side."

The gray-haired man trembles and the raunchy scent of piss ruining my edge of bloodlust. Red droplets flow down my fingers in thick rivers.

It's warm.

Wet.

And breaks my will.

"You should have taken the silver supplements like your master said," I say before sinking my teeth into his neck.

I forget humans don't have masters, not like vampires do.

My father was the coven master and now he is dead. Remembering him and the rest of my family has my anger reaching new heights. I want revenge. All we ever wanted was peace. I hold the human tighter until his ribs break, latching my fangs deeper in his jugular. I sift through his memories to see if he is the one responsible for my father's death, but he is just a stupid man who joined the hunt last minute.

The sigh of his last breath leaves his lips, but I drink his blood until he is dry. When I'm done, I'm stronger. I know the new burst of energy won't last long. The venom will eventually win in the end.

Ripping a chunk of my kill's throat out for the hell of it, I toss his body to the side and spit on him.

Curling my lip, I growl at the unmoving mass and then remember my brother. I jerk my head where the commotion is and see him fighting a werewolf. The beast is huge, the size of two grizzly bears, and werewolves can walk on two legs if they prefer. They have long claws, dark grey skin, and glowing yellow eyes.

And I can't wait to tear him limb from limb.

I try to use my advance speed to get to Atreyu, but my new strength fades and I slow. My limbs are sluggish as I drag my feet through the garnet ridden leaves, twigs, and mud.

My fangs drop again but I can't attack, I am too weak. I catch myself against a tree, the bark scratching my palm. Gasping for breath, with sweat dripping into my eyes, I watch in horror as the werewolf sinks his teeth into Atreyu's shoulder.

"No, Atreyu!" I roar as loud as I can, my voice booming for miles.

Atreyu doesn't even cringe as his veins begin to pulse black, the venom working its way into his system.

He uses the bite to his advantage. Atreyu grips the werewolf's jaws and begins to pull them apart. The wolf whines and his black irises widen when he realizes just how fucked he is.

I smirk. "Maybe next time, asshole."

Atreyu takes a bite of the beast and with a new rush of rage, he rips the wolf's head in half, throwing the bottom jaw across the forest.

Another animal will feast well tonight.

Atreyu's chest heaves and droplets of ruby flow from his chin as he stares at his kill. "He killed mother," he informs me, fists clenching by his side.

I swallow to coat my throat again, trying to take a step forward through the puddles of death to get to my twin. "Atreyu—" What he said about mother dying doesn't hit me yet. There's so much of me that can't believe it, that refuses to accept this is our reality.

"—I know." He cuts me off. He stares down at his arm, watching the venom slowly work its way through his body. He is resigned, as if he accepted his death a long time ago. "It will be okay. Let's get to the catacombs. If we can get there, there's hope."

I don't know who he is trying to convince. Me or himself.

He spits onto the carcass lying headless on the forest floor. "I fucking hate dogs."

I snort. He reminds me so much of Greyson and my reminiscing is interrupted when I notice how silent the forest is.

Silence can be good, but in moments like this, the quiet is too loud.

There's no one left to scream.

"We need to hurry. There are a few hunters left a few miles away and they are coming." Atreyu places a hand over his shoulder, red leaking between his fingers.

"I can't go. I'll just slow you down. The venom has taken me," I groan, leaning against another tree, closing my eyes as my stomach turns and bile rolls up my throat.

Atreyu gripping my face awakens me. His fingers dig into my cheeks and I'm left staring at a warrior, blood and bone on one side of his face, and exhaustion on the other. "Hell no. You don't get to give up on me. We will make it, but you can't quit on me. I need you. You hear me?"

"Atreyu—" I choke, my heart slowing as we speak.

His good eye waters. "I need you. Don't go."

My brother is a lot of things, but a begging man he is not.

"You know we won't make it out of this. You know what will happen."

He is grim, pressing his lips together in a firm line. "I know." Still, he holds me by the arm and hauls me through the trees and low branches. It's like death is reaching out to clutch onto us, but in the nick of time, we escape.

As we get closer to the estate, I smell blood and smoke.

Vampire blood.

And that's when the grief and loneliness sets in. Now that I can focus on something other than surviving, I feel the loss. There is no connection, no thoughts colliding with mine, no warm buzz of home and protection.

I feel my brother, but compared to the power of the coven, our connection is low and distant, like he is yelling at me from a thousand miles away.

No one has survived.

Only we remain.

Fog begins to set in, sweeping just above the ground, a tinge of red in the ominous clouds.

So much death and no time to mourn.

We stumble through the tree line and fall to our knees. The mansion is before us. Our home. Our sanctuary.

And it's nearly been destroyed.

We take a moment to look around, stepping over dead bodies. I can't recognize them. They have been torn apart limb from limb.

"We don't have time to burn them. We have to get underground, now."

"Atreyu," I gasp his name on an emotional breath as I look around, but he drags me up the steps of the front porch. "We have to—"

He slams me against a wooden beam, not hard enough for it break but enough for it to crack. His eyes change from a light blue to a shimmering silver, he's always had unique eyes. "We have to leave them. You don't think I feel it? It's like my chest has been hollowed out. If we want to live, we have to ignore them. We have to. Plus, you're growing weaker." He places his hand on the back of my neck and squeezes. His forehead falls on mine and we share a single thought.

"*La Fale brasken ini ou sanguila.*"

It's an ancient language vampires don't speak anymore. It's old and outdated, only known by our kind.

The Fallen forever in our blood.

I nod and he leans away, stepping through the front door that is nothing but splinters on the floor. Windows are broken and as we walk, small red ponds cause my boots to stick to the hardwood.

I feel sick.

The bite is eating away at my soul, and it won't be long until it falls asleep, leaving me in the hands of my beloved, wherever she may be.

I bet she hasn't been born yet.

I don't look around the house. I can't. I know it is wrecked and death is a cloak around me. The fan is on and somehow blood got on the blades, splattering against the wall with a soft static sound that will haunt me in my coma.

Atreyu opens the library door, and he lifts me over his shoulder to go down the steps. I groan to try to protest but this is better. I don't think I can walk.

I hear the grind of a bookcase as Atreyu opens it with one arm. When we step inside, he slams his fist against the wall and the case shuts, leaving us in musky darkness.

It's been decades since anyone has come down here.

He continues down the dark hallway, nothing but night and dust around us until he runs into a wall.

"Ow," I bitch, not really feeling anything but wanting to make the situation lighter.

"Shut up." He lifts a trapped door hidden in the ground, disguised as dirt and stomps down those steps next. When we are shut in, there's another door below us.

I fall from his shoulder and throw up the blood I had earlier from the hunter.

Atreyu lights a torch. "Your blood is black. It's thickening and eventually it will stop flowing. And soon..." His face is pinched, the flames of the torch allowing me to see him work his jaw and look away from me. He exhales and tilts his head back, blinking at the ceiling.

His lashes are wet, glistening from the pearly tint they have.

His worry for me has my heart hurting.

I spit, rubbing my mouth against my shoulder. "Yeah." We know what that means. There's no need to talk about it.

"Come on. The catacombs are below us," his deep voice echoes through the tunnel.

He slings me over his shoulder again and my eyes hood, barely seeing the dancing shadows the flames cast from the torch.

Atreyu hisses. "Fuck. I forgot about the pin prick."

That's right. Growing up we were taught the only way inside the catacombs was to sacrifice blood, hence the needle on the door.

"You okay?" I slur, trying to make a joke.

He has gotten bitten and clawed by a werewolf. He can handle a pin prick.

Saying nothing, a scratch accompanied by a knock against the wall has me dragging my eyes open. Atreyu has placed the torch in its iron cast, freeing his hands and illuminating the forgotten room.

There are only two stone mausoleums that have seen better days but are strong and protected by magic. Again, no one can open the doors unless they are a vampire or a beloved.

Atreyu bites his hand and swipes his palm over each door. Cobwebs stretch and dust flies in the space after being disrupted.

They open to darkness, showing what eternity will hold for me.

I'm going to die in the dark.

As I prefer the night, it shouldn't scare me.

But I'm terrified.

Atreyu grunts as he opens the grey lid of the coffin, the stone scraping against stone. It's thousands of pounds, but since my brother is infected, a thousand pounds is more like a million.

"Alright. Come on." Atreyu runs out of the mausoleum and wraps my arm around his shoulder before lifting me into his arms.

I want to tell him when we see each other again, he must never speak of this moment, where I was too weak to walk, but I don't have the strength in me to say it.

He places me inside the cold, damp coffin.

I glance up to see the mangled side of his face covered by the shadows and the untouched side illuminated by the flame.

"*Brother, brasken ini mi sanguila,*" I whisper my goodbyes.

His jaw flexes and he bends down to press our foreheads against one another for what is probably the last time.

Brother, forever in my blood.

He shares the endearment through our minds. He's never been the kind to share his emotions. "I'll see you when I see you," he replies on an emotional hiccup.

Something unlike him as well.

This is devastating. I'll never see my brother again after this.

"I'll see you," I say, the final farewell.

His eyes swirl the hypnotic silver, his emotions raging inside him.

Atreyu huffs as he closes the lid, our eyes never leaving one another. His face disappears as darkness dominates. The stone grinding loudly until it suddenly stops, leaving me in a tight, small space.

He got me to safety just in time.

My heart descends to a near stop and my coma tangles my soul around its fingers, pulling me deep.

Death is always stronger than a man's will, but a beloved is stronger than the two combined.

All that's left to do, is wait.

Chapter One

MAVEN

Present Day 2021
Salem, Massachusetts

My life has been simple and there is nothing wrong with simple. There's a beauty to it, a calmness, a silence.

Simplicity can be a gift, but after living with it for so long, I'm tired. You know what else comes with silence? Loneliness.

Not that I'd ever complain because my life with my Pa is everything I could ever want. It's been me and him since the day I was born. My mom, his daughter, gave birth to me when she was fifteen and wanted to give me up for adoption. He stepped up and said he'd take care of me.

My Mom, Meredith, didn't wait for him to change his mind. She handed me over and never looked back. She left town that day and we haven't seen her since. I never found out who my father is and when I ask Pa, he just shrugs his shoulders. He says, "I never knew your mom was dating."

Unlike some kids, I didn't continue to ask about my mom or dad. I asked once and when I got my answer, I moved on. I don't need them. I have my Pa and, as long as I have him, I have everything I need.

My grandma died when I was two years old, so I don't remember her, but Pa has pictures hanging around the house of her holding me, smiling wide while I drooled on her like babies do.

Love surrounds me. I know that and it's enough. Everything else in question, all the what ifs and maybes, they can go straight to hell.

Nothing is better than the family I have.

"Maven, come get this dang cat. It's ruining my couch," Pa shouts from the living room.

I grin and toss the blue covers off. "You mean the couch that's already ruined?" I tease, slipping on a tattered grey robe that has seen better days.

"I'm not getting rid of this couch! It's just now worn in. Sits me just right," he huffs.

I roll my eyes and head out of my bedroom door, gathering my long red hair from where it is trapped between the material of the robe and my body.

"It sits you because your ass has left an indent in the cushion, Pa." I slide my hand down the worn wooden rail that leads downstairs and the steps creak from my weight.

"And that's what makes it perfect." He greets me at the bottom of the staircase, his gray hair wild and in need of a good brushing. His shirt is buttoned wrong making the lengths uneven, but his smile is always the same: bright and cheerful. He gives me a kiss on the cheek like he does every morning. "How did you sleep, Fireball?" He rustles my flame red hair.

"Good. How about you?" I ask, waiting for him to lie to me again. Something has been going on with him, I don't know what because he won't tell me. The dark circles under his eyes tell me he didn't sleep again though.

He waves me off. "Don't worry about me. These old bones have gotten plenty of rest. Come on, I made us breakfast."

I bend down and pick up Barney, the menace cat that usually stays outside because he wrecks everything. He hisses at me, jumps out of my arms, and lands on Whiskey, my Pa's Newfoundland.

He lets out a grunt and Barney hisses again before making a beeline out the door, Whiskey doesn't move. He won't until Pa cracks open a bottle of whiskey.

He's Pa's companion, best bud, ride or die, partner in lazy crime.

I pat his head. "Morning Whiskey." His fur is as soft as a blanket right out of the dryer.

"Come on, now. Before breakfast gets cold." Pa ushers me into the kitchen and pulls out a chair for me. It scrapes against the ancient wooden floors. There are grooves in the floorboards from how many times he has pulled this chair out over the years.

The scent of bacon fills the small kitchen causing my stomach to grumble. "Thanks, Pa. It looks delicious." The first thing I go for is the cup of coffee, black, just how I like it.

Bitter like my soul.

While I take a sip and let the warmth sink into my palms, I watch Pa for a minute. He scoots around the kitchen, cleaning up the mess he left on the stove, and I look around the small space. This house, it isn't much. It's a two bedroom, two bath old country home. Everything is original. Pa hasn't updated a thing. The oven is black and white, the left burner doesn't work, and the sink is this ugly yellow color.

Everything creaks and groans and when it's windy, everything shakes. Pa never had a lot of money and since he retired from the steel factory, money has been a little tighter, but we do okay.

I work too, but from home since no one in town will hire me. All because my last name is Wildes, like the "witch" who burned at the Salem Witch Trials. Stupid town and its paranoia.

I don't have a magical bone in my body, and I'm not even related to her. Luckily, in today's world, working from home is accepted. I'm a bookkeeper for a fancy law firm. They pay decent but not enough.

I give Pa money for bills and then I put the rest into my Monreaux account. If someone goes into my checking account, that's what they will see it labeled as.

I'm obsessed.

Ever since I was a little girl, there has been this property on the outskirts of Salem called the Monreaux Estate. It's abandoned, half crumbled, and needs a ton of work, but I've been saving for it ever since I saw it when I was ten years old. I don't know what it is about it. Maybe it is the fact that there is a mystery surrounding the place. There are rumors, but nothing evident.

People in town say a cult used to live there. Others say it belonged to witches and that's where they would hide, hoping the Salem Witch Trials would end soon. I've heard werewolves and vampires, which always makes me laugh, but I'm not dumb enough to rule it out.

I think anything is possible and I keep an open mind.

It's been for sale all these years, and no one has bought it because apparently the energy on the property is malevolent.

I have only ever felt welcomed when I'm there.

I've worked my entire life, saving every penny I can in hopes I can buy it one day and make it mine. Just the thought makes my heart race. It's where I am meant to be. I know it.

But money doesn't grow on trees and I'm thousands of dollars away from making my dreams come true.

The dream gets further away every year.

From putting a dollar into my piggy bank after walking the neighbor's dog, to putting a hundred aside as an adult with a real job, I'm no closer than I was when I first started this crazy plan to save. I have a good chunk of cash. I could buy a new house for me and my Pa, and then we could have a better life.

Maybe it's time I give up my dream.

"Hey." My Pa's fingers grip my chin and turn my head. His eyes wrinkle on the sides and his silver stubble glistens in the morning light peeking through the windows. "What's going on in that head of yours?"

I know better than to lie. Taking one last sip of my coffee, I put the mug down on the table and grab the fork, pushing my eggs around the white plate. "I think it's time I stop saving for the Monreaux Estate, Pa. I could work for the rest of my life and I still won't have enough. I can buy us a house or upgrade this one with how much I have saved. I think it's time to move on." Even the words break my heart and I have to stop myself from saying anything else. My eyes water, and I clear my throat. "It was a stupid dream to have."

Pa grips my chair and yanks me closer to him, the wooden legs grind against the floor once more. He takes my hand in his and his lips are flat as he ponders. When his aged brown eyes meet mine, I know he's going to give me an earful.

Never once has Pa belittled me for wanting that Monreaux house. He is a firm believer in what is meant to be will be. He's always cheered me on, encouraged me, and tries to help in any way he can for me to have my dreams. He wants this for me.

He opens his mouth, then closes it, his teeth clanking together. Standing, he wipes his mouth on a napkin and tosses it on the table. "Come on, we're leaving."

I look down to remind him what I'm wearing. "Leaving?"

"Yep. You don't have to get all dolled up to go where we are going." He grabs the keys to the 1960 Ford truck that was passed down from his father. He walks away and I'm still sitting there not knowing what to do. "Well, come on. We don't have all day."

I snag a bite of bacon and run after him, the savory sweetness bursting over my tongue as I slip on my boots by the front door. Good thing I'm not trying to impress anybody.

We step outside and the wind kicks up. Autumn is in full blast as the yellow, red, and brown leaves drift across the lawn. The tire swing sways, and the wind chimes sing as the rods bump against one another.

I love it here.

And hate it.

I love it because it is what I know.

I hate it because it's all I've known.

Tucking the bottom of my robe in my boots so the hem doesn't drag on the ground, I go to head down the steps when Whiskey barks, scaring the life out of me. I hold my hand to my chest and take a deep breath. "Jesus, Whiskey. You gave me a heart attack." I open the door and he bolts, jumping over the steps to catch up with Pa. He jumps into the bed of the truck and the entire frame bounces from his weight.

"Fat ass," Pa grumbles as he opens the passenger side door for me.

Always a gentleman and setting the bar really high for the men I date.

Which is laughable.

Dating.

I've never even been on a date but there is hope, that fickle bitch.

I run across the yard, my boots slapping against the mud since it rained last night and stop right before I get into the truck. "Where are we going?"

"Don't worry about it," he mumbles.

I roll my eyes and slide in, buckling the seatbelt before he tells me to. The hinges of the door squeak as he shuts it, reminding me how old this vehicle is. The truck itself needs a new paint job, but other than that, the engine runs as if it is new. Pa makes sure of it.

The tires spin against the dirt and gravel as we reverse out of the driveway. I glance over at Pa as he puts on his glasses. It makes me wonder if I should be the one driving. He kisses his fingers and places them on the photo of Grandma that's taped to the dash, then puts the truck in drive.

Whiskey barks and I peek into the side mirror to see him perched up and the wind is wobbling his cheeks. I chuckle, witnessing drool flying everywhere.

"Now, I don't know where this silly notion is coming from to give up on your dreams. I know I never taught you that, so you better stop that nonsense right now. I know Dottie would slap you silly."

I cringe when I think of my best and *only* friend. She's brutal with the truth and does not accept self-doubt. Dottie is my other biggest cheerleader, but right now, she's at school since she's a teacher. She's unable to go with me everywhere. Dottie is tough since she teaches high schoolers. She refuses to let them walk all over her, and I don't know how she handles those hormonal teenagers.

I wouldn't make it as a teacher. Kids are brats.

"Pa, it isn't self-doubt. I'm being realistic. There are other ways to be happy. I'm okay with that." I'm not but sometimes the truth is unsettling, and it hurts.

"I refuse to believe that, Fireball." He grips the steering wheel hard until his knuckles turn white. "I know I haven't been able to give you everything and maybe if your mom stuck around—"

I reach for his arm and lie my hand across the old tattoo of an anchor that has lost most of its color. "Don't. You give me a life that people should be jealous about. I love my life. You have given me everything I could want. This isn't on you, Pa. Don't for a second think it is."

"I just wish I could help more."

"You help me in all the ways that matter." I give his arm a reassuring squeeze before looking out the window, watching the red maples and black cherry trees blur as we pass them.

There's a sign up ahead that says, "Salem 3 Miles" but we are bypassing Salem.

We drive for about twenty minutes, enjoying the gorgeous scenery before we take a left down a dirt road with potholes the size of Texas in it. Overgrown weeds invade the sides of the road. The truck crunches them as we surge forward.

My heart thumps when I realize where he has taken me.

Black iron gates stop us a few yards ahead, the brakes squealing. Something makes me get out of the truck. A pull, a force, I don't know how to explain it, but I listen to it. I climb out of the vintage vehicle, not bothering to shut the door, and my robe snags on a few pieces of long brown grass.

Hypnotized, I move forward until I'm in front of the iron gate. It's locked. No one has been able to get inside since the city locked it up, plus the bad energy always sends people away. Not me. I only ever want to be closer. I feel like my heart is here.

I'm home.

The iron gates circle the entire 200 acres. They are impossible to climb because of the height and the vines that have nearly taken over the metal.

I want inside so bad it physically hurts my chest.

I grip the bars and shake them, but they don't give way. I sigh as I head to the side where a concrete slab is. I break the vines and weeds, moving them out of the way so the black plaque can shine.

Monreaux Estate.

That's all it says, but I reach out and touch the M, tracing it with my finger. The concrete scrapes against my skin and I swear in the distance I hear my name being whispered by a deep, commanding, yet tired voice.

It's all in my head.

I look to the left, the mansion is the size of an ant since it's so far away, but I see it.

"How do you feel?" Pa asks.

I turn around, gasping. I forgot he was there.

"I feel like I'm home," I admit, hoping he doesn't get mad.

"Not a lot of things can give you that feeling, Maven. When you experience that feeling, hold on to it. Remember this moment, remember how you feel, and why. When things get hard and exhausting and that doubt starts to trickle in, remember why you're doing it. You're working toward your home. That's a beautiful thing. I'm proud that you see the beauty in this estate when everyone else has given up on it. You see things differently, Fireball. It's my favorite thing about you. Dreams are meant to drive the human soul. If we don't have dreams, we don't have anything."

I take a long look at the house in the distance and grip the gate until the vines dig into my palms.

I'll be back.

And I'll finally be where my heart is.

Chapter Two

MAVEN

"How's my favorite redhead?" Dottie asks as we sit down at the local coffee shop, Witch's Brew.

It's been a week since I was at the estate, and it is still weighing on my mind.

"Oh, I know that look. What's wrong?" She sips her pumpkin spice spell latte, leaving a red imprint on the rim from her lipstick.

She's a classic beauty with long brown hair, big blue eyes with long lashes, and has a plump pinup model body type. She's perfect.

A few people glance my way and begin to whisper, souring my mood further. I stir my black coffee for no reason other than I need something to do. Dottie on the other hand isn't coy.

"Hey!" She gently places her mug down against the polished cedar tabletop. "You got something to say? Don't whisper it like a little bitch, say it to my face." She stands up and flicks her hair over her shoulder, towering over the gossipers. At five foot ten inches tall, with two inch heels on to boot, she towers over most people.

They quiet.

"Oh, yeah. Not so tough now when the object of your obsession has backup. Shut the hell up and get out of here." She shoos them with her hand, and they scurry out the door, curling their lip at her as they leave.

Well, she's nearly perfect.

The girl has a temper hotter than Hades.

She sits down and smiles as if nothing happened. "So, tell me what's on your mind?"

Dottie is always saving me.

When the hell am I going to be able to save myself?

"Pa took me to the Monreaux Estate again. It's been a while since I've been there."

"Yeah because you work yourself to the bone to save for that property." She doesn't cringe at the name of the estate but the people at the next table over give us a little more room.

Hearing the Monreaux name in this town is like being cursed, but Dottie doesn't feel the same. Or maybe she does and doesn't care.

"It isn't realistic of me to buy it. I'm trying, but it's so hard, Dottie. Eventually, the house will sell."

She snorts. "Girl, that property has been on the market for over a hundred years. I doubt it. Why don't you make an offer on it? Maybe the bank will take it."

"The mansion itself might not be worth a lot but the land is worth more than I have. No way they will take what I have."

"I can pitch in. I don't mind investing in your dreams."

My heart melts at her offer, and I reach over the table and take her perfectly manicured hand in mine. "While that's so sweet, I can't have you do that. You're on a teacher's salary. I know how much you make."

"Strike a bitch where it hurts why don't you?" Dottie puffs out her bottom lip. A waiter passes by us with a newspaper tucked under his arm and Dottie stops him in his tracks with a look.

The power she must hold. If anyone is a witch in this town, it's her.

"Can I have that?" She points to the newspaper.

He smiles, holding out the paper as if it is the answer to the all the earth's problems, never saying a word.

"Thanks, sweetie. I appreciate it." Dottie is the only one I know that loves the paper. She likes the crosswords in them and the arrest report. She likes to know if she knows any of 'the caught.' That's what she calls people who get arrested.

He spins on his heel and hurries away, keeping his red face down.

"Aw, sweet little baby." Her bottom lip pokes out for a second, holding a hand to her heart as she watches him leave.

"You're cruel," I chuckle.

She lifts a shoulder and shrugs. "I only asked for the paper. It's not my fault he doesn't know how to talk to a woman." Her eyes wander across each page as she flips through, her expression transitioning from happy to intense. Wrinkles form above her mouth as Dottie pinches her lips together.

"What?" I mumble around the rim of my mug.

She turns the newspaper around and flattens it out on the table, pointing at the headline. "Maven. Today at three o'clock an auction starts." Her brows crinkle together, and I set my coffee down to see what has got her rulers in a twist.

I gasp, my fingers curling into the paper so hard the edges tear. "No! No, no, no. This can't be happening." Tears quickly burn my eyes and spill over onto my cheeks.

Monreaux Estate is finally being auctioned off. Come with your wallets and checkbooks!

"This can't be real. I... no. No! That property is mine, Dottie. It has been since I was ten. How could I have not known? How last minute is this? Who put this together? Why now?" I can't contain my confused, rage-filled questions. I ball up the newspaper and throw it across the room, covering my face with my hands to hide my emotion. "You don't understand, Dottie. That's ..." I take a deep breath "That's my home." I place my hand over my heart as it begins to thump in agony.

"I know, Maven. I say we go. For all you know, we could be the only ones that bid on it."

I sniffle and slowly bring my hands to the table to grab a napkin, wiping the wetness from my cheeks. "You think?"

"Hell yeah. No one wants that place. Everyone thinks it's haunted. No one wants anything to do with it. It's as good as yours. If you offered a dollar, they would sell it."

She's right. Out of all my time here in Salem, I've heard nothing but negative things about the estate. It's about as voodoo as I am in this town. Maybe I'll get lucky.

I look at my watch to see the time. It's two o'clock now. By the time we get across town and get checked in, we will have barely made it. I have my checkbook and a pen. I'm ready to drain every cent I have ever earned.

I don't even need to think about what to do next.

"Let's do it."

"Yeah?" She claps in excitement.

"Yeah. I'm not going down without a fight. I have to call my Pa, though."

"I'll drive." Dottie slides out of the burgundy leather booth and loops her arm through mine. She flips her hair dramatically gaining a few longing looks and the bell above the door rings as we push through.

I think a part of me knows she chooses me as a friend because she doesn't get as much attention when she's paired up with the outcast. I should take offense, but it doesn't bother me to be a shield.

We all have armor to protect ourselves with, some are more dented than others, and I think Dottie's quick temper is one of those dents.

I hold my phone to my ear and on the third ring Pa answers, "Yellow?"

I grin when I hear his voice. "Hey, Pa," I greet, trying to hide my fear.

"What's wrong, Fireball?"

Damn, he's good.

"Pa, I won't be home for a while. There is an auction today at city hall. They are auctioning off the Monreaux property." My breath hiccups as I try to explain, but the fear of losing my dream has emotion welling up all over again. What if Dottie didn't ask for the paper? What if I never found out?

I can't even think about it.

I knew I'd have to face the truth one day, either I'd have the house or not, but I didn't expect it to hit me from out of nowhere.

"I'll be right there. Okay? Save me a seat. Me and Whiskey are on the way."

I nod, forgetting he can't see me. "Okay, I love you."

"I love you too, Fireball. It will all be alright. We're going to make those dreams come true. You just wait and see." He hangs up sounding so confident, but I feel the dread settling in my bones.

The wind dries my tears while tangling my hair. I tug my black beanie over my head and open Dottie's car door.

"Hold on tight," Dottie warns before I have a chance to buckle up.

Her tires burn rubber as she speeds out of the parking spot, nearly hitting the car behind us. A loud, drawn-out honk pierces the air.

Dottie rolls down the window and flips the guy the bird. "Fuck off. We have a house to buy, asshole."

So much rage in such an elegant looking woman. Looks really can be deceiving.

The car does a 180 before she presses on the gas, and we zoom down the road in her Honda Civic.

The smell of rubber still invades my nose as we travel through town, passing the antique shops that have been here since before I was born. As much as this town hates me, I love it. I love how it looks. So quaint and beautiful. The buildings are historic, each one unique down to the brick.

It doesn't take long to get to the big gray concrete building of city hall built in 1838. The steps seem to get higher the longer I look at them. The American flag waves, the red and white nearly blending together the longer I look at the stripes.

My palms begin to sweat, and that doubt begins to kick in, but I remember what my Pa said.

I think back when I stood in front of the gates to the estate, the feeling of hope and belonging that coursed through my system. The urge to break the iron with my hands, to run inside the mansion, to call it my own.

To save it from destruction while saving me from self-destructing.

A few people are heading up the steps and for all I know, one of them will outbid me.

"Are you ready?"

"No," I say honestly. This is all very quick and happening last minute. I have no idea what I'm doing. I never thought of what the process of buying the property would actually be like. I imagined it a million different ways just not like this. "But it's now or never, right?"

Dottie grins as if she has no doubts. "Thatta girl. Come on, let's go."

We open the doors at the same time, and I stare up at the large building, swallowing the nerves climbing up my throat.

The feeling of home tugs at me again, and I run up the steps, not wanting fear to rule my life anymore.

"Wait for me." Dottie's heels click and clack against the steps.

I open the heavy solid oak door and a security guard is standing at the metal detector, eyeing me once before I plop my purse on the conveyor belt. I wait for the guy ahead of me to step through the detector, and when he is in the clear, I walk through next.

"Wildes, right?" The guard questions as he runs the wand down my body.

Great. Is he not going to let me in because of my name?

The wand doesn't go off and I grab my purse. I sling it over my shoulder and hold my chin high. "What of it?"

"I just wanted to say, I don't think it's bad if you're related to a so-called witch. Whatever you're here for, good luck."

He's handsome, but the thought quickly turns into guilt for some reason.

Weird.

"Thanks."

He smiles. "No problem."

"Listen, it's pepper spray. You know, to protect myself."

I sigh when I see Dottie being asked questions and responding like she is being interrogated.

"Well, can I get it back when I leave?" She yanks her purse out of the other guard's hold. "Be lucky I don't spray you," she mumbles under her breath. "Come on, Maven. Let's go get you that house."

I yelp when she snags me by the arm and yanks me with her quick strides. I give the kind security guard a wave before entering a large conference room through heavy oak doors.

The ceilings are high, and the windows are large and square allowing enough light in the room, so it doesn't feel like a cave. There are cheap, foldable chairs ready and lined up one next to the other.

"We sign in there." Dottie points to the table across the room where two old ladies sit and greet people.

Great. One is Ms. Houser, and she hates me.

My chance of getting this property dwindles by the second.

"We need a seat for Pa too."

"Duh. Like I'd leave Grandpa sitting alone." Dottie loves Pa, as if he were her own Grandfather.

Dottie's heels echo in the hall and when we get to the table, Ms. Houser gives me a once over, her jaw flexing.

"We'd like to sign up for the auction," Dottie says, chin held high. "And we need a seat for Walter. He's on his way too."

"Sorry. We don't allow—" Ms. Houser begins to say when Dottie interrupts.

"Listen, you old bitch. I didn't ask for your opinion. We're doing business here. If you don't like it, you can go cram that stick up your ass higher when you get home." Dottie places thirty bucks on the table and she snags three paddles with numbers on them for us.

Ms. Houser turns red with anger. "You wait till your father hears about this."

"He hates you too, lady. You judgmental, arrogant, wrinkly hag!"

This time, it's me dragging Dottie away before she gets arrested for assaulting a senior citizen.

I sit us down in the front row and place my purse on the chair next to me for Pa. "You have to stop picking fights because of me. She will always hate me."

"I wish you were a witch so you could turn her into a frog." Dottie crosses her arms and taps her foot against the ground. "Okay." She takes a deep breath. "How much money can you spend?" she asks.

"About eighty-thousand. It taps me out," I say sadly, a nervous sweat wetting my palms.

"Okay. I have about ten thousand, so that puts us at ninety. I think we have a good chance."

"No way am I letting you do that."

"I'm my own woman. You can't tell me what I can and cannot do."

"You're so sweet and infuriating all at the same time." I throw my arms around her in a tight hug. "Thank you. I'll pay you back."

She squeezes me tight. "Your dreams are just as important as mine."

"Okay, how are we doing today?" Mike Wilson stands at the podium, gripping the sides with his hands. His dark hair is parted neatly to the side, his red tie perfectly in place. "Let's get the party started with the biggest item on the agenda. I know we will be happy when this monstrosity is taken care of. The Monreaux Estate."

The lights turn off and the projector turns on to show a faded black and white picture. The aged photo is hard to see.

"Built in the 1600s, the Monreaux Estate has always been a part of Salem history. Over the years, it's become a sore thumb sticking out in the gorgeous town of Salem. We were hoping our friends at Hills Construction would tear it down, but apparently, according to an old will we found by Severide Monreaux and witnessed by Alexander Monreaux, it must go to auction. And we are honest people, so here we are..." He clears his throat as if he is annoyed.

My heart leaps when I hear the name Alexander and a fuzzy picture begins to form in my mind.

"Shit, you're betting against a construction company. I bet they already have plans for that land," Dottie says, an edge of despair in her voice.

"We will start the bidding at fifty-thousand," Mike announces.

I raise my paddle and look around the room, no one else is bidding besides some man in an expensive suit. He must own the construction company.

Ass.

"Do I have sixty?"

We both raise our paddles.

"Seventy?"

"Eighty?"

"Ninety?"

I can't go higher than that, but the man in the suit doesn't seem nervous. I bet he could sit here all day.

"A hundred thousand?"

My soul shatters when I can't lift my paddle and the man in the suit does. I bet he could drop a million bucks on the ground and walk away without batting an eyelash.

It's like someone has ripped open my chest and squeezed my heart. I think about Alexander and how I failed him. I don't know him, but something inside me recognizes his name, and I let him down.

"Going once, twice—"

I sob, my home being torn out from under me.

"Two hundred thousand dollars!"

I gasp when I hear Pa's voice. Dottie and I turn around at the same time.

"Cash." He ends his dramatic entrance with everyone's favorite word.

The crowd murmurs in shock but my eyes are glued to Pa. He sends me a wink as he casually walks around the seats.

The man in the suit doesn't raise his paddle. I guess tearing it down and building something has to be more profitable to him.

Slowly, my heart gets stitched back together. This can't be happening.

"Okay, okay, quiet down," Mike says, slamming the gavel on the podium. "Two-hundred thousand, going once—" he looks around the room. "Twice—" he waits for someone to speak up. He stares at the man in the suit, hoping he will save the day, but the man stands and walks out. "Sold for two-hundred thousand to the crazy old man who has no idea what he is getting into."

Pa finally sits next to me, and I have no idea what to say. I'm at a loss for words. I had no idea he had that kind of money.

"I told you, your dreams were going to come true."

I hug him as tight as I can and cry, shoulders shaking as years of questions and doubt lift off me. "I love you. Thank you. Thank you so much."

Home is just a key turn away now.

******

Alexander

The shadows become lighter but the dark still overhangs. Life is still out of reach, but it's closer than it has been in a long time.

I think.

Everything is hazy.

I'm pushing against a restraint of some sorts. I'm bound by heavy weights underwater and I'm trying to get free.

I'm drowning.

Something has changed.

I see red.

Flames.

Hope.

Yet I'm frozen.

Beauty stirs me.

But beauty fades and time always stands still.

Darkness awaits.

Chapter Three

MAVEN

"Do you want me to go with you?" Pa asks, looking too comfy in his recliner. He seems a bit pale and green around the gills. It's been a hell of a day. The auction went by quicker than I thought it would. It's all a blur.

Honestly, it feels like more of a dream than anything. If it weren't for the heavy, centuries aged key in my hand that allows me onto the estate, I wouldn't believe it. There is a faded orange gem in the middle of the weighted iron. The key is gorgeous, and I have a feeling it has experienced so much in its life. I wish I could know.

On the car ride home yesterday, I cried, thanking Pa over and over until I hiccupped, and my throat hurt. My eyes are still puffy from all the tears.

"No, I think you should rest. I need to do this alone." I sit down on the well-seasoned couch he refuses to get rid of and play with the key in my hand. It's large, nearly taking up my entire palm. "Pa..." I furrow my brows as I think, letting the rust and bumps in the iron key scratch my skin. It's as if I have found the key to my restless heart and I'm finally able to open it to give it the rest it deserves but there is one question burning the back of my mind. "How did you get that money? I thought we were strapped. I'm confused."

He coughs, the sound is wet and unhealthy. "We are, but I never once thought about going into my safe to give you your inheritance." He holds up his finger and presses the leg lift of the recliner down to stand.

"Inheritance? Pa, I don't expect a thing like that. Use that money for you." I get to my feet and help steady him.

"Fireball, I don't need it. I want to take care of you when I'm gone, and this is my way to do it. Follow me." He shuffles his feet across the floor and Whiskey grunts as he follows Pa down the hallway to his bedroom. His chocolate brown fur looks like a floating rug as he sticks against Pa's legs.

I follow behind, trying my best to keep a clear head. I've never thought of the day where I'd have to be without Pa, but it's going to happen. He won't live forever and somehow, that enrages me. I can't be without Pa. My heart can't take the pain it will bring.

The bedroom door groans open, and I crinkle my nose as I enter. The musky smell of an elderly man and stale air overwhelms my senses even though Pa has always been a clean man. The bed is in the middle of the room, crisp white sheets and a wrinkle free blue blanket lies on the bed, the pillows perfectly fluffed.

On the left side where the nightstand is, a picture sits of my grandma in her wedding dress. It's been there for as long as I can remember. Nothing has changed in this room over the years.

Not even the lace curtains hanging over the windows that have turned yellow over time.

He grabs each side of a pretty painting of Salem, then takes it off the wall. My eyes round when I see a vault. A round circular black notch clicks as he turns it. "Now, I know it's hard to accept, Fireball, but I won't be around forever. It's going to hurt and upset you, but just know I'll always be with you. This is my way of always being with you, okay?"

"Pa, I don't like this. I don't like how you're talking." Tears begin to brew, overflowing like a boiling cauldron over a fire.

"I'm not going anywhere anytime soon. I'm just letting you know, okay?" A louder click sounds, and he swings open the vault. "Now, in my will, it says not to give this to you until I die, but I think now is a good time. You need it." His arms reach inside the vault, and he pulls out stacks of twenty dollar bills.

"Pa!" I gasp and turn to look over my shoulder to make sure we're alone. We're always alone. "What is this? Did you rob a bank?"

He snorts. "I'm not a criminal, just a smart businessman." He snags a bag from beside the bed and stashes the cash inside the red duffle. "I've saved for years. I started the moment your mother was born, but when she left and I had you, I knew this money would go to you and you'll do well with it. You'll be smart. You'll make it last. And you'll make your dreams come true, just like this Monreaux Estate. This allows me to help you in the only way I can. My bones aren't built like they used to be, so I can't help you build, but I can help you pay for someone who will bring your visions to life. Add this money to your bank account, the one you've put all your savings in." He empties the vault besides one stack of cash, then zips the duffle bag shut. "That's about seven-hundred thousand dollars, Fireball. It's everything I've ever saved for you. I hope this helps create a home you can live in forever."

He tries to hand me the bag and I stare at it. I can tell it's heavy since the material is stretched and the zipper looks like it's about to burst.

"I can't take this," I say breathlessly, the air leaving my lungs in one full whoosh.

He takes my hand and closes my fingers around the black handles. "You can and you will. I want you to. I want you to make this home everything you've ever dreamed about since you were a little girl. This is for you. Either take it now while I'm alive or accept this money when I'm dead."

This is a dream that wouldn't have come true without him. I drop the bag and throw my arms around his neck, tucking my face against his shoulder while squeezing him tight. The key digs into my palm as I hold onto him. He smells like his room and I'm finding that scent more comforting than ever right now.

"You've always taken care of me," I manage to whisper through the tightness in my throat.

He hugs me in return. "I will always take care of you, for as long as I'm breathing, Fireball. You can count on that." Pa leans away and brushes the tears off my face. "Now, go see your home. I'm going to kick back and relax. Go to the bank first," he suggests with a stern tone warning me I better listen to his suggestion.

I snicker. "You can count on that. I'm not walking around with this much money." I wipe under my lower lash line to gather the rest of the tears. "Are you sure about this? This is so much, Pa."

"I've never been surer about anything in all my years. Now, go on. I'm tired of the mushy stuff and I want to nap."

Whiskey barks in agreement, then yawns as if that was too much work.

I stand on my tiptoes and give Pa a kiss on the cheek. "I'll never be able to repay you."

"You've repaid me just by being you, Fireball. Go on, before it gets too dark out, maybe take a few candles just in case."

Oh, yeah. That's a good idea since the Monreaux Estate doesn't have electricity. "I'll grab a lantern instead," I tell him, thinking about the lantern in the garage that hasn't been lit in years. It's sitting there next to the mower.

"Be careful. Call me with updates and let me know if it's haunted. Oooooo," he mimics a ghost wiggling his fingers at me.

I roll my eyes at the silly thought. "I can't wait to call you with no exciting news." I tuck the key in my back pocket, then grunt as I lift the duffle in my hands, the cash feels as heavy as bricks.

"I wouldn't be too sure," he says under his breath and it has me kicking up a brow at him.

Salem has always been a paranoid city, filled with myths and what ifs. Everyone believes in witchcraft and paranormal creatures, or at least fear the *possibility* of them. Me, I don't know what I believe. I'm good either way.

The world could use a little excitement and so could my soul.

I decide to drag the duffle across the floor, making my way to the living room. The end of the rug curls as the money stuffed bag slides over it. The door is open so I'm able to push the handle of the screen door with my butt and open it. As I go down the steps of the porch, the bag thumps heavily.

I begin to sweat.

Who knew dragging so much cash could be such a workout?

Whewie.

The dead grass crunches under my feet and when I get to the truck, I open the passenger side door. Remembering to lift with my legs, I toss the money into the seat, then lean against the side for a breather.

This cannot be happening. I can't suddenly be rich.

It doesn't feel real.

Once my arms stop shaking, I push off the truck and run into the garage to grab the lantern and the matchbox.

"Alright, Pa. I'm going to the bank, then the estate. I love you!"

"Love you, Fireball. Be safe."

I grin, feeling better than I have in a long time. There's hope. Something big is on the horizon and I'm going to grab it. My entire life is about to change.

I run to the driver's side, and with a smile on my face, my journey to the bank seems like the final stretch to all the hope I've ever held onto.

Cranking the lever against the door, the window rolls down and the evening breeze flutters into the cab. I rest my elbow against the side and take a quick look at the bag sitting in the passenger side seat.

Time moves so fast when I'm not ready for it to, yet so slow when I'm waiting for it to speed up.

I think about everything I want to do to the estate. I definitely want to clean up the property and the inside probably needs to be completely gutted.

Oh, I know.

I really want sparkly paint, maybe an accent wall in the kitchen. A pretty light mint green that glistens when the sun comes through the window.

I'm so fucking excited! I can do whatever I want, but I also want to find pictures of the property to keep its originality.

I'm so lost in thought, I don't even remember pulling into the parking lot at the local bank. When I park, I lace my arms over the steering wheel.

Everything is changing. I close my eyes to take a moment to myself when blue eyes sear my mind. Gasping, I snap them open and look around, wondering what just happened. Confused, I jump out of the truck and try to think of someone I know with blue eyes.

There's Dottie, but I wouldn't be thinking about her, would I?

That stops me in my tracks, my hand sliding over the warm hood of the truck and then I begin to laugh. My cackles bring attention, but I don't care. It isn't Dottie I'm thinking of.

Gathering my wits about me, I lace the duffle bag handles through my arms and carry it like a backpack since I can't lift it the other way. The straps dig into my shoulders and bites into my skin.

"Ms. Wildes?"

I turn to look over my shoulder and grin when I see the familiar face of the handsome security guard. "Hi? I'm sorry, I didn't catch your name at city hall." I gather my hair from under the bag and it tumbles down my shoulders. His brown eyes slide down my body and the security guard doesn't bother to hide his desire before meeting my face.

"Hall. Brenden Hall." He holds out his hand for me to shake. He has a friendly smile, the kind that can charm a woman right out of her panties, but my panties are very secure.

I shake his hand and inhale a sharp breath when I envision blood and death. I let go quickly and take a step back. My mind must be fucking with me.

His grin fades, but something else lurks in his features. "Is everything okay? I didn't mean to startle you."

"Sorry. I haven't been sleeping well," I lie, feeling uncomfortable all of a sudden.

Run, My Sweet. Run.

A voice whispers from the depths of my mind and I shake my head, insanity gripping hold. What the hell is wrong with me?

"I'm sorry to hear that. I'm glad I caught you. I heard you won the bid on the Monreaux property." He fishes out his brown leather wallet and hands me a card. "Congratulations. I think it's an amazing piece of land. It needs some work and I also happen to own a lumber and construction company."

Don't you dare take that card.

"I know what you're thinking. What is a security guard doing owning a lumber company?"

I wasn't wondering that at all.

"I'm a part time security guard and I'm transitioning to my new company. I'd love a chance to work on this estate. Selfishly, it would be great for me considering the historical value of it, but I swear, I'll make your dreams come true." He smiles then releases a deep breath after his speech.

Why do I feel like there is more to that last sentence?

I take it because my subconscious is suddenly a sexy male voice screaming superstition. I need all the help I can get. Making sure not to brush against his fingers, I snag the card from him, then stare at the matte black cardstock with gold letters.

"I'd love to help you restore it. It would be great for my business and you. So call me some time." He gives a sideways smirk and scratches the back of his head, the light catching the amber flakes in his brown eyes. "For anything."

A growl snarls next, rumbling loose my ability to think.

I'm a crazy person.

Yep.

That's what is happening.

"You know, I might take you up on that." I tuck the card in my pocket "Well, I have to go deposit a check. It was nice to meet you Brenden." My converse scuff against the sidewalk as I hold onto the straps of the bag.

"I look forward to hearing from you, Maven," he shouts.

I give a friendly smile and wave before opening the door.

"Welcome to Salem Credit Union. How can I help you?" A teller with puffy brown hair and smudged lipstick on her teeth asks.

"I need a private room to deposit a large sum of money," I say, feeling more uncomfortable by the second. They are going to think I sacrificed a life for this money.

"Absolutely, right this way." The big haired woman saunters around the counter. Her skirt hits her knees, and her purple blouse is tucked in with a rhinestone belt that wraps around her waist.

She walks with her hands up, wrists back, and fingers curled, sashaying her hips quickly while her heels kiss the black tile floor.

I hurry after her and when we enter the room, I drag the straps off my shoulders and the bag hits the floor with a hard thud.

"I'd like to deposit seven-hundred thousand dollars."

She grins, unzipping the duffle to begin placing the money in a counting machine. That's when I notice the wrinkles on her face. She hides her age well with her young-dressed appearance and makeup.

I expect her to say something sly and rude to me like everyone else, but besides a few curious glances, she doesn't say a word to me while she counts the money.

I shiver and give a tight smile while she blows a bubble with her gum. We remain in silence for the rest of the time, and I decide to put most of the cash in my savings account with a large chunk in checking, then I might invest in some stocks to be safe.

"Have a great, *non-witchy* day, Maven."

Ah, there it is.

I don't even know this woman's name. My eyes flick to her nametag. "I'll think about it, *Beth*." With an empty bag, I hurry to the truck.

When I push out the door, the sun has set and an eerie feeling washes over me, as if I'm being watched.

Come home. Come to me, where you will be safe.

"Losing my goddamn mind," I grumble under my breath before hopping in the truck.

I tap my fingers against the wheel, glancing around. Someone is watching me. Not wanting to stick around and find out who, I do what I planned on doing the moment the iron key fell into my hands at the auction, and head home to the Monreaux Estate.

The truck grumbles from the old exhaust and I take a peek in the rearview to make sure I am in the clear.

I'm the only vehicle in the parking lot now. A ghost town is all that's left.

And the further I get away from bank, the further the headlights burn against the pavement, the darker the night sky gets, the better I feel. This town suffocates me without understanding me. People fear what they don't know and for some reason, that's me. The only place I know where I am accepted is with Pa and at the estate.

The stars are millions in the sky and trees are trying to wrap the constellations in a tight hug as they soar to space. My surroundings get prettier as the buildings diminish, which is just how I want to live.

I flip my blinker on out of habit and turn down the dirt road that leads to the mansion. These overgrown weeds engulfing the driveway lead the way to my only dream since I was a little girl.

The brakes squeak as I come to a stop. My nerves shake my hands as I try to grip the wheel. The yellow headlights beam against the black iron that's stopped trespassers for the last one hundred years. The M in the middle of the gate hypnotizes me.

On autopilot, I step out of the truck, and dig into my pocket for the key. I can't get over how heavy it is. My boots crunch against the grass and vines. I stand in front of the gate for a few minutes, that feeling in my soul tugging me home again. As I slip the key through the hole, the metal clanking against iron, I notice the vines seem greener.

Or maybe I'm imagining things, but I swear, they seem more… alive.

"This is it," I whisper, my words a cold cloud in the night. My fingers clutch the handle of the key, the only one out of the original three that has been found, and I forget what to do next.

I need to turn the damn thing, but I'm frozen.

Once I step through these gates, my life changes forever.

The vines creep closer to the lock, as if they have come to life, and I know I am losing my mind because the orange gem in the key begins to glow.

Closing my eyes and taking a much needed breath, I twist my wrist and the key turns to the stopping point. With a hard shove, the gates swoop open, presenting me to the Monreaux Estate.

I stand in the middle of the headlights, staring as far as they can show me. A few Spanish Oaks line either side of the drive next to the Red Maples and Eastern Red Cedar. The moss hangs down low from the branches, almost dripping to the ground. A few red and yellow leaves scatter, blowing across the tops of my shoes.

I'm home.

Even if it does look a little creepy right now.

I hurry back to the truck and hop in, slamming the door just before I press my foot on the gas. I forget the gate behind me and leave it wide open. It's not like anyone ever comes on this property anyway.

Squealing in excitement, I can't help but turn my head in every direction so I can see every inch of the property I can. It's hard to since it's so dark, but it's gorgeous. The trees go on for 200 acres and one day, I'm going to walk through every single inch of this place and explore.

The moss drags over my windshield, scraping against the top of the truck while my tires dip into a steep pothole which causes the frame to shake.

Another sheet of moss blinds me again and when I pass through it, I slam on the brakes, seeing the front of the house up close for the first time.

I hold my hand over my heart as it jackhammers against my chest. In slow movements, I slip out of the truck and gently close the door, afraid I might wake the dead in the stunning silence around me.

The house itself can't speak, but right now, it's screaming at me to come inside. I reach into the bed of the truck to grab the lantern, the autumn night cool against my skin, the air suddenly still while crickets sing their lullaby into the distance.

An owl hoots and I dart my eyes around to the left to catch a glimpse of the bird. His large orange eyes stare like two glowing embers ready to launch at me. He ruffles his feathers, his long nails dig into the bark of the tree while his wings spread, lifting himself into the air and flying away until he is nothing but another star in the sky.

A moan comes from the house, the beams rotted and barely supporting the roof. I continue to glare inside where a door used to be. All that's left is empty space. The left side of the porch appears burned, but it doesn't look like it reached the house. It must have rained the night it happened for it to have done so little damage. I shiver when I think about the disaster that could have happened if it had reached the rest of the house. Carefully, I climb up the unreliable steps, swirling the key in my left hand before switching it for the matchbook that's in my pocket.

Stopping at the threshold, chains rattle to the right of me and I see an old swing trying to rock, but half of the body grinds against the ground. Placing my palms on either side of the doorframe, the broken paint pinches my skin. I chew my bottom lip, debating if I want to take the final step inside.

If I do, I know my entire life will change, but my life changed the moment the keys were in my hand.

And now I'm here.

I'm too nervous to take the final step after all this time.

I have to.

I'm *meant* to.

With an uneven breath, I take a small step forward and gently set down the lantern. Opening the matchbook, I grab a stick and strike it against the box, the flame but a speck in the void of this house.

I swallow. "You can do this, Maven." I bend down and pick up the lantern, lighting it on the inside. Sparks fly as the wick ignites.

Welcome home, My Sweet.

Chapter Four

ALEXANDER

I wake with a start and a thirst in the back of my throat.

Why is it so dark?

The next time I blink, I'm standing outside the mau-soleum. Why on earth would I be down here in the cat-acombs? The memory tickles the back of my mind, but I can't remember. It's all… blank.

I need to find Atreyu and the others.

He'll know what to do. He always does.

I think about mother and father, needing to find them and tell them how disgusting it is down here. We need to take care of every inch of our estate if we want to be taken seriously.

The Monreaux's are better than this.

As I walk down the hall, a dreadful feeling sets in my fangs, and I stop.

Something isn't right.

Someone is here.

Rushing to the top floor, I bypass all the steps and I'm suddenly standing in the middle of my living room.

What the fuck?

"Atreyu!" I shout to figure out how I'm in one place one minute then another the next, but it isn't the only thing I seek answers for. "Greyson! Uncle Luca?"

Silence replies, mocking my anxiety with tension. The living room is a wreck.

It's filled with dust, beams are broken and lying across the floor, some of them scorched. I tilt my head back and see a hole in the roof, moonlight casting down on me. I try to inhale to sift through memories through scent, but I can't smell a thing.

My home is destroyed.

I run from the living room to the kitchen, to the bedrooms, but they are all the same. Empty and dilapidated. Where is everyone?

Why am I alone?

The sound of something humming outside captures my attention and I head to the window, well, where a window used to be. The porch sags and my heart begins to ache.

Something... bad has happened.

I don't know what, but I'm all alone and the house is in shambles.

Grief washes over me.

What I'm grieving over, I don't know. I just know I need to.

I wish I understood.

A vehicle comes to a stop in front of the house. The car is oddly shaped with a bed of some sorts attached to the back.

Hmm.

I try to scent the air again, but my attempt fails. My fangs throb though and my cock aches, filling to the point of pain. I watch from the window as a woman steps out of the weird looking car.

A human.

Immediately, I'm on defense.

Why?

She looks up at the house and smiles, the moon catching the fire in her wild locks of hair.

I hold my breath as I watch this woman walk up the creaking steps to my home. Anyone else, any other human, I'd tear from limb-to-limb, but this one is different. I want... I want...

My thoughts come to a halt when she steps through the doorway, the lantern making her eyes greener than summer grass, and she peers into the living room as if it's everything she's ever wanted.

"This is my home," I speak clearly, ignoring the lust coursing through me. "You are trespassing. Leave." I point toward the door again, but she pretends she can't hear me.

Me!

Alexander Monreaux.

No one ignores me.

"Get out of my house at once," I snarl, pushing aside my want for her.

"I can't believe it," she speaks, her voice sounding of honey and an easy flowing river.

Two of my favorite things. I love listening to the calm trickling of water drifting.

She's a witch. She's bewitching me with her voice. It makes sense with her odd car and flaming hair.

My talons free and I hiss, preparing to launch.

"It's finally mine. After so many years, it's mine. Oh, I have so many ideas. I need blueprints. I need to keep to the original plan. I wish I knew what it looked like before so many years have nearly ruined it. They have to be here." She runs by me and into the kitchen, then again to bolt into the dining room, the lantern swaying back and forth. Her reckless behavior is on the verge of causing a blaze.

I curl my lip and stomp after the maddening intruder. "This is not your property. I don't know what the hell you think you're doing, but you need to leave!" I watch as she touches the broken chandelier on the floor, rubbing the dust and soot off the crystal. "I don't know how that got there, but clearly I've been gone for too long. You need to stop touching things that aren't yours." But all I can think about are her hands touching me, running down my body because I want to be hers.

It's ridiculous.

"I wonder what happened here," she mumbles, placing a gentle hand on the wall as she floats to the next room connected to the foyer.

The library.

I follow after her, getting annoyed about the feelings coursing through me. I want her gone, but I want her here. Nothing is making sense. "Maybe you can tell me. Why is my home in shambles? Did you do this?" I want to kill her all over again.

A few books are strung across the floor, open, the pages face down. She lifts one up, the imprint of the book left behind on the dusty hardwood. She puckers her lips, red as a rose petal, and blows, sending debris everywhere. She coughs, then sneezes, her eyes watering.

Humans.

So weak.

I cross my arms as I watch her try to read it. She can't. It's in vampire language.

"Wow." She rubs her fingers down the spine and I swear, I tremble. It's like she caresses every vertebrae of mine as well. I can almost feel it.

I clear my throat, not liking how intimate this is starting to feel. "Miss, I think there has been a mistake. You need to go. This is my home and while I don't understand any of this—" I run my fingers through my hair, a part of me worried I'll never figure it out "—I am still here. Please, respect my wishes and go." I tuck my hands in my pockets and head to the library door. I glance down, noticing piles of ash on the ground.

So many piles.

I step over one, being careful not to bother it.

"Like I said, there is the door, don't let it hit you on the way out." I try not to sound rude, but the bitterness can't be contained.

This woman is a nuisance, standing there curious about my life and my home, looking as beautiful as the first snowfall in the winter. That doesn't matter, she needs to get out.

She ignores me once again and I growl, a deep vibrating rumble that has made human men piss themselves in fear.

The woman begins to hum, dragging her fingers along the books lining the wall until she finds one that has the darkness inside me brewing to the surface.

She sits down on the worn chair in the corner, the expensive Victorian lounge I liked to sit on as I wrote in my journal...the same journal she has in her hand. The pages are bound in leather and the strings are tied around its body.

This witch places the lantern on the end table but ends up placing it on top of a book.

"Have you no manners? Who places objects on books?" The audacity.

She wipes the muck off the front cover, and she smiles as if she notices something. "Alexander Monreaux."

I walk closer to her, kneeling on the floor and stare up at her curious face.

Who is this woman? Why does she call to me? The way she says my name, it's as if she has known me forever.

"I am Alexander Monreaux. What is it that you want?" I ask gently, hoping my new tone sounds more welcoming.

Yet, she ignores me as if I'm not there.

"I feel like I've known you all my life. You have no idea how much I've dreamed about this moment."

"What moment? I have so many questions, please," I sound desperate as my voice breaks. "Help me understand why you are here."

Help me understand *anything*.

She tugs on the strings of my journal to read before pausing. She inhales a shaky breath and looks around. I wave my hands as her green eyes pass right by me. "It doesn't feel right reading it," she states, wrapping the strings around the journal. She sets it back on the shelf between two books. "I know you're dead, but it still feels like an invasion of privacy."

"Dead? I'm right here! Stop ignoring me. Pay attention to me, damn it. Answer my fucking questions!" I yell, but she stands, wiping the dust off her waist overalls.

They are tight too, scandalous in a way I've never seen before. They hug every curve. From her hips to the lean muscle of her calves, I can't look away.

My eyes fall to the shake of her ass, so round, so succulent. I could sink my fangs into the thickness of her cheeks and drink.

I shut my eyes and inhale, a slight rumble rattling my chest.

But what has me opening my eyes is how I can't smell her blood. I nervously peer into every corner noticing she's no longer in the room, but I catch a glimpse of her red hair as she takes a right down the hall.

"You menace. Where are you going now?" I follow the mysterious woman and she stops, cocking her head at a picture on the wall. The only one that is still hanging. The rest are in shambles on the floor. She gently plucks it free and takes the end of her shirt to clean off the glass.

She holds a hand over her mouth as she gasps.

"What is it?" I ask her, then roll my eyes at myself, as if she'll actually answer me. I peek over her shoulder and grin. "Oh, yeah. That's me. I graduated the top of my class. Master, my father, was proud. He's around here somewhere. A human shouldn't be here, you know. You've walked into a vampire den. You're bound to get feasted on." In more ways than one if she isn't careful.

Just the thought of another vampire tasting her sweet blood has me ready to fight.

Why?

"Alexander Monreaux. You were very handsome. Look at that dark hair and your blue eyes... they are piercing. Your skin is so pale, like milk," she says to me.

Well, to the picture.

Nearly the same.

"Hey, we aren't all fair skinned. That's just a myth. I got the pale genes from my mother," I grumble, displeased that she thinks I'm pale. I've happened to enjoy the sun a time or two.

"Beautiful," she whispers. "Why do I feel like I know you?" The green-eyed beauty asks the picture. "Why do I feel like I'm meant to be here?"

"I don't know." I steel myself as I squeeze my jaw tight. "But you don't. This is no place for a human." There's a voice in the back of my head that is telling me she does belong here, that this is her home, but how can I welcome her when I don't understand anything that is happening?

She holds the picture to her chest and a tear escapes from the corner of her eye. Not liking that she is crying, a woman so gorgeous should only ever smile, I reach up to wipe her tears away when my hand vanishes through her.

Gasping, she takes a step away from me, wide-eyed and fearful as she sets her sights everywhere but on me.

I stare at my hand, stunned, and reach for her again, my hand disappearing once more.

"What. The. Fuck!" I scream at the top of my lungs so loud, the house begins to shake. Pieces of glass on the floor tremble, clanking against the ground.

Her red hair flows left and right as she seeks the force causing this, like she can't believe what she's witnessing. She traps the photo of me against her breasts as if it is a lifeline.

Nothing can save her from me.

She did this.

She is the reason why my home is ruined and why I am... *this*.

"Can you see me?" I grit through my fangs.

She doesn't look at me. Tears continue to spill down the tops of her freckled cheeks.

I want to kiss them away while at the same time tear her to pieces and bathe in the warmth of her blood.

I raise my voice. "Can you hear me?"

The stranger rushes by me, without answering my questions, stepping on the piles of ash along the way.

A well of pure rage ignites inside me. "Do not step on those!" The boom of my voice quakes the house again and she rushes outside, jumping down the steps.

"Don't ever come back," I roar, banging my fists against my chest.

The car starts and she speeds away, leaving me aching in my own despair.

I *want* her to come back.

And I *never* want to see her again.

My knees become weak and hot searing agony rips me apart, stealing my breath. I fall, catching myself on the floor as I try to breathe.

There's a pile of ash below me and I try to grab it, but I can't.

A soul wrenching cry escapes me, one sounding more like a beast than a man. The moment she leaves the property, I succumb to the darkness that I've always feared.

Chapter Five
MAVEN

So much pain.

All the screaming, it hurts my ears.

Kill them. Kill them all! Keep their fangs.

"I can't go. I'll just slow you down. The venom has taken me."

"You can't quit on me. I need you. You hear me?"

"Did mother make it? Sister? Father, Greyson, Uncle Luca?"

So many conversations morph as memories switch quickly.

Death.

Pain.

Torture.

Howls.

I toss and turn in bed, sweat covering my entire body. I feel their will to live, the fear, the grief.

It's all too much.

A man, tall with dark hair and blue eyes takes over my nightmare. He's beautiful. Wide shoulders, muscles I want to explore, and a smile that would send any woman into a sexual frenzy.

"I need you to come home. Come to me, Maven. I need you."

"Why?" I ask, taking a step closer.

"I've waited for so long to be set free. Come home."

"Alexander?" I ask the mirage.

"Save me," he pleads before he tilts his head back and screams. The veins in his neck protruding and blood coats his entire body. Tears drip down his face, leaving clean glowing lines in the red staining his cheeks. The guttural sound shaking the roots that set my heart.

I jolt awake, gasping for breath as I hold a hand to my chest. My heart beats in wild tandem and I cringe when I feel the sweat coating my skin. I take a minute to gather my thoughts, wondering what the hell just happened.

I lick my lips to wet them and taste the salt of sweat, then toss the comforter off my body. It's damp, as if I ran a mile in my dreams or was roasted alive.

My imagination is really getting the best of me. It has to be because I went to the Monreaux Estate just a few short hours ago. Whatever happened there definitely scared me and obviously my subconscious is still bothered.

The house shook. I felt it. I heard a roar. A horrible, painful sound that when I think about it, I feel the anguish and tear up.

The dreams aren't real, I know that, but the ghost? That had to be real. I felt it touch my cheek, but instead of cold, it was a warm, caressing touch, as if the ghost was trying to wipe away my tears.

Impossible.

But what other explanation is there for the quaking of the house? I've watched enough movies to know ghosts can do some unbelievable things. How can I get the ghost to leave?

I swing my legs over the bed and sway, feeling sick and dizzy all of a sudden. It's the same feeling I had in my dreams, as if the man talking to me was ill.

And the man... good god, he was gorgeous.

"You're a crazy person thinking this ghost is good looking. You really don't have a dating life," I mumble to myself in the darkness.

The only light is from the moon beaming through the windows. I yawn, stretching my arms above my head as I stand, staring through the glass to the round white circle hanging in the sky. My brows crinkle together when I hear a howl reverberating in my mind and a clear hatred for the moon surfaces.

I pick up the picture on my desk and stare at the young man in the photo, Alexander Monreaux, the person who seems to be haunting my dreams. An idea hits me, a realization really. I rub the fragile glass with my thumb, staring into the ice colored irises. "Are you the ghost in the house?" Maybe these dreams are a way for him to communicate with me. It's a long shot, but the man in the photo is the same man in my dreams.

It's the only thing I have to go on right now.

I gently place the photo next to my laptop and pull out my chair. My damp hair gets on my nerves as it sticks to my neck and I throw it in a messy bun on top of my head. A lone piece dangles to the side and taking one last look at the photo, I do what any sane woman would do when she's being haunted.

She researches a way to get the ghost out of her home.

I type into Google, "How to get a ghost to move on," I say it out loud as I type. I scroll through the results and most say the ghosts are bound there and have unfinished business. Until that business is complete, they aren't going anywhere.

I see a few "spells" and the usual sage to help cleanse the home, but the thought of forcing him to leave upsets me and it doesn't feel right.

"Okay..." I say unsure and begin to bite my thumbnail as I think. I blow out a breath and begin typing again. "How to communicate with a ghost." I type.

A Ouija board.

I jump out of the chair and run to my closet, digging through the different board games until I come across the Ouija board I got for my thirteenth birthday. "Hmmm, does it matter if the board glows in the dark? Does it make the results less likely?" I ask myself. I bet this isn't even a real board, but it's all I have.

I sit down and shake the box until the top pops off and settle on the floor. Unfolding the board, I stifle a laugh when it begins to glow.

Yeah, this isn't going to work.

I close my eyes and place my hands on the planchette. "Is Alexander here right now?" I ask and wait for a few minutes to see if it works. After I don't feel anything, I peek an eye open to see the planchette hasn't moved.

"Damn it." I drop my hands and stand, heading to my laptop again. I tap my fingers on the desk and click my tongue while I think of why it didn't work. Granted, I only asked it one question, maybe that was it, but it was a pretty important question. He obviously isn't here.

I begin typing into Google again. "Do ghosts leave their home?" I press enter and begin to read. "Ghosts can travel, but some are bound to where they died."

My brows hit my hairline but a pang in my heart blooms thinking about Alexander dead.

I don't even know this damn ghost.

But I don't want him to be dead. I don't know why. Maybe because it's sad and heartbreaking. He must be so confused as to why I'm there. That's what the shaking had to be about. He wanted me out of the house.

I snort. "Tough titty, ghost man. That's my house now. We either learn to live together or your ass is out of there," I say confidently. I know what I need to do now. I gather the Ouija board and place it on the bed, then begin to get dressed. Nothing fancy, just a pair of skintight leggings.

Because I have this sick thought that I want this ghost to check out my ass.

"You're mental," I sigh in disappointment. I throw on a purple shirt that says Witch's Brew across it, gather the board, slip on my shoes, and head out the door.

There's a light on downstairs as I ease the door shut. I look over the rail and see Pa in his recliner, watching TV. Whiskey is lying on the rug in front of the fireplace and Pa is flipping through the channels.

"Pa, why are you up?" I come down the steps, holding the board to my side, cocking my head in worry.

"Ah, just can't sleep. Nothing but damn ads on this time of night. I swear, I've almost bought a damn blender ten times in the last hour. I don't need a blender."

A chuckle escapes me. I bend down and give him a kiss on top of his head. "Pa, try to get some sleep."

He ignores me. "Ouija board, huh? Got a ghost in that Monreaux mansion? Doesn't surprise me. It's ancient. I'm sure a few people have died there."

"Do you know any stories about the estate?"

He scratches his chin. "Nothing you don't already know, I'm afraid. Why? Did something happen when you went there?"

I sit down on the couch and forget the cushion nearly hits the floor. I feel a spring pinching against my right butt cheek. I wiggle to get comfortable, placing the board on my lap. "Someone was there with me. And I swear, I felt him try to touch me, but then he got so mad that the house shook. I heard the cry, Pa." Emotion chokes my throat. "It was so horrible. So much pain. And then I woke up a little bit ago with the oddest dreams. Flashes of... what seemed like memories, but my imagination is running wild. I need answers before I drive myself crazy." It's hard to believe it has only been a few hours since I left the Monreaux Estate. I feel like it's been ages since those dreams made me feel exhausted.

"Did you say dreams?" His face hardens and leans forward in the recliner. "What kind?"

I lean back, not liking the tone Pa is having with me. "Nothing to be concerned about. Why?"

"What was said? Who was in your dream? What was it about?" He throws question after question at me.

"Pa, you're scaring me." I get up and head toward the door, his hand wrapping around my wrist to stop me. "Pa..."

"Maven, I didn't know you were drawn to the house because—"

I yank my arm from his hand. "Because nothing. That's my home. I don't care what I dream. I can't believe you're trying to talk me out of this, after all this time." I shake my head in disappointment, giving him one last look before grabbing the keys and running out the door.

"Maven! Maven, we need to talk. There are things you need to know!" He shouts after me, Whiskey barking behind him.

I wipe my cheek, heartbroken that the one person I thought I could count on would try to stop me from figuring out my destiny.

Yes, this house, this ghost, I'm meant for this. I don't know how or why but I believe there is a reason I've been drawn to the estate my entire life.

I'm going to find out why and I don't care if the news kills me.

I throw my arm over the passenger seat and turn my head over my shoulder to watch where I'm going as I reverse. I throw the truck in drive, ignoring all the potholes that are bad for the frame.

Pa would have a fit right now.

The headlights illuminate the night as I travel.

There's a loneliness that hangs in the dark, a type of solitude that feels like I'm alone in space. It's as if I'm waiting for someone to reach out and grab me, only to miss because they can't see.

I rub my chest with my fist, wondering where these emotions are coming from. They aren't from me.

I don't pass another car the entire ride to the Monreaux Estate. The weeds are already flattened from earlier so driving is a bit easier. When I get to the iron gate, the large M in the middle along with the keyhole seem bigger while I stare at it.

There's that feeling again, the overwhelming need to be here.

It reminds me of crippling anxiety mixed with butterflies and anticipation, fear, and love.

There are different types of love, I just haven't figured out what type I'm feeling yet.

With a tired sigh, I open the truck door and an annoying ding sounds. I slip off the seat and the weeds crunch under my shoes as I walk to the gate. I haven't fought with my Pa in ages and as I insert the aged key, I know it's because this estate has already changed me.

With a hard click to the right, the lock opens and by flattening my palms against the M intertwined in the gate, I push it open, gasping when an image rushing to the forefront of my mind has me stumbling back. I hit the warm hood of the truck and hold the side of my head. Flashes of someone running through the woods in pain has me clutching my side.

Is it me?

No. I'm seeing from someone else's perspective.

I fall and it causes me to hit the ground in real time, my knees digging into the thorns weaving across the driveway.

My heart is racing. I hear something in the distance...howls? I cry out in turmoil, my side on fire and my vision blurring.

Blood.

I taste blood.

The gates groan and it yanks me out of my dream. With a large inhale of air as if I haven't been able to breathe for minutes, I fall forward on my hands. I'm present. I'm no longer running. I'm here. The ground is beneath me.

I curl my fingers against the dirt needing to feel the grains.

"I'm okay," I say, pushing myself onto wobbly legs. I stretch my arm to reach for the truck and use it as a crutch while I try to decipher what the fuck just happened. Am I losing my mind? Maybe this estate is vile. Maybe I'm slowly going mad because of the curses that live in the ground and trees like so many people say.

Specks of dirt and small bugs flutter in front of the headlights. I follow the glowing yellow as it tunnels toward the mansion I've wanted my entire life.

After everything, fear is still the last thing I feel.

The tug on my soul begins again. My heart is a puppet, and the ghost in my house has to be the puppeteer.

I need to cut the strings, but I have a feeling not even that would be enough to get away from the force that this Monreaux estate has.

I hurry into the driver's seat and don't bother to buckle up. Slamming my foot on the gas, the tires spin as they try to gain traction. Rocks fly and hit the ground behind me, and the truck fishtails for a split second before surging forward.

Large, willowing trees with sagging branches line each side of the driveway. The leaves have all but nearly fallen to the ground, decorating the path in array of colors, but the majority are bright red.

As if I'm driving through a river of blood.

When I get to the front of the house, I jerk the truck into park and stare at the condemned estate.

It's so gorgeous, but in this moment, it looks like a fear come to life. The white paint is chipped from years of weather and the wood is rotted. The porch sags and the steps are broken. The Victorian home has had better days. The windows are shattered or completely missing, letting me peer into the abyss inside. The roof needs to be replaced and I'm starting to think I'm a mad woman for wanting this property.

What hold does this place have on me?

I snag the Ouija board, then the small flashlight Pa keeps in the glove compartment since I left the lantern here earlier. Slamming the truck door, I stomp up the steps with determination. I might have stomped a little too hard on the unfaithful wood and snap it in half, nearly tripping up the stairs.

Not letting it stop me, I ignore the slight pain in my ankle and march through the doorway of the house. A few leaves have made their way into the living room, and they swirl, scratching against the ground, but not from the breeze.

"Okay, so you're here. Awesome. Listen, buddy. I'm not in the mood. I think you're fucking with me, and I don't appreciate it. So come out come out wherever you are. It's time to have a little talk. I'm tired, need to shower, and I fought with Pa. I never fight with him." Not that this ghost cares about my personal life. I plop down on the ground and cross my legs, then unfold the Ouija board, placing the planchette in the middle.

From this moment on, I refuse to have my heart manipulated, whether it be by unrealistic dreams, selfish desires, or a damn sexy ghost.

Chapter Six

ALEXANDER

I don't know how I got to the living room. One minute, I'm trying to grab a pile of ash, then there is darkness, and now I'm here, watching this beautiful mad woman.

This human has lost her damn mind.

I stare down at her with my arms crossed. I can't stop admiring her beauty. Her hair is up, settled on top of her head in a messy nest of sorts. There's one waving piece that's framing her face. Her eyes remind me of the emerald gems my mother used to wear. Only the best and most expensive for mother.

This woman's skin seems soft and there are freckles all over her body that I want to explore the longer I stare at them. My eyes drift to her neck, the vein there begging for my attention. I'd lick and suck, drive her wild until she's begging for me to sink my fangs into her while I drive my cock inside her too.

I shake my head.

Why am I having these thoughts? This stranger invades my home, says its hers, and nearly reads my journal.

And then has the nerve to call me dead.

She's infuriating. At the same time, she can't hear me or see me. I can't touch her, so maybe I am dead.

She's brought a Ouija board, but it glows in the dark. Amateur.

She's has obviously never met a real witch. Their Ouija boards are the real deal. My family had a family witch long ago. I'll have to look in the records for her name, but she was the strongest witch for centuries. No one dared to challenge us, but then she was captured by werewolves and burned at the stake.

"Okay. I'm not here to fight, okay? I just want to talk and maybe we can learn to coexist."

Not a chance, but I'll play along. I sit down on the other side of the board, and I'm caught in her stare, as if she can see me, but she looks through me instead. It... hurts, I find, the longer I think about it, the more I wish she could see me.

My soul is screaming at her to save me, but from what?

She places her hands on the planchette and I do the same, out of habit. I place my hands on top of hers and she lets out a shaky breath. I jerk my eyes from our hands. She can't see me, and my hands disappear within hers, but she feels something.

"Can you feel me?" I ask her.

"Are you touching me?" she replies with a question.

"Yes," I answer, forgetting she can't hear me, and I move the planchette across the board to the Y.

She grins and a giddy squeal leaves her. "I knew it. Your touch, it's warm, you know. It makes me feel... safe. It's the only way I know how to explain it."

I can't explain it, but I know she'll always be safe with me. I'd start and end wars for her. I'd protect her with my life.

"Did you touch me earlier when I was crying?" She asks again, and I move the planchette to the left for a split second before moving it back over to the Y.

She rolls her red lips together, wetting them with her tongue next and I memorize every curve of her mouth, wishing I was a man so I could take her, to fill this need building in my chest.

"I'm sorry I ran. It was unexpected."

"It's okay," I reply, remembering to spell my response out on the board.

Her smile is bright enough to cast the loneliness out of the dark.

I find it's the only night light I'm wishing for.

"Am I talking to Alexander Monreaux?"

I nod, then roll my eyes. How do I keep forgetting she can't see me? I force the planchette to the Y.

"I knew it! Well, it's nice to officially meet you, Alexander. My name is Maven Wildes."

Wildes. Where do I know that name?

"It's nice to meet you, Maven." I make sure to spell out my response, watching as her lips form the words with each letter.

This human woman is very intriguing. Dare I say, I'm obsessed?

"I'm so happy we can communicate. I'm sure you were upset when you saw me before. I'm guessing that's why you yelled at me?" Her cheeks tint as she looks away, nibbling her bottom lip.

Guilt eats away at me. "Long response," I spell out, wanting her to get ready.

She nods and another piece of hair comes loose. Automatically, I reach out and try to tuck the unruly piece behind her ear, but my fingers brush against her cheek, a hint of sparks coming to life between us. Her eyes flutter shut, and she leans into my hand. While there's a centimeter of space between where we could touch, I can feel her warmth.

My heart rate speeds and the bitterness in my soul unravels as I become closer with Maven.

She's the answer to everything.

I just need to figure out what *everything* means.

I jerk my hand away and her eyes snap open, her long red lashes curling with every slow blink as she comes back to the present. She reminds me of when my brother has too many glasses of wine.

He's a lightweight.

"Wow." Her throat moves up and down as she swallows. She rubs her neck and laughs as if she's embarrassed. "Sorry. It's just this entire experience."

The fact that my touch felt amazing, because I felt the connection between us, has awakened something inside me.

"Anyway, back to the question?" Maven tries to get us back on track.

Right. The question.

I begin spelling out my reasoning for yesterday, keeping my movements slow. "I apologize for scaring you," I start with. "You came to me as a surprise. I don't remember anything. It's like I woke up from a very long nap and found you here, my home a wreck, and my family gone." I pause to take a minute to gather my thoughts and emotions. "Everything is black. I tried talking to you and I thought you were ignoring me. It was very frustrating as I am not the kind of man that is ever ignored," I end on a chuckle.

She rolls her eyes. "Cocky, much?"

"Confident," I correct her, remembering to spell it out. I sigh. "I realize you weren't ignoring me. You honestly couldn't see me or hear me. When I touched you, that is when I realized something wasn't right, that I wasn't present, not really, and I shook the house because..."

"You realized your reality," she completes my thoughts for me.

I slide the heart-shaped piece of wood to the Y.

"That's awful. I'm so sorry I disrupted you. Maybe I can help you?" she offers.

"I don't know how," I respond, wishing she could hear the sadness laced in my voice.

"Hmmm," she stares at the board. "So you're a ghost, let's start there."

I shout in protest and shake the house, cringing when a piece of glass shatters in the distance. "Sorry," I apologize.

She snickers and I find it adorable, wanting to hear it again. "So you aren't a ghost, is that what you're saying?"

"In order to be a ghost, you've had to die. I haven't died." I don't know how I know that; I just do.

"You have to be," she corrects me, and I begin to get agitated.

I know what I fucking know.

"The year is 2021."

I remove my hands from hers and gasp, holding a hand over my heart when I realize it's been 121 years since I've last lived. What happened all those years ago?

"Alexander? Are you still here? My hands got cold." She looks around for me even though she can't see me, a sweet endearment that should make me feel better.

I press my palms against my forehead and try to breathe. 121 years. I let out an excruciating yell, the kind that holds pain and anger, the kind that hurts the lungs and the throat just by how loud it is.

The entire house rumbles again, the piles of ash being disrupted by the vibrations in the air. When I run out of breath, I inhale and roar again, a singular tear breaking free.

"Take my hand. Take it, Lex. Hold onto me," she begs, desperation swirling on her tongue. "I know it hurts. I know."

I can't grab onto her, but I try anyway, those same sparks igniting between us at the attempt. I feel her warmth, the goodness in her soul, the thrum of her steady heartbeat, and I focus on that. The rumbles slow until they eventually stop. I try to catch my breath, shoulders rising and falling.

Instead of answers, I'm only more confused.

"I'm here. It's okay," she shushes me as if I'm a baby needing cradled, yet her attempt to rub her thumb over my hand helps soothe me. "Do you see that?" She points to the golden sparks between us.

"Yes." I stare at the planchette to will it to move to the Y.

It works.

"Your pain... I feel it." She taps her chest. "Right here."

I remove my hand from hers and press it against her chest, her heart beating in the same untrusted rhythm as mine.

She gasps, her lips parting in invitation.

I lean in, then stop myself. We can't kiss.

"If you're upset about it being 2021, what year do you remember last?"

Her question yanks me from my sinful thoughts, wishing I could dip my tongue into the heat of her cavern, feeling the silk of her against me.

Removing my hand from her chest, the soft mound of her breast grazing my palm, I hold her hand again. "1900." The planchette scratches against the board.

"Oh my god." Her hand shakes as she covers her mouth. "How old are you?"

"Seventy." I answer, then change it. "Plus, 121."

"You're 191 years old." She laughs in disbelief.

"Vampires live a long time," I answer, watching her smile fade to shock.

"V-vampire?" she stutters. "The rumors are true?"

"I'm unaware of rumors."

"This would be a lot easier if I could see you," she says, seeming a bit pale from the news. "Vampires are real?"

"So are werewolves," I add to the shock.

How is it that I remember those details, but I can't remember events or reason? Why am I like this? Why do I find this woman so enthralling?

Maven clears her throat. "Not anymore. At least, I don't think." Her brows furrow.

"We always exist. You just haven't seen us yet."

I'm not sure how she feels about it. She isn't passing out or crying, but she looks like she might throw up. It's better than most humans.

Shaken, she asks the million dollar question. "What's the last thing you remember happening in 1900?" Maven stares at the board waiting for my answer as I think.

"I wish I could remember. Everything is dark. When you leave, it's like I don't exist. I fade into the nothing. When you're here, I come to life again, but that's all I know. Everything is uncertain. Maybe I am dead, but in my time, ghosts remembered how they died. They stick around for unfinished business or revenge. I don't feel either of those things," I say. "It's like I'm stuck."

Maven remains silent as she thinks, nibbling her bottom lip. "I'll find a way to help you. I promise. I..." she suddenly seems nervous. "I bought this house at an auction, Lex."

Lex.

My brother calls me something similar. I hate it when it comes from him, but I find I like it when the nickname falls from her blood-colored lips.

"I've wanted this property ever since I was a little girl. I've been drawn to it. Maybe it's because I was meant to help you."

I let out a built-up breath. "While, I hate my home went to auction, I'm glad it is you who bought it. I hear you have plans?"

"Yeah, but I'd like your help to restore it to the way it was?" She asks, once again staring at me as if she can see me.

I get lost in her eyes, the way they glitter in the moonlight casting down from the hole in the roof.

"I'd like that," I admit, my instincts telling me to pull her close and never let go.

She tucks her hair behind her ear and her cheeks turn a bashful shade of red. I wish I could feel how warm her skin is, experience the rush of blood rushing under her flesh like a raging river.

If I didn't know any better, I'd think this woman was meant to be mine.

In another life, in another form, in another world, I'd bind her to me. I have this life, this ghostly form in this world, and she deserves more than an apparatus.

She stands and wipes the dust off her odd waist overalls. "I guess I should get going...." She sounds unsure.

She doesn't want to go, and I don't want her to.

I reach out, taking her hand in mine and her head tilts to where we touch, the sparks of the veil between the living and the unknown colliding. "Don't go. I only exist when you're here," I admit, not wanting to fade into nothing. My heart isn't ready for her to leave either.

Her eyes widen, the whites of her eyes as big as moons. "Say it again?"

"I only exist when you're here," I repeat, watching as emotions I don't recognize rush over her face.

"I heard you."

I feel stronger every second she is here. Maybe that's why.

"I heard you, Lex!"

I smile, wishing she could see the relief on my face. "Thank goodness. Talking through that board took ages," I joke.

Not that I had anything better to do.

"Yeah, but I would have waited all my life anyway," she admits.

I cup her jaw with my hand, the sparks stronger and brighter.

It's a barrier I intend to break. I don't know how, but I will. I need to feel her in my arms.

Pressing my forehead against hers, I drag my other hand down her arm. The sparks tingling my fingertips. I don't say anything and neither does she. Saying something might ruin everything. This moment is too hard to believe.

A vampire's ghost and a human falling for one another?

It isn't possible.

Yet, here we are.

"Stay?" I finally say after what seems like hours holding one another.

"You wanted me out yesterday."

"And now I never want you to leave." I only wish she could see me now, so she could see the want and need I have for her as I stare into her eyes.

"This is my house. I'm not going anywhere."

I correct her, "*Our* house because I'm not either."

With hesitation, she lifts her hands and tests the waters of touching me, hovering them right over my chest.

"Higher," I say to her.

She slides her palms up to my neck and the glow the sparks create give her an outline of my chest, illuminating my form. She continues up, trailing her delicate fingers across my neck until she reaches my face.

She can finally see me, granted it's through light since our veils are hitting against one another, but it's how she reacts when her eyes land on mine.

"I've dreamed of you." Maven has a look of wonderment and astonishment on her beautiful face.

If I could dream, I have a feeling I'd dream of her too.

Chapter Seven
MAVEN

His lips are on mine, the fiery passion in his demanding kiss has me submitting to his every want and need. His hands caress my sides, gripping my hips with such force I'm sure he's about to break me. I tangle my fingers in his hair, gripping the strands for dear life as he kisses down my throat. The scrape of his fangs has my back arching, my breasts pressing against his chest. He's warm and inviting, unlike the myths of vampires being cold and dead.

Alexander is very much alive. I feel his warmth just as I feel my own.

"You're sure? Once I do this, it can't be undone," he gives one last warning, one last chance for me to back away.

I shake my head. "Make me yours," I beg.

With a vicious snarl, he sinks his fangs into my neck at the same time he thrusts himself through my virginity, claiming me as his.

He drinks, sucking long drafts of my blood from my heart. Pleasure rockets through me as an orgasm rushes over my body.

I open my mouth to scream—

And I awaken on the hard floor with a crick in my neck. My body still hot and flushed from the dream. It felt so real, like it actually happened. The man in my dream was my ghost, Alexander. His lips were on mine though, his tongue sliding against mine, tangling as if he couldn't get enough of me. I felt the tips of his fangs pricking against my lips and I felt his large, heavy cock thrust inside me.

I *felt* him.

How? I can't see or touch him, really touch him.

My body is on fire, my nipples tight against my shirt, and my pussy is wet, slicking against my underwear as I press my legs together to ease the ache.

"Good morning," Alexander's deep voice booms from somewhere in the room and I scream, forgetting for a second that I spent the night on the floor of this rundown house for him. "Hey, woah, it's just me," he soothes. He's close.

I can feel his energy, his arms wrapping around me and pulling me close.

"You're okay. I have you."

It hurts. This hurts. And it shouldn't because I don't really know the man, but this pull I've experienced that brought me here, it's settled with him.

I stand up and stretch, wincing when I feel the pain in my neck. I redo my hair and throw it in a ponytail. "I think we should talk about renovations today," I say, wanting to change the subject and atmosphere of being affectionate.

I can't fall in love with a man that doesn't exist.

"I have to go and get supplies. I'll be back." I need to get out of here, away from him. Take some time to think.

"Maven, what's going on?" he asks, the baritone of his voice soothing, washing over me like armor meant to protect me.

What's wrong? I just found out vampires and werewolves exist. This ghost is a vampire, and this house held a coven. I have wanted this house not because of the property but because of him. I've lived my entire life for someone else, someone who doesn't truly exist.

"Maven." The way he yells my name on an impatient bite has me jumping. "Talk to me."

"I'm afraid of you. I'm afraid of what this means. I'm confused about vampires existing and werewolves. I'm wondering what else there is in the world, things you can't tell me because you can't remember. I don't know how to make you remember, but I also don't know why my heart wants you and my mind is screaming at me to run. We don't make sense. This makes no sense. I can hear you, I can almost feel you, I dream of you, and it's like you're here, but you aren't, not really. It's only been a night of this and already I'm in pain."

"Maven—"

I hold up my hand and wipe the tear away from my cheek with the other. "I need to go. I'll be back." I walk out the door, my heart breaking while the dream races through my mind of him owning my body.

Dreams are dreams for a reason, they aren't real. They transform wants into fantasy. I need to rebuild the house and set Alexander free and then maybe I can live my life.

Living with a ghost isn't a way to live.

I hear another roar and this time it's so loud, the ground shakes under my feet.

I'm outside and the pain laced scream matches how I feel on the inside. I open the truck door, knowing I'm being irrational as I start the truck and head down the driveway. That damn tug begins to pull me back and this time it hurts, as if my heart is being ripped out of my chest.

I ignore the pain, knowing I need to do human things, like bathe and eat. I do need to go to the hardware store with Pa so I can start this renovation. I want us to fix the place up together. I hope he can forgive me after I left the way I did last night.

So many things happened.

I was able to communicate with Alexander, then hear his voice. Oh god and the way he spoke, he had an old English accent to him, elegant and sophisticated. I could listen to him speak for the rest of my life.

Since I'm not on the property, I know Alexander is in his nonexistent state. I don't know what that means, and I don't know why he is only awake when I'm there. Another question to add to the long list.

Guilt eats away at me for not being there, for being the reason for his nonexistence.

Maybe I shouldn't go back for a few days. What if this is all in my head? I'm so wrapped up in my thoughts, I don't know how I made it home so quick. I'm putting the truck in park and lacing my arms over the steering wheel as I try to figure out what to do.

I've never been more confused.

I hear the front door slam and snap my head up to see Pa standing on the porch, two cups of coffee in his hand, Whiskey right by his side. Guilt eats away at me with how I left things last night.

I'm all messed up inside ever since I stepped foot inside the Monreaux mansion.

I get out of the truck and walk with my head down, the sun warming the back of my neck. The air is crisp from the morning, and I can smell the bacon cooking from the kitchen since the window is open. Whiskey's tail thumps against the porch and Pa is relieved when I step closer.

He holds out a mug for me to take. "Hey, Fireball."

"Hey, Pa." My chin wobbles as I fight back tears.

This... I can't talk about this. I can't talk about Alexander.

It's all too unbelievable.

"I think we need to have a little talk," he says, ushering me inside.

I nod, sniffling as I take a sip of coffee. The warmth does nothing to thaw the frozen parts of me since I'm away from Alexander.

"You look like you haven't slept all night."

I guess I haven't. Lex and I stayed up talking and getting to know one another. Is it possible to fall in love in one night?

With a ghost?

My head begins to pound with a headache.

"I fell asleep on the floor." I plop in the chair at the dining room table.

"Did you talk to your ghost?"

I turn my head and nod, looking out the window instead of meeting Pa's eyes.

"Is it Alexander Monreaux?"

"Yeah, it's him, but I don't think he's a ghost."

"The Monreaux's weren't ghosts. They were vampires, Maven."

I gawk at Pa. "How did you know that?"

"I know a lot of things, things I probably should have told you ages ago but I didn't know how."

"What do you know?"

He holds up his hand when he hears the edge in my tone. "I don't know a lot about the Monreauxs. They were a large coven, but that was before my time. I really only know of rumors, but Maven, it's our lineage that I've kept from you."

The chair squeaks, adding to the grooves in the floor and Pa unlocks the cabinet where he keeps his whiskey out of reach. He pulls out all the bottles and Whiskey begins to wag his tail, barking at Pa to give him some.

"You damn alcoholic. This moment isn't for you." And Pa never gives Whiskey alcohol, but he does steal a few licks from Pa's glass when he can. I caught the giant bear red-handed. Now, Pa never leaves his glass unattended. All because of Whiskey.

Whiskey grumbles, then circles the floor before plopping down with a grunt.

Pa pulls out an old worn book. He gives me an unsure glance, pausing as he rethinks his decision, then shuffles to the table again. The book is a dark green, the edges torn, and in the middle there's a large W.

But next to the W is an M.

"What's this?"

He sighs. "Please, don't be mad at me," he begs. "I didn't tell you because I wanted you to have a normal life. I knew that was close to impossible when you had your eyes set on that estate. Maven, the Wildes' and the Monreauxs go back centuries." He places his hand in the middle of the book and the metal clasp opens.

I jump out of my chair and point to the book. "What the fuck was that? What was that? How did you... how did the... when..." I'm at a loss for words.

"The rumors of us being related to Sarah Wildes are true. We are from a long line of witches and warlocks. After Sarah burned at the stake, that's when everything started to change for us. She died in 1692 when she was the coven witch for the Monreauxs. She helped protect them, but when she died, so died her protection and that's when vampires started to dwindle. It was said when a Wildes witch and a Monreaux reunite, our magic will awaken. I didn't think anything of it, but when you said you had dreams, I knew they weren't just any dreams. They were visions. You were reliving something, weren't you?"

I shake my head. I don't know if I want to hear anymore. My entire body is trembling in betrayal. All this time, I've been lied to about who I am.

"Your magic is coming to life, Maven. I didn't think it would be possible. I truly thought the hope for our kind was gone, that our magic had died, but when you started wanting that estate, a part of me wondered. You want to know why people point fingers at you? They are afraid of your power."

"I don't give a fuck about power!" I yell, grabbing the damn book that links me and Alexander. "I don't care about magic. I don't want to be a witch. You think all these years, I cared about that? Don't you think my life would have been easier to understand if I knew why I was such an outcast? People fear me, Pa. It isn't because I'm powerful, it's because they know what I could be capable of. You're saying I'm related to a witch, that I'm meant to be the witch for the Monreauxs again, but how can that happen when Alexander isn't real? I don't even know how to cast a spell. I don't even know a spell. I spent my entire night talking to a vampire and you're telling me I'm a witch who is coming into her powers?" I cry, slamming the book on the table, my face red as I stare into his eyes. "You don't think I had a right to know? I want nothing to do with that estate now. I'm not going to be a part of some predestined plan."

"But you already are. I don't know your role with Alexander, but I do know magic, Maven Wildes. Magic isn't something you can ignore. It's set in the ground, the trees, the dirt, the house you want so bad, it's in your blood. It's rooted. You are pulled to that house because that's where your magic belongs." With a flick of his wrist, the book opens and flips to the last page. "This is the last thing Sarah wrote before she died. No other witches have written in it since. She had the gift to see into the future. She said a witch of her lineage will change the path for us and all paranormal kind. She'll have long red hair, green eyes, and her heart will belong to the one she's meant to protect." Pa closes the book and stares at me, but I look away, not knowing how to accept this information. "Her written word is stone, Maven. She wrote everything down. This book was supposed to be in the hands of the coven, but they vanished, and we've protected the book since. I don't know what happened to them, but perhaps Alexander will know."

"He doesn't even know why he's there," I grit. "He has no answers. You think this... book will help? I just learned my life was never my own. It's been meant to serve. The last thing I want to be is a servant."

"Being a witch to a coven is the greatest honor a witch could ever receive."

"What coven?" I scream, throwing the book across the room. "They are all dead. No one is left." I sob, thinking about how lonely Alexander must be. "You're saying my heart belongs to a ghost. There isn't magic powerful enough to bridge that gap, Pa."

"Magic is as powerful as you want it to be. You might not like that you were destined for that estate instead of having this dream that it was meant to be yours. Isn't that the same thing? Isn't it better that it is literally meant to be yours, Maven? Fate has brought you to that abandoned estate to bring it back to life."

"And then what?" I ask, resigned, my tone flat. "I bring it to life. I breathe magic into it and what then? Alexander is still a ghost."

"Maybe he won't be if you accept what is, Maven." The bright blue escapes his eyes, and he flops down into the chair, exhausted. "I'm not the warlock I used to be. Flipping pages in a book is all I can do. I am not powerful. I never was. Magic barely lives in me, but witches become stronger when they have a coven, not because of other witches. It's other witches who drain a witches power. Having the strength of a coven to protect you... it's beautiful."

"It's pointless. The Monreaux Coven is dead. And I don't know why I keep talking about this with you. I am having none of it." I head to the door and pause, staring out at the rolling plains. "Sarah was wrong." I run out the door without looking back at the man I thought never lied to me.

My entire life I felt different, and he had all the answers. All this time, all the long talks about the Monreaux estate, and he knew. Maybe knowing earlier would have changed things for me, but right now, I want nothing to do with it.

I don't want to be the thing the people in this town have whispered about. I've yearned for acceptance and maybe that's stupid and naïve of me, but what hurts now is knowing I'll never get it.

If Dottie were to know this, I know I'd lose her.

I'm alone in this.

Alexander doesn't count, because in the grand scheme of things, he isn't here.

Love can't be born out of magic, it's not real then, it's just... a spell.

Chapter Eight

ALEXANDER

Her distress beacons me like a light from the dark.

I don't know how long it's been since she has been here, but she's wearing a new outfit, what I now know are called leggings and a shirt that hangs off the shoulder. Even from upstairs and as I look out the window, the ridge of her collarbone meeting the elegant curve of her neck entices me.

I want her, but she wasn't wrong about what she said. What kind of life would there be for her with me? It's best if I remain in the night, quiet, so she can live her life the way she wants. It will hurt to watch her live without me, but maybe if I stay in the void, I'll become the void, and she won't have to worry about me again.

She stares up at the house, her flaming hair drifting in the slight breeze, standing stark against the gloomy sky.

I want to be closer to her, I need to be, and just the thought has me outside on the porch instead of upstairs.

The sudden transportation with a mere thought must be a ghost thing.

Her hands grip her hips as she continues to look at the house, but I continue to watch her, every part of my soul calling out to her.

To *save* me.
To *fix* me.
To bring *me* out of the cold.

My fangs lengthen when she lifts her hair up into that messy bun, showing the delicate sides of her neck.

She's mine.

She knows it.

I know it.

I just have to respect her space until she realizes that fighting me is useless. I always win.

Dead or alive.

I remain quiet as she walks around the truck and grabs a toolbox, carrying it to the bottom of the porch. I can't help myself, I stand next to her, needing to be close and she freezes.

Leaning down, I close my eyes and relish in her warmth. I feel how uncertain she is, the confusion, the restless in her heart. I want to know what happened to the curious woman who walked through the door to make her into the scared woman standing in front of me now.

"Alexander, I know you're here."

I keep my lips shut and take a step away, respecting her boundaries.

"Don't even think about staying quiet. I know you're here. I feel you. You're all around me. There's a buzz hovering over my skin and that only happens because of you. Answer me."

I don't.

A flash of disappointment crosses her face, the sides of her mouth curve into a frown. I don't like the sadness pinching her eyes, but she wanted space, so I'm doing what she wants. Isn't that what matters?

Sighing she changes the subject, "I have a friend coming over today to help me rip the porch out. I found a picture of the estate and I think I can replicate it." She pulls out an odd device from her pocket and places it on the hood of the truck. I peer over her shoulder and on the surface is a picture of what my home used to be. The photo is vivid. I can't believe it fits on that little device. How do they get images in there?

Grinning, I reach out and try to touch the picture. The house looks like it was built recently. The colors are so bright and clean. The pictures I'm used to are blurry and the color was dull, if the photo had color at all. The mansion is painted white, the shutters black, but the door is a deep blooming red.

The porch in the picture had just been built and now half of it lies on the ground. I loved this porch. Atreyu and I sat on these steps many a nights, laughing as we drank blood martinis. We've told many stories to one another on this porch. I've stopped him from attacking father, from running away, and there are plenty of times where we have physically fought right on those steps.

I experienced my first kiss on that porch.

Tears.

Heartache.

Everything happened on those steps.

The house is a memory and when I look at the trash that has become of it, it pains me. I don't know what Maven saw in this estate, but maybe it's best if she cut her losses.

I'll sink into oblivion anyway. What's the difference?

Why is it I can remember that, but I can't remember the events leading up to me being a ghost?

"You're sad," she says, cutting through the silence. "Your energy changed."

Rolling my lips together to keep myself quiet, I disperse into the house, finding myself in the library. The comfort of books was where I always went when something was bothering me when I was alive. Why would that change because I'm dead?

Well, dead-ish. A part of me still doesn't believe I died.

"Alexander!"

I grind my teeth together from her constant pushing. "What?" I bark, rushing out to the living room where I see her with her chin held high. "What do you want, Maven? You left, remember? *You.* I'm only staying quiet because it seems like that's what you need. Actually, you should go. This might be your property, but it was my home first. You need to leave."

"We need to talk. I'll explain why I haven't been by in a few days."

"You were able to be gone for days?" The question leaves my lips before I can stop it, but what I really wanted to ask is how she could be without *me* for days. If I was able to notice how many days had gone by, I'd be aching for her.

"It wasn't easy." She rubs her hands down the front of her thighs. "I learned a lot about myself when I left here. You're very overwhelming, Alexander. I've always been a simple person with simple wants. I don't have many friends besides Dottie, and I've never dated. I worked from home and lived with my Pa. I only ever wanted one thing with every fiber of my being and it was this estate. But come to find out, my life wasn't simple, and I didn't want this property because I actually wanted it." She begins to walk around the mansion, her arms folded under her breasts. She turns suddenly and I nearly run into her, not that she knows that, but I grab her shoulders from habit. It isn't the first time I've nearly run into someone.

"Do you really not remember anything?" Her eyes dart around the space I encompass.

"I remember plenty of things just not the things that matter. I remember my brother, Atreyu. My parents. My coven. I remember what blood tastes like. I remember this home being pristine. I don't remember what happened when I died. Everything is black and numb. I don't know what happened to my coven and I don't know where my twin brother is. I'm here alone, like you."

She searches the bookcase, looking the shelves up and down. "Do you remember anything about witches?"

My brows raise, not that she can see. I stand beside her as she searches for something. I'm sure she'll know when she finds it. Our coven witch slams into the forefront of my mind. I remember her name now. I nod. "We had a coven witch. Her name was Sarah. She was very protected but eventually the werewolves caught her and burned her in the trials. My grandparents knew her, but I was raised with stories. We didn't have a coven witch since. We were constantly vulnerable. It's probably why this house is such a waste now."

"My Pa told me—"

"Maven?" A woman's voice interrupts us.

"Your Pa told you what?" I urge her to finish her thought, cursing the intrusion.

"I'm meant to be here," she whispers. "I'm the descendent of Sarah Wildes. Pa told me I am coming into my power and that's why I wanted this estate so much. I'm your coven's witch apparently."

"Maven!" The impatient voice grows louder, and I hiss at the intruder, wishing I could scare her away.

"Which means you are the reason why the coven will exist again," I say with hope.

"I don't know how. I have dreams but that's it."

"Dreams? What kind? Talk to me. Maybe it will help me remember."

"I have to go talk to Dottie and rip out the porch. I promise, we will talk later." As she leaves, a book falls from the shelf and the title tells me everything I need to know.

Monreaux History.

"Idiot. Of course, the answers are here." I try to pick it up or turn the page but fail. I attempt to will the book to open since my efforts worked with the Ouija board.

Nothing.

Frustrated, I leave the book behind, following the pull tugging me to Maven. When I see her friend, my vampire instincts roar. Something isn't right with her. I can't smell her to tell, but she isn't all human.

I growl and Maven glares in my direction.

"Jeez, did it just get really cold?" Dottie rubs her hands up and down her arms.

"No, I'm warm," Maven replies.

I lean into Maven and whisper into her ear, "Because you're so fucking hot. You have no idea how much I want to sink my fangs into you, taste you, and have you beg for me." I'm not sure why I'm wanting to make her uncomfortable around her friend, but I do. All I have is time on my hands and ruffling Maven's feathers is fun.

I'm a ghost. What else am I supposed to do?

I smirk when Maven coughs, holding a hand around her throat. An image of me manhandling her with my grip around her neck, throwing her onto the bed while drinking from her femoral artery has me weak in the knees.

"Maven, are you okay?" Dottie asks, her painted pink lips pinch.

I need to get this woman out of here. She can't hear me or see me which is a benefit I can use to my advantage.

"I'm fine. It's just been a long few days. Come on, let's go rip out this porch. I have a delivery of lumber coming in a few hours."

Dottie claps in excitement. "I'm so proud of you for going through with this. It's such a huge project."

Okay, the high praise doesn't make me want to rip her throat out. A supportive friend is a good friend.

I stay near Maven, walking side by side, staying close to protect her in the only way I can. She feels it too because she reaches for me subtly, the veil between her world and mine colliding again, the bright orange color reminding me of a million fireflies.

That's new.

I wonder what that means.

"Thanks, Dottie. It finally feels like mine."

"As it should. You worked your ass off for this. Hey, where is Pa? I thought he'd be here with you." Dottie surprises me by ripping into the porch with her bare hands and tossing the ruined wood to the side.

Super strength, questionable for a human woman.

But she isn't human, is she?

Maven doesn't notice, but perhaps she's used to her friend's unique ways. Maven, my sweet, struggles with one piece of wood but with a grunt she finally rips it free.

"Good girl," I praise her and a blush forms on her cheeks.

Oh, she likes that.

Noted.

"We got into a fight," Mavin admits, and I reach for her hand, wanting to bring her solace. Her world must be turned upside down right now. We talked nearly all night the first night we met, and I know how much her Pa means to her.

"What?" Dottie stops tearing apart the porch as if she's an animal feasting on her kill. "That's unlike you guys."

"Yeah, well, he hid a big thing from me my entire life. I'm allowed to be upset."

"Can I ask what?" Dottie becomes nosey. She doesn't lift her eyes from the porch, instead, she waits to see if Maven will answer.

I sneer and it turns into a hiss, my fangs at the ready… ghost ready.

Maven rubs my arms, well, tries to, and picks up a hammer to get an unruly nail out. She remains quiet and I can tell she's debating on telling this woman the truth. I could always try to kill Dottie if she doesn't accept Maven.

Maven is mine to protect. She will only ever need me at the end of the day, everyone else, they are just temporary.

I'm for eternity.

The word eternity stirs a memory or tries to wake it up. It's on the tip of my tongue but eventually the feeling fades.

Maven laughs. "Apparently, I'm from a line of witches. Sarah Wildes to be exact. So everyone has always been right to point fingers. I'm here because my magic is tied in with the Monreauxs. I didn't truly want this property. I was made to. Forced to." I don't like the bitterness in her explanation.

I take a step away, feeling like I've been punched in the chest. It's in the molecules of my cells to believe in fate and when someone doesn't, it always surprises me. Especially, since it is coming from Maven.

Dottie doesn't seem surprised. She keeps working. And almost has her half of the porch ripped open. "I think it's awesome. I mean, you're a witch. You're truly meant to be here, which means this place is yours by blood right. What's so wrong with that?"

Yeah, I actually agree with her. "What's so wrong with that?" I repeat, crossing my arms at Maven.

She glowers in my direction before turning her attention to her friend. "He lied to me. I knew nothing about myself. Only to find out I'm supposed to be a coven witch?

A coven that isn't even here? With powers I don't even have?" She snorts in disbelief. "Sounds like a bunch of hocus pocus."

I'm here. Did she forget about that?

"Hmm," is all Dottie says as she continues to work, throwing bits and pieces of wood into the air. Something about the anger in her eyes reminds me of... of... something.

God, I hate this. I need to remember.

"What, do you think I shouldn't be mad?"

"I get it, but how was he supposed to break something like that to you? He must have seen some type of sign, right? Give the guy a break. Don't throw such hard stones, Maven. You have your dream house and on top of that, fate intertwined you with it. How cool is that? Stop being such a glass half empty." Dottie pauses and pulls out a tube of lip gloss and slathers the glittery substance on her mouth while she's working.

What a weird creature.

"Yeah, I suppose you're right."

"But that can't be the only thing bothering you," Dottie pushes. "You aren't the type to get so worked up." Dottie has made her way to Maven's side of the porch and Maven finally notices how quick her friend worked.

"Not fully human," I whisper in her ear to let her know.

Maven's mouth falls open and I go to shut her jaw by lifting her chin, but it doesn't work. I keep forgetting I'm on another plane.

"I'm not ready to talk about it. I'm still figuring it out."

Meaning, she's still figuring out me.

"Okay, girly. I get it. When you're ready, I'll be here." Dottie gives a bright, sincere smile and tosses the last piece of the porch to the side. "Whew, what a workout, right?" There's barely a sheen a sweat on her skin.

Maven barely got three planks out of the porch. "Yeah, crazy." She gives me a confused look as if she doesn't understand how Dottie can't be human.

How can she hear me, but her friend can't?

Sometimes, things just can't be explained.

"Well, I have to go. I have a tutoring session starting in an hour and I need to get cleaned up." Dottie kisses Maven on the cheek. "If you need me, call me. I know you said you were staying here tonight, but if you need company, let me know."

Knowing she told her friend she was staying here has me tingling all over. I'm excited to know we will have another night together. I can show her how much I need her and prove to her that *we* are home. Not the house or the stories, but her and I.

"I will. Thanks for your help. You were... so fast."

"It felt good to get some of that anger out. That must have been why. See you later and be safe. Oh, and don't think I forgot about Mr. Hot Security Guard dropping off the lumber. A protector and a businessman? Don't do anything I wouldn't do," Dottie winks.

My talons unsheathe and my eyes flip to a crimson hue. My fangs descend and anger rips through me, a roar causing the house to shake again.

Who the fuck is this security guard? The thought of another man touching her has me wanting to raise from the grave.

I'm going to kill him.

"What the hell was that?" Dottie stares up at the house and takes a few tentative steps backwards.

Maven tries to shove me with her elbow to get me to be quiet. "The... wind?"

"That's a piss poor excuse, but I'll take it because I'm not mentally prepared for the truth. Love you." Dottie waves and gets into her car that doesn't have a top.

Interesting. So much has changed since the 1800s.

Maven waves in return as Dottie speeds off and when Dottie can no longer see us, Maven spins around, kicking up dirt that floats in clouds around her feet. "What the hell was that? Seriously?"

"Another man wanting you like I want you makes me want to be violent."

"It shouldn't. I don't care about him. And what do you mean you *want* me?" She cocks her head and tilts her hip to the side, but I ignore that question and decide to answer the others.

"No? You mean a man, one you can see and feel the way I want you to see and feel me, is coming here? How can I not be mad and jealous? It's like every time I think we take a step forward, we take a step back. I can't fucking touch you!" I yell, my eyes burning at the raging thought. "Do you know how bad I want to hold you?" I take a step closer, my heart thrumming inside my chest, my voice bouncing off the empty space of the fields. "Do you know how bad I want to feel your lips on mine? Taste you?" I run my nose down her neck and inhale, not smelling a thing and my bones ache for it. "To scent you? For vampires, scent is everything."

"Lex—"

"—And we shared a perfect night. I held you the only way I knew how, then you left. I know I'm not enough like this." I place my hand against the apple of her cheek. "But even knowing that, I'm selfish enough to admit I don't want you to be with someone who is enough. I want you to settle for this, for me, for this house, and what you're meant to do here. Settle for me."

A stray hair floats in front of her face and she blows the wayward strand out of her line of sight. "We barely know each other."

"That statement means nothing when we feel everything." The wind kicks up and the leaves rustle together, a few falling onto the ground from the force. "Tell me you don't feel it and I'll go back into the caves of this house."

"Feel it?" She says in such a low whisper I can barely hear it. She lets out a half chuckle mixed with frustration. Her green eyes brighten, bolts flickering in the emerald irises, and I can't tell if it's my imagination or if her eyes are electrified. "I've felt it since I was ten years old," she yells at me, the sky darkening as she lets her emotions rule. She spreads her arms, and the wind gathers around us, sending the leaves rolling along the ground. "I'm furious that I'm here and you're nowhere to be found. Settle? It wouldn't be settling when I feel more than I ever have when I'm here, with you, in this house." A tear breaks her lash line and rain begins to pour at the same time, lightning striking in the distance.

A dangerous glow fills the clouds, the electricity veining through the ground as if it is chasing Maven. Her hair becomes impossibly redder, and her eyes have crackles of gold.

As the droplets of turmoil roll down her face, the rain bullets against the ground, the road quickly becoming mud. Watching the magnificent sight before me, I witness the tree branches dancing in Maven's power, the day disappearing behind the storms building above us.

Even though she can't see me, I wrap an arm around her waist and the crashes of the veils jolt like the lightning in the sky, warming me, almost as if I can feel the sun again.

Impossible. A man in my state shouldn't be able to feel a thing, but one look at Maven, it's as if I feel everything at once.

Having enough of the fucking what ifs, maybes, and fear, I grip her by the back of the neck hoping she can feel me. I tug her close, the rain becoming perilous, and the wind becomes stronger and untamed.

I stare into her eyes, wide and glowing as a solar eclipse in the night, directed straight at me.

"I see you," she shouts over the static of the storm she's causing.

A storm that's also raging within me, it only makes sense the environment matches the chaos inside.

"What?" I lick the water off my lips, darting between the gold flecks blazing in the green grasses of her eyes.

It's when I notice the fireflies of the veil are gone and I notice a faint white glow. Instead of warm colors, I'm reminded of snow with how the sparks slowly drift around us.

She lifts her hand to my face, the warmth of her palm restarting the nerves that have lied dead in my skin. "I see you," Maven repeats, bringing her other hand to my cheek to cup the edge of my jaw.

The clouds above us wring together, drenching us in heavy sheets of water. I can barely see her through the haze it causes, but I still see her emerald shards combined with flickers of flame, and chunks of gold.

"You see me?" I ask desperately, wishing she could feel the way my heart pounds in my chest.

She grins, her red lips painted wet, and I suddenly feel a thirst in the back of my throat. Maven nods, finally answering my question. "You're beautiful," she admires me, her tongue peeking out from her mouth for a split second as she looks me up and down.

I want…

To taste.

To devour.

To savor.

I rub my knuckles down her face, tracing the freckles sprinkled across the high cheek bones. "You can hear me, you can see me, but can you feel me?" The words are a strangled choke in my throat as I force them out.

Her lashes flutter shut as she leans into me, the snow heavier between us the harder she presses against me. Her hair is drenched and clinging to her head and shoulders, her clothes sticking tight against her body, leaving nothing to the imagination.

Her brows furrow as she thinks, and I want nothing more than to rub the wrinkle she's created away. "Almost. I can and I can't. You're so close," she whimpers, taking my wrist in hand and dragging my hand down her neck as if she's aching to feel me.

A roll of thunder shakes the ground beneath our feet.

Once. Twice.

Then a lightning strike.

It does this again.

And again. A catastrophic cycle on repeat.

When Maven flattens my palm over her heart. "I wish you could feel what you do to me," she says, raising her voice over the power she's created around us.

Thunder quakes in the rhythm of her heartbeat.

"You're showing me. I don't need to feel you when I can hear it all around me." The next wave of thunder is louder followed by a strike of lightning that would be dangerous to anyone else. "This is all you, Maven."

"I want to feel you," she screams on a broken sob. The scream has another bolt piercing the sky, hitting a nearby tree. A branch cracks and falls to the ground in a smoky heap.

My hands drift up her breasts, settling on either side of her neck. "You do, Maven. Just as I feel you." I smash my lips against hers, groaning as the veils bends to the point I think it will break, but it remains, keeping us just out of reach.

But that doesn't mean the closeness, the heat, the want, isn't there.

It is.

And I'm torn apart with it all.

I move my lips, turning my head as I control the kiss and she does the same. A whimper escapes her lips that I try to drink down.

She's right.

I can almost feel her, it's similar to being cold to the point of freezing, the chill settled in the bone. Then, the sun beams its warmth onto the flesh, and you melt, yet you can't reach out and touch flames, you just have to trust it's there.

And I trust Maven is here.

Because she is the sun on my frozen bones.

I break the kiss and press my forehead against hers. She holds onto me, clutching me, willing this veil between us to fade, but not even a Wildes witch is strong enough to break the planes of life and death.

The rain eases and the wind dies which stops the leaves from swirling in the air. The thunder grows distant, but the overcast remains.

She takes a step away from me and the snow fades between the veils as she takes her touch out of reach. Maven grins, opening the driver's side door and snagging blankets and a pillow.

Without one word, she marches to the house, her boots squelching over the wet ground. I follow, not making a sound, staring at the way her shirt sticks to her curves. I can see the milky flesh beneath the wet material and want nothing more than to peel the clothes away.

I want to drink her down, her moans, her whispers, her secrets, her skin, her orgasms.

Her blood.

I fucking need all of her to survive.

She heads to the library, stepping over the piles of ash, that have gotten smaller since the last time I've seen them, and that I've deemed so important. It's like the house stayed suspended in time, only to unfreeze when she walked through the door for the first time, allowing the ashes to finally dwindle away. It means everything that she's stayed mindful. I rub my chin, hiding a smile, glancing at the muddy shoe prints she's left behind.

The floors need to get replaced anyway.

She passes through the archway that leads to the library, the doors broken and off to the side. Maven piles the blankets on top of one another before tossing the pillow on top last. With a nervous smile, she strikes a match and lights the lantern she left the other day.

The glass burns with fire, and she sets it on the nightstand next to the Victorian chair I loved to read in.

"I want more," she breaks the silence between us, my lips still tingling from the kiss we shared moments before.

"I want everything," I reply, stepping into the room.

She crosses her arms over her torso and grips the hem of the wet shirt. Inch by inch, I'm graced with the view of the flawless skin of her stomach.

Images assault my mind imagining her pregnant with my child, her stomach round, my hands caressing the beautiful bump, and the baby kicking against my palm.

I don't know how to make that happen, but I will.

She tosses the shirt over her head, her cascading locks flowing with the material before it's far enough away for her hair to fall to her sides. The tips reach her hips, perfect for wrapping around my wrists and using them as reins to fuck into her tight heat.

God, I bet she's fucking perfect and made just for me. I bet every inch of her body was created and sculpted for me. My hands, my chest against hers, my cock gripped by her cunt, we will fit like missing puzzle pieces.

I swallow to coat my dry throat as I stare at her. Her undergarments are very different than what I was used to seeing. Her brassiere is a delicate plum-colored lace, dipping into a low V and her breasts are pushed up. My fangs ache to sink into the soft and giving mounds. I trail my tongue over my teeth, licking the tips of the sharp points.

Delectable is the word I'd use to describe her.

The lace is sheer so I can see the faint outline of her rosy nipples. My mouth waters.

And I wish I could feel her.

There's that feeling again, the chill in my bones.

I blur closer to her, hearing her breath catch from my sudden nearness.

"Are you afraid of me?" A question I should have asked when I met her.

She nods, her throat dipping as she gulps, casting her eyes downward.

"You should be. If I were alive, you have no idea the things I'd do to you."

The faint brilliance of the lantern emphasis the auburn in her lashes as she lifts them. "Show me," her breathless voice sounds timid, but attempting to be brave.

In a motion quicker than she can blink, I take my shirt off.

She gasps, her hands landing on my stomach, the damn veil glimmering from our touch.

Mark my words, I'll break this damn thing by the end of the night.

"What happened?" she rubs her fingers over a horrid scar. It's pink and ugly, eerily familiar to a bite mark.

"I don't know," I say honestly, the weighted regret of not remembering heavy on the words.

Because I don't know anything about myself other than I'm supposed to be here with her.

"I want to find out for you." She bends down and I move her hair out of the way as she kisses the wound. Maven is careful, her lips just a whisper against my skin so she doesn't hurt me.

I close my eyes and enjoy the bending of the veil once more, her warmth, the buzz it brings, it floods my veins with hope.

"You're gorgeous, Lex," she states, standing straight and undoing the clasp of her brassiere.

My vision flips to crimson, and she inhales a sharp breath, her movements slow as she slips the straps off her delicate shoulders. She pinches her lips together and lowers her arms, letting the seductive lace hit the ground at my feet.

The growl leaving my chest permeates, shaking the dust into the air as it loosens from the floor.

"I love that sound." Maven slides off her leggings next, along with her panties, revealing soft legs I can't wait to drag my tongue down.

"Good. You seem to bring it out of me often." In her next breath, my pants are off as well and her eyes land on my long, thick cock.

Enough playing nice, I remember how I moved the planchette and focus on moving her.

She yelps when I send her to the ground, hands pinned above her head, the damp tendrils of her hair splayed around the pillow.

"You're a goddess," I whisper.

We're in a library, after all. We can't be too loud.

I roam my eyes down her body, focusing on her nipples that have pulled tight into mouth watering points.

Our bodies align.

Our chests press together.

My cock is settled between her legs, the crown nestled in the copper hair above her sweet cunt. Another rumble of pleasure singes my insides. I run my right hand down her side, keeping her left arm pinned above her.

The veil explodes with light, the familiar luminacin multiplied by thousands as every inch of our skin touches.

Her eyes flutter shut and her back arches. The lights of the house flicker and black roses begin to grow from between the wooden slates, the green vines circling all around us.

Maven is bringing life to a dead place.

That's her power.

I should know, since death is what I am.

I roll her nipple between my fingers, the sparks wrapping around the pink morsel, touching her in ways I can't.

Bending down, I rob her of her next breath and use it as my own, slanting my lips over hers. Tingles spread throughout my body as her hands wrap around me, her fingers tracing the muscles along my back.

When did I unpin her wrist?

I can't remember.

I break the kiss, wrapping a hand along the side of her throat while trailing my tongue down the vein I want to use as my own life source.

If only I could break through this veil, then maybe.

She turns her head more, submitting to my urges, telling me it's okay to take if it were possible. I press a kiss to the side of her throat and keep skating my tongue down her body, wishing I could taste her flesh.

How unfair to be so close, to want so bad, to need to the point of tears, and not be able to enjoy the body and soul meant to be mine.

I suck her nipple into my mouth, and she cries out, scratching her nails down my back. The pain is a sharp tingle, closer than I've ever felt before.

"I feel the veil vibrating," she says in a breathless moan, her cheeks a gorgeous shade of pink.

"Funny. I thought it was you," I smirk, pressing open mouth kisses along her ribs.

She runs her fingers through my hair, the inky tresses falling into my face. It's like a barely-there caress. It's the only way I know to describe it.

When I get between her legs, they fall to the sides, and I kiss each supple thigh.

Each petal of her pink lips.

"Alexander?"

"Maven, my sweet?" I don't take my eyes off the glistening sheath before me.

"I've never..." she takes a breath. "I've never been with a man."

Everything around me fades to roseate as my vampire sight takes hold. My talons grow and try to dig into her hips, but the veil protects her from being marked.

I press my forehead against her stomach, clutching onto her tight as I try to breathe.

As much as I want to dive into her and claim her, I know I can't. The circumstances aren't right. She deserves more than that.

And I'll beg a dark witch with magic illegal to use to be brought back to life so I can experience Maven to the fullest degree.

"I'm the only man you'll ever be with, Maven." I wrap her legs around my neck and delve into her depths, the curtain that keeps us apart shocking her from the inside out.

Pleasure is to always be found even when everything is out of reach.

"Lex. Oh god, that... that feels..." she grips the covers in her fists, those black roses continuing to snake around us. Her mouth drops open on a silent scream and one blooming flower turns red.

"Let me hear you, Maven. I've spent too many years in darkness and silence to be denied the pleasure of hearing you scream." I kiss her core before latching onto her pearl, her legs shaking on my shoulders, the veil trembling at the same rate.

"It's like static and needles and boiling heat all at once." She tosses her arm over her eyes, her breasts jostling from the move.

While flicking my tongue across her bundle of nerves, she becomes louder with every stroke. I reach down between my legs and wrap a hand around my girth. Pre-come leaks from my slit, and I use it as lubricant to fuck my fist.

God, I want to come. I don't even know if it's possible.

I feel nothing while feeling everything.

Just like she is.

"Lex," she pants. "Oh, god, Lex." Her legs tighten around me one last time just before the veil blinds us as she orgasms, embers smolder snowing down around us like pieces of paper on fire.

My claws dig into her hips and she gasps, but not from trying to catch her breath from the orgasm.

"I feel you," her voice shakes, the white of her eyes as big and bright as the moon.

"You feel this?" I rock my hips and my cock glides across her sensitive bud.

She cries in response, and I hold out a hand as ash from the veil floats onto my palm.

We broke it.

But I know it won't last forever, I hold onto her like a dying man in need of sanctuary. Lifting her arms and legs, I wrap her around me. Her feet cross and lock behind my back. Her arms laced around my neck. Her breasts against my chest.

And I cherish every second of this embrace.

I thought I'd want to tear her apart when I finally got her in my arms, but I don't. I've wanted to feel her body and taste her lips. I could sit here all night just like this if it meant feeling the tickle of her hair, her wild breaths, and the heat of her skin.

"I feel you too," I say quietly, my eyes landing on her lips just as a tear outlines the side of her mouth. My hands grip her jaw, my palm and fingers too big for such delicate features. "I fucking feel you, my sweet, sweet Maven." I press my lips against hers again, but it's the first kiss.

Our mouths move as if they have been destined to. Our tongues duel, hers timid and submissive while I tangle mine with hers, needing to dominate, needing everything in the short amount of time we have.

She clutches onto me, her nails digging into my skin just as my talons claw down her back.

I draw blood.

The scent hits my nose.

She smells of rivers in winter and honey when it's warm. I rip my mouth away from hers and her green eyes are glassy as they stare at the monster before her.

I don't let her give me her neck willingly like she did last time.

I take because that's what monsters do. I bend her neck to the side and strike, sinking my fangs into the pumping vein filled with magic.

A memory slams through me.

Beloved.

I squeeze my eyes shut and wrap my arms tighter around her as another orgasm rips through her, her wetness dripping onto my cock.

Tasting her, feeling her, knowing she's the other half of my soul, sends me spiraling. I latch onto her neck harder, holding onto dear life as I come, hot seed shoots from me and lands between her thighs, marking her.

God, she tastes like nectar straight from the flower, the finest champagne, the perfect combination to sate my hunger. I can taste her magic, the spice, the strength, like the finest top shelf bourbon that doesn't get made anymore.

Exquisite.

I'll never be able to feed from another again. She'll feed me.

My life will be in her hands for the remainder of eternity.

Before I take too much, I retract my fangs and lick the wound shut. Two small dots remain.

She's mine.

"My beloved," I whisper, kissing the middle of her chest, smiling when I hear the strong pump of her heart.

"What's that mean?" she asks as we struggle to breathe.

"We are meant to be together. You're my blood mate, the better part of my soul." There's a piece of the story missing, I just can't remember it right now.

"Make love to me, Beloved." She runs her fingers through my hair, and I tilt my head up to look at her.

"I want to, but as a man, not... this," I say painfully. "Not on borrowed time."

"That might be all the time we ever have," she says honestly, with sadness turning the corner of her eyes.

"I want you like this if the other option is not at all. And if you can drink my blood, then you're here on this plane now, which means, this..." she reaches between us and wraps a hand around my cock. She squeezes it tight, and I can't remember how to breathe. "This can be used too." Maven's fingers can't wrap fully around me, but she slides her small palm up and down the engorged shaft, using my come to help her hand glide. "Now, Lex, before there's no time."

She climbs off my lap and lies down on her stomach, her round ass swaying in the air as she opens her mouth. Maven's tongue wraps around the flared crown before stretching her mouth wide as she sucks me into her soft cavern.

A vicious snarl rips from me and my fangs lengthen. I yank her by her hair, pull her off my cock with a soft pop and flip her onto her back before covering her with my body.

I kiss her, tasting myself on her tongue before I line myself up to her wet heat.

"Take me. Make me yours, Beloved, just as you are mine." Her hand gently presses over my chest and a stinging has me flinching.

When I look down, I see her mark on my skin like a tattoo. A W with a black rose intertwined around it.

"How did you know to do that?"

"I didn't," she says, confused. "I just followed my instincts."

Instincts.

The ones telling me to fuck her into oblivion.

And also the ones telling me not to claim my beloved in this body.

Would fate be so cruel to give me my beloved on borrowed time?

I kiss her instead, tasting her spice and not a minute later, the veil stitches itself back together. The glowing light blocks our skin from touching and now I crave her more than I ever had, reminding us that borrowed time is all that we will ever have.

Chapter Nine
MAVEN

I see Alexander running through the forest. The inky black hair bounces with every hurried step he takes. He looks to into the dark behind him and that's when I see the teeth marks on his side.

He is bleeding.

"Lex!" I scream his name, but he doesn't hear me.

He runs right by me, tripping over a tree root.

"Fuck," he curses, holding a hand to his side. "Goddamn werewolves."

A wolf howls in the distance with screams and he closes his eyes, one lone iridescent tear escaping his eyes.

I reach to wipe it away but can't touch him.

"Lex, get up. Run! Don't give up. I need you," I yell at him, checking every corner surrounding me to make sure we are alone.

My dream changes again.

This time, I see Alexander with someone who looks just like him. This must be Atreyu. I wince when I see his injuries. The long bloody claws marks on his face seem painful.

"He killed mother."

"Atreyu—"

"—I know. It will be okay. Let's get to the catacombs. If we can get there, there's hope."

The dream switches again.

I'm in front of the house and Atreyu is carrying Lex, who looks like he is on the verge of death.

He is pale from the loss of blood, weaker by the second.

Wait, I've seen that wound before on his side.

I follow curiously, seeing where Atreyu goes, but with every step I cry silently, seeing the dead bodies of their coven in pieces. Blood everywhere I step.

I hold my hand over my mouth and weep for Lex.

I cry for his brother.

And I follow them into the dark hallways and basements. The smell old and stale, cobwebs lingering in the corners.

I'm cold and my breath is coming out in frozen clouds.

I watch as Atreyu pricks his hand and opens an iron door. The room is dark, and the air is hard to breathe. I hear the scratches of nails against the ground.

Rats.

He places Lex in a mausoleum, the only light is from the torch on the wall. "Brother, brasken ini ou sanguila," Lex tell his brother as they touch foreheads.

The tomb closes, the grinding of stone has my teeth aching when it closes, locking my beloved inside.

I catch a moment with Atreyu that Lex would never witness. Atreyu covers his arms across the top of the tomb and cries, the sobs heart breaking and loud. They echo in the small space.

Tears leak from his eyes, streaking down his face. He throws his head back and roars, the power trembling the foundation of the house again.

I can't help but mourn with him.

"Please, if not me, have his beloved come. He is too good and undeserving of darkness. I will die in my two hundred years happily if it means he lives." Atreyu presses a kiss to his hands and places it on the stone.

That's when I noticed the emblem on the top. I take a step closer as Atreyu opens the second crypt with the blood on his hands. He walks forward to his fate, the wound on his shoulder telling me he has the same destiny as Lex.

Running to the tomb, I notice a raised W with a rose intertwined.

The same mark I've left on Lex.

Did Sarah make these crypts? Is that why they are protected?

Atreyu closes the door to his resting place, and I'm yanked away from their horrible reality.

I wake with a sob in my throat... I was having the best night of my life and then the veil came back.

It was like someone forced their hand in my chest and ripped my heart out. To be so close to having him, to not at all, is a torturous agony. I'm thankful for the moments we shared, but I want more.

I want so much more.

I want the eternity he explained to me.

He's here. Alexander is here and he is waiting for me.

"Maven? Maven, what is it? I'm here, Beloved. I'm right here," Alexander says, wrapping his arms around me.

That damned veil in our way again.

I push him away and get to my feet. "Where are my leggings?" I ask him, glancing around desperately. I find my bra and put it on, then slip on my shirt.

"What's wrong? What's going on?" he asks, worry laced in his voice. "Don't leave me again."

The pain in his eyes has me bending down to kiss his forehead. "Never," I reply, the guilt vanishing as I flip the blankets and find my pants crumpled into a lump. "Found them!" I say way too excitedly. I pop them in the air to straighten them out and jiggle my legs in the spandex, then jump to get my butt covered.

"Tell me what is going on! Don't leave me," he repeats on a growl, his eyes changing from ice blue to red.

He'd stop me if I ever tried to leave again, not that I'd want to.

I belong right here with him.

I shake my head and invade his space, holding his face in my hands, the veil stronger than it was before. I can barely feel him now. Instead of a kiss on the forehead, I explain myself. "Never. I'd never leave you, but I think I know what happened to you, Lex. I've been having these dreams and I thought they were my imagination getting the best of me because you were so heavily on my mind." I smile hopefully. "They were answers you've been seeking.

You and your brother, you got injured." I placed my hand on his side to remind him. "There was a war, between werewolves and vampires. You barely made it to safety. Atreyu carried you through this house and I think I know where to find you. You've been waiting on me. Your spirit didn't wake because I'm the coven witch. It woke because I'm your beloved. Only beloveds and vampires can open the tomb, at least, that's what Atreyu said in my dream. Do you remember yet?"

He shakes his head, the black brows showing confusion as he looks away.

"I'm not wasting any more time." I take his hand in mine. "Show me the catacombs."

"Your dreams make no sense, Beloved. I think they are just that... dreams."

I don't know why his doubt pisses me off so much but lightning cracks outside, lighting the room for a split second. I take my hand from his and clench my fists to my side. "I said show me the catacombs!" My voice booms as loud as thunder and the same black roses begin to twine across the floor, showing me the way. "Fine. If you won't, they will." I point to my roses, which I still have no control over. I don't understand my magic.

And I don't know if I even believe in it yet, even though I should. Magic surrounds me.

My feet crunch against the soft velvet of the thornless roses. "Show me the way to him," I whisper to them, and they bloom more, covering an old door with a broken handle. The vines and leaves twirl, turning the gold rusted doorknob. The hinges cry out as it's forced open after so many years of unuse.

The roses cascade down the steps, padding the way for me, they bloom under my bare feet with every step, the magic in tune with my thoughts. The room opens up to what looks like another sitting room. The green vines climb up a bookshelf, forcing their way down behind it. I grab the bookshelf and pull it away from the wall. It swings easily on a hinge, exposing a darkened hallway.

I can't see.

"Bring me light," I tell my roses, following my instincts once more.

Each begins to glow, their middles pulsating with gold to show me the way until I run into another wall. I look around, searching for a door, until I notice the vines circling a spot on the floor.

"Open it," I order, and the vines strangle the handle.

The door lifts, breaking cobwebs that are attached. My roses lead me down more steps, to another tunnel like hallway.

It's a maze.

"What are you doing?" Lex stops in front of me, his eyes begging for me to stop. "The dead can't be brought back to life, Maven. I'm sorry you are stuck with a mate you cannot have," he says with so much sadness and disappointment, I can't decide if I want to kiss him or slap him.

"You aren't dead. You're in a coma from a werewolf bite." I shove him out of my way the best I can, which doesn't work since he can poof out of sight. "You won't be able to use that trick much longer," I warn.

God, if he isn't in a coma and I have to fight with a ghost for the rest of my life, I will be salting the doorways to keep him trapped so he can't vanish.

"I hope you're right." His voice comes from behind me.

I know I am.

The roses travel down the sloped dirt hall and take a right.

"Your magic is becoming stronger. It's beautiful," Lex compliments.

"It's because of you," I admit.

I have a feeling my magic would have lied dead forever if I had not met him. And my Pa would have never told me. I would have lived the rest of my life completely unfulfilled.

The roses stop at a large iron door with a needle protruding out where the handle is supposed to be.

"I think I prick my finger on this," I say to Lex, but only silence is returned.

I turn around to see what he is doing but he isn't there.

"Lex?" My lone voice reverberates off the walls.

Not wanting to wait a second longer, I hold back a groan when I press my finger on the needle. The drop of blood flows down the metal and disperses into a thin river in the nooks and crannies of the door. The rods of roses and leaves begin to move, the clanking of iron causing my ears to ring.

It unlocks and I have to throw my weight into the door to swing it open it's so heavy. The fresh roses follow me inside the cold room, the familiar cold breaths puff in front of me.

"I remember this room from my dream."

"I'm in here." Lex stands in front of the crypt. Monreaux is carved in the marble above him. "I feel it. I'm being forced to come back," he snarls. "I won't have death take me from you."

"It isn't." I press my hand against the door, the droplets of blood proving I'm a beloved gives me access. "Creepy," I say softly as I look around the small space. A stone coffin lies in the middle of the floor, designs of a W and roses capturing my attention.

"It's definitely not the royal treatment."

I chuckle at his remark, but the moment is fleeting compared to the seriousness of the situation. I hover my hand over the W engraved on the coffin, hoping that this fixes everything. Changes everything.

My whole life lies before me.

If this doesn't work, I choose coma too.

"Don't be upset if it doesn't work," Lex informs me. "I'm happier than I've ever been."

"You don't remember other moments of happiness because you're stuck where you are. You're meant to be with me." I press my bleeding finger against the stone and the blood turns black, darkening the cement. The stone begins to move on its own accord, a sandstorm of dust blinding me.

I cough, waving my hand in front of my face and when I can see the lid of the coffin moving slow, I use my own strength to push it away faster.

It doesn't work.

I will my magic to help, the roses circling around the lid, moving it effortlessly.

When the dust settles, I gasp when I see Lex's face. "My beloved," I whisper, running my hands through his hair. Whatever magic this tomb possesses has kept him frozen in time. For the most part, he looks healthy.

His clothes are disgusting, his shirt tattered and stained red, but I don't smell anything rotten, and to be honest, I expected more of a skeleton and soggy... bits.

His lips are full and pink, his dark lashes curl and frame his eyes. I tug on the useless shirt and see the wound, dried blood coating the teeth marks.

Feeling his body, his real body beneath my fingers is different than his ghost.

"I told you." I look over my shoulder to smile at Lex, but he isn't there.

And quickly my happiness fades. "Lex?" I search for his spirit everywhere, my eyes seeking every corner of the room.

Nothing.

I grip his face in my hands and cry, rubbing my fingers through the stubble on his cheeks. "Come back to me. I'm here, damn it," I raise my voice at his still body, watching his chest rise and fall. "I followed the directions. I'm here! Wake up," I beg.

No, I plead.

I rub my bleeding finger over his lips and blood red moons stare back at me suddenly, a madness etched on Lex's features as he licks his tongue over his lips. I watch as he inhales, his fangs longer than I remember.

His eyes roll to the back his head, and I slowly remove my hand, fear thudding my heart instead of blood.

His hand snakes out in a blur, gripping my wrist with a powerful hold. He sucks my finger into his mouth and moans, my nipples tightening against my shirt in response.

Before I'm able to take my next breath to try to speak to him, my back is slammed against the wall and Lex is towering over me, his talons wrapped around my throat in a deadly grip.

We stare into each other's eyes and right as he bends down to kill me, no doubt, he sinks his fangs into my neck instead, taking long swallows of my blood. He moans, trapping me against him with his body. I have nowhere to go.

I'm his for the taking.

Warmth spreads in my lower belly and with another suck against my neck, I explode, stars swimming in my vision as I come from the pleasure of his bite.

His mark.

It's been so long since he has had a drink, I'd let him have every drop if I could.

Alexander snarls viciously, like he is fighting not to tear me apart. His vampire strength can be felt in my bones as he holds on tight, my neck bent at an odd angle as he takes.

He breaks the kiss against my throat and flattens his tongue against my skin, licking every smeared drop along my flesh.

People lick their fingers when they are done with their meal. So right as I think he is about to call it quits, he bends my neck to the other side and sinks his fangs into my jugular.

Another explosion sends heat through my body as another orgasm hits me. He grunts, groaning as if he just came as well. I snake my hand out to feel the front of his pants, gasping when I feel his hard length. The material is wet from his release.

He's here.

In the flesh.

He is real.

He finally pulls away, his lips red from my blood, his fangs dripping from their meal.

I reach up and lick a stream from his chin, the iron metallic taste not as delightful as he seems to think.

"Beloved," his voice is so close, so deep, the marrow in my bones calls out to him.

I didn't realize how far away he actually sounded while on the other side of the veil. His words are crisp, an old accent twists his tongue making him sound sophisticated.

"You've found me," he finally says, but then he staggers away from me. His hands run through his long, unkept hair and he tugs before screaming, a nightmare unfolding before me.

My blood drips from his cuspids while prismatic-hued tears stain his face. I have to cover my ears the roar is so deafening.

It breaks my soul.

"Everything is gone. Everyone is gone," he states, staring out the door. "Brother."

He remembers.

But he remembers everything as if it happened yesterday.

For him, I suppose it did.

He runs out of the tomb and bangs on his brother's mausoleum. He cracks the door, and the stone breaks the skin of his hand. Blood smears and the stone opens. Lex dashes inside and falls on his knees beside the coffin so similar to his own.

"I'm here, Atreyu. I'm here. I'm here, brother. Come back," he begs, placing his hand on top of the W. "I can't live this life without you. Everyone is gone." He bends his head and sobs, a powerful creature, a broken man, succumbed to the pain of losing everyone he has ever known all at once.

I don't know why I didn't think about that before I released him from his coma. I was hoping our reunion would be magical, hot, and forbidden, but like a fool, I turned a blind eye to his past.

A past that feels like the present to him.

I step forward, feeling like I'm cornering a wild animal.

Tears fall from his jaw onto the floor, and I take one of the roses, ripping the petal off and wipe his cheeks with it.

"You are not alone, beloved. I am here and we will protect your brother. I swear it."

He blinks at me, as if he forgot I was here, his lashes sticking together from the tears, turning them into spikes.

Lex gathers me in one arm, tugging me close, while one hand remains on the coffin. His talons dig into the rock, scraping five lines down the side before his arm circles around me.

I hold him in return, my knees aching from the hard surface of the floor, but I don't care.

I have him in my arms.

And my vampire has so much healing to do.

"Maybe we can try to bring him upstairs?" I ask, hoping the idea makes him feel better.

"No, this room, these crypts are protected by Sarah's magic. They were the last two that survived the war before she was burned. He has to stay in here. So I know he is safe."

I nod, understanding his worry.

"But you're a Wildes, maybe your magic can wake him?" he asks hopefully, placing my hands on the top of the W in the middle of the coffin.

His eyes are round with faith. "Please."

I know it won't work, but I'll do anything for Lex. I kiss his cheek and lift my hand to his mouth for him to bite.

He doesn't even drink. He bites making me inhale a breath, but the pleasure is short lived as he retracts his fangs and I gently push my hand on top of Atreyu's resting place.

The blood doesn't soak into the stone like it did before. My magic doesn't buzz in my veins.

Just stillness.

"I am not his beloved. My magic won't work. I'm so sorry."

He seems lost as he stares at my hand. He lifts it in the air and licks it clean, closing the wound with his saliva. "It's me who is sorry. I should have known better. In my haste, in my broken emotions, I had hoped for something I knew was impossible. I just thought, I found my beloved after 121 years, she woke me from a poisonous coma, and she's a descendent of one of the strongest witches that has ever lived. Hope is a fickle thing," he mutters. "You awakened me." He takes my hand, and my heart skips a beat when the heat from his palm seeps into mine.

"Come on. Let's go get you cleaned up?"

He kisses my hand before bending down and whispering, "Brother, brasken ini mi sanguila."

"What's that mean?" I ask in a soft voice, remembering the words from my dream.

"Brother, forever in my blood." His fingers drift down the body of the coffin before his hand falls to his side as he walks out of the door.

I follow close behind and instead of a dark stillness in the room, I give the room life. My roses fill the walls and bloom, hoping they will keep Atreyu company.

Lex snags me by the waist, and everything is a blur as he runs as fast as he can to the library where our little home away from home is.

The joy and excitement leave his eyes as he squats, picking up a fistful of ash and watching it fall from his hand. "These piles of ash, they are my coven. It's why I didn't want you stepping on them."

I run to him, throwing my arms around his neck and hold on tight, burying my nose in his shoulder. There are a few cobwebs in his hair, but I don't mind. "We will bury them. I'll create a new place for them to rest and be at peace."

He leans away, his thumb outlining my bottom lip. "You will?"

"Anything for you."

"I had hoped all those years ago, I would have met you, but when I got bit by the werewolf, you were my only hope. We can only live for 200 years without our beloveds. And it has been 191 for me and my brother. He has 9 years left." His forehead falls to mine. "It took me so long for you to find me, what if his beloved doesn't come?"

"She will. I'll find a way to bring her here. I don't care how many books I have to read. How many spells I have to try. I'll make sure he wakes soon."

"I can't live without him," he admits, the glowing streaks on his face reminding me of pearls. "Just as I can't live without you." He glances around the house, a home of so many things that used to be.

I make note to ask about the uniqueness of his tears. I've never seen anything like them before. An answer to that question isn't important. His stability is first.

There's no need to rush his process of accepting his reality.

We have forever.

His coven did not.

He has waited 121 years to mourn.

And what is worse is, not only can't he mourn in a place he knows, but he also has to grieve in a new world he doesn't.

Chapter Ten
ALEXANDER

"We're going to have to go to Pa's," Maven, my fire-haired beloved states.

I shake my head, staring at a broken picture on the second floor. I bend down and pick it up. It's an image of me and Atreyu as teenagers, standing in the sun, and soaking wet from taking a swim in a nearby lake. "I can't leave him here alone. He never left me. He fought for me. He's in a coma because he was protecting me!" I throw the picture down the hall and right before it smashes against the wall, it stops.

It begins to float back to me, and Maven snags it out of the air, smiling when she sees the picture. Her magic is getting stronger. The photograph is black and white since I'm from another time.

"I understand your worry. We are only going to Pa's to get cleaned up, to shower, and to get you some clothes. Tomorrow, the first thing we will do is try to update the plumbing and electrical. Still, it will take time until we can be here every day. He will be safe here, Lex." She tries to reassure me.

"We will be right back?" I say, unsure. My brother is my everything besides my beloved.

"Yes. You haven't bathed in a while," Maven crinkles her nose at me while plucking a cobweb from the tangles of my long hair.

I lift an arm and sniff, the smell pulling me from my depressed thoughts. "My god," I cough. "How have you been able to be around me? The stench is making my eyes water."

She giggles, standing on her tiptoes to give me a kiss on the cheek. I have to bend down for her to reach me, but gladly will I bend for her even if it means I break.

"The last thing I wanted to do was tell you that you stink when you're still processing so much. It isn't a big deal."

"Maybe not to you, but I want to hold my beloved without her holding her breath," I grumble. "The magic in the tomb preserved my body but I'm afraid the smell is finally catching up with me."

She leans on her tiptoes to kiss me, and I lean away. "I haven't brushed in 121 years, beloved. Please, don't kiss me yet."

Maven seems heartbroken for a second before her long hair sways behind her as she tosses her head back to laugh. "That's fair. Come on, let's go. The sooner we leave, the sooner we can come back," she informs me.

I nod, taking one last look at the picture of my brother and I before I take her hand and leave. Her palm is warm and small, her skin soft as a flower petal. I got to experience her body once as the veil broke but even then, it wasn't the same. The experience was dulled, muted since I was in another form. Even her blood, it didn't do anything for me like it did when I woke from the coma and attacked her.

I *attacked* my beloved.

Guilt settles in my stomach. I have never lost control, but I smelled her, and her blood was all that mattered. My life, my need, it all zeroed in on Maven. I had to taste her, I had to feel the flow of warmth down my throat as her iron liquor encompassed my body.

I'm about to apologize when her foot goes through a step. We freeze, her eyes round with fear, an emotion I never want to see.

Everything happens in slow motion.

Her eyes, her gorgeous gems round in shock, and her hair sways from the force of gravity. Our eyes lock, a small gasp escapes her sweet lips, a sound of fear.

Something I never want to hear again.

The step gives way, the sound of wood splintering. She begins to fall, but I run, blurring at the speed of light and snag her before her body vanishes below the staircase. I hold her tight until we are in the living room, livid at myself that I let such a thing happen.

"Are you okay? Are you hurt?" I pat her body, checking for any wounds and inhale to see if I scent blood.

A low growl forms in my chest when I smell her ambrosia. Squatting, I grab her leg carefully and notice a few cuts along her ankle from the wood. The blood beading in small circles, gathering for me.

"I'm okay. You saved me before anything could happen," she says in a broken breath.

"I'll always save you. As long as I'm awake," I add, knowing I can't do much if I'm in ghost form again. Even then, I'll haunt whoever harms her.

I bend down and wrap my lips around her cuts, closing my eyes as her blood rolls over my taste buds.

Delicious.

Making eye contact, I kiss her ankle before I lower her leg.

She'll be able to heal when we fully mate. She doesn't know, but me drinking from her is only half of it.

We have to have sex first. Blood surges south, hardening my cock and my hand drifts up between her thighs.

But then I remember why we are leaving.

I need a bath.

I yank my hand away as if she burns me, which in a way she does, being around her is like a constant sear to my self-control.

"Let's go," I grunt, grabbing her arm and speeding toward the car.

"You know, we don't have to do the sonic speed everywhere we go." She holds her stomach, seeming a bit pale.

"Beloved, I'm sorry. Are you okay?" I push her hair back and my nearness causes her cheeks to pink. Her eyes begin to swirl, the electricity whirling from my presence. The wind picks up and I smirk, seems like I'm not the only one who can't control myself.

She could cause catastrophic storms if she isn't trained to control her power.

I'll put it on my 'things to do after 121 years' list.

I open the driver's side door for her. "I'd drive but it's been a while and this car is different than what I am used to." I peek inside the cab, unsure if it's safe.

"It's a truck," she giggles as she slides into the seat. "And it looks like you didn't lose your manners while you were... sleeping." Maven bites her lip, and her heartrate kicks up a notch.

The breeze decides to blow and carries the scent of her arousal to me. I moan as I inhale as much as I can. "You like it when I'm a gentleman?"

She nods.

I spread her legs with my knee and wrap a hand around her throat, elongating my talons until I press one against her bottom lip. Her breath catches and the pink flesh gives under the sharp point.

"I bet you'll like it when I'm not." The baritone of my voice deepening as the beast inside me surfaces.

Her nipples tighten under the layer of her shirt, the peaks dying for me to scrape my fangs across them.

Oh, to drink from such a sinful place would be demonic.

It's a damn good thing I'm on demon time.

I swing her legs in the car, then shut the door, making my way to the other side. "Drive. The earlier I shower, the earlier I can show you the plans I have in store for you."

She swallows and my eyes catch the movement of her throat. I want nothing more than to scoot closer and kiss her neck while she drives, but I'm a bit self-conscious about my scent.

I was always a clean-cut vampire, one that exuded wealth and an amazing scent. Maven has only ever seen me at my worst, I just hope she doesn't mind me when I'm at my best.

"I'll need to trim this moss. It's gotten out of hand," I say, knowing it's bad small talk, but I feel comfortable talking to her about nothing.

"I love it. Don't, please," she says, taking my hand in hers. "It gives the property character." The moss covers the windshield, blinding our line of sight for a second.

I bring her hand to my lips and kiss her knuckles. "Whatever my beloved wants," I reply as we exit the iron gates.

The truck squeaks when we come to a stop, and she peeks in the rearview mirror. Curious, I turn to the side mirror and watch as the gates close. Roses engulf the metal until it can no longer be seen.

"So cool," she whispers in astonishment.

"Very impressive for a beginner. How did you do it?" I lift a brow, wondering how she's gaining so much power so fast.

"I just thought about it. I feel like it's never happened before though. Not until I came here."

"Like me, your magic woke up here."

She falls quiet as we drive. I take the time to memorize our surroundings, so I always know how to get to her Pa's. I used to know Salem like the back of my hand, but I'm afraid I've gotten a bit rusty with my sense of direction.

Anxiety begins to pour from her in rancid waves.

"Maven? What's on your mind? You're nervous."

She chews on her bottom lip, another habit she does that sends my lust into a frenzy. "I haven't spoken to Pa."

I stare off into the night, my vampire vision spotting an owl swooping down to snag a mouse. "He's family," I say simply. "Life is too short to have so much pride to not forgive the ones you love."

"I'm sorry. I didn't mean—"

"—Don't ever apologize. It's okay." I push aside my sorrow. "My family is dead. Nothing can fix that, but you have a chance with your grandfather. Don't let it go to waste, Beloved."

She nods and I tuck a piece of her hair behind her ear. "So stunning," I whisper. "Such a beauty."

She presses her thighs together while ducking her head bashfully, the two movements combined contradict themselves. I love it.

My cock turns to steel in the flimsy century old material. I want nothing more than to scoot over into the middle seat to be closer to her.

I can wait another hour to be inside her, where I belong.

I've waited so many years, surely sixty minutes won't kill me.

"Can you tell me more about vampires? Can you go into sunlight? Does garlic bother you? Why are werewolves your enemy and why can't you heal from wounds inflicted from them? Can you see your reflection?" She rattles off question after question, bouncing in her seat from the excitement.

I chuckle, forgetting how new the paranormal world is to her. I keep a hold of her hand, stroking my thumb along the velvet skin of her knuckles. My nerves igniting from the softest stroke.

"Let's see," I begin to think about where I want to start. "We only drink blood. I can eat normal food, even like it, but I don't need it. Blood is what sustains us. We can go out into sunlight, which I can't wait to feel. We have a heartbeat, it's just a little slower than a human's. I happen to love garlic, but pure silver is a real bitch." I sneer when I remember the arrow that lodged into my leg. I rip my pants and see the scar. It looks like it happened just a few hours ago. It's hard to believe it's been so long. "We can heal from silver; it just takes time. This is from a silver arrow, but I was already infected from the werewolf bite, so it made my healing abilities non-existent. I'll heal over time, but the scars will always remain. I don't know why werewolves affect us. It's said it is because the species do not mix, others say it is because werewolves are meant to be vampires, but the gene mutated. There's always a power struggle between the two of us. And to answer your last question, I can also be in pictures. We do not live forever, regardless of what you've heard. We live for two hundred years and if we meet our beloved, that's when we will live forever, if not, we die. Back in the 1900s, our kind only survived because vampires turned humans or vampires decided to mate and form a bond extending their lives by a thousand years. That's the only way children are born from us. Now," I blow out a breath. "I'm afraid I'm the only one alive. There will be no coven." Thinking I'm the only one left of my kind sends a loneliness to my reignited soul.

Having a connection with Maven is a gift, I adore it, but the connection of a coven is different.

It's power.

It's home.

It's... a settlement in a vampire's nature.

With Maven, I'll truly be happy for as long as eternity, nothing will change that. But there will always be that longing pain that will rear its head, reminding me I do not have a connection to others of my kind.

"Until we have kids," she adds.

I slam my fist against the door and run my knife sharp talons along the leather, ruining it. "You can't say things like that when I can't have you like I want."

A smug, playful smile teases her lips and plumps her cheeks. "I know, but you can soon," she says, taking a left down a long dirt driveway.

I pinch the bridge of my nose to try to gain some self-control. "How can I meet your grandfather when I am like this?" I point to my cock, wanting nothing more than to sink into her virgin heat, drink her blood, and begin building our coven.

"Just think how much I'll take care of you later," she whispers, which does not help my case.

I think about death, pain, howls, and darkness, which wilts my want instantly just as we park in her grandfather's driveway. It's a nice home, nothing large like the Monreaux Estate, which is massive because it held so many coven members.

"This is where I grew up," she says, pride in her voice and a slight edge that wants her to dare me to say otherwise.

"It is beautiful." It's true. The acreage is small, but wide and open. There's a tree with a tire swing hanging from it that looks like it hasn't been used in years. The rope tied to the branch is tattered and torn, unravelling with every passing year. There's a garden full of different herbs and flowers, taking me back to when I accidentally set fire to Mother's flowers.

I wince internally.

Sorry, Mother.

I climb out of the truck and hurry around the other side, opening the door for my beloved. I never want her to have to lift a finger again. I want to do everything for her. As long as it is in my power to give it to her, I will.

I sniff the air, the smell of dog overwhelms me for a second before I smell something else, something close to death. I spin around and step in front of Maven when I see an older man on the porch with a damn bear by his side.

The bear barks.

Ah, I see.

That's the dog.

This must be her grandfather. He stands there with his arms crossed and a toothpick between his lips.

"Pa," Maven begins, walking slowly toward him.

His eyes move from me and that's when I see that familiar spark in his eye, the magic Maven contains. "Fireball." He holds out his arms and she dashes from my side, wrapping him in a tight hug.

A possessive sound rings from my chest and Pa chuckles, uncaring how much I want to yank her from his arms and pull her into mine.

"I'm so sorry for getting upset," she says, blinking up at him with teary eyes.

"I should have told you the truth long ago, Maven. Your anger was justified." He turns to me. "You must be her ghost?"

"Pa, yes. This is Alexander Monreaux," she introduces me with a big smile on her face.

I hold out my hand, then think better of it. "I apologize. I would shake hands but I'm filthy. I haven't bathed in some time."

He laughs so hard he coughs and that's when I smell it again, the rancid scent coming from him.

Does Maven know the man who raised her is dying? I doubt it or she wouldn't have stayed angry.

"A vampire as I live and breathe. I'll be damned. Never thought I'd see the day. I only have books on your kind now."

"I'm afraid that's all I have too," I state sadly as Maven's fingers intertwine with mine.

"I'll have Maven catch me up on everything. Why don't you go take a shower?" He offers.

"Thank you...?"

"Walter Wildes."

"Mr. Wildes. I'm indebted," I tell him, giving a curt bow of my head. The Monreauxs owe everything to the Wildes' anyway.

"I'll find some clothes for you and show you the bathroom." Maven's cheeks pink and I know not to disrespect a man in his own home, but I think that's the only way I'll make it till tomorrow.

"Maven, I'll wait for you in the kitchen. Alexander, it's a pleasure to meet you." His eyes fall to Maven, then back to me before scooting his feet along the floor, disappearing into the kitchen. The putrid scent of death lingering in his wake.

Maven takes my hand and leads me up the stairs. I look at pictures of my redheaded beauty that are on the wall. From the time she was a little girl, to her most recent picture of her and Dottie.

Something is off about that woman; I just can't figure out what.

The steps are lined with carpet and the walls have a vintage floral pattern that's peeling from the corners. The house is old, but it's stood the test of time.

Unlike mine.

Maven clears her throat and opens a door. "This is my bedroom and that door over there is the bathroom," her voice cracks, her hand pausing at the base of her neck, her fingers stroking the skin. Her scent changes, arousal thick which makes it hard to breath. Beads of perspiration gather along her hairline and her fingers rub back and forth along the droplets. I lick my lips, my gums tingling and my mouth watering to lick and suck.

I can hear the whoosh of her blood pumping under her unmarked flesh.

Hearing the life in her veins is a song I'll never get tired of listening to.

Her bed is small and there's a window with a bench to the side, perfect for reading and admiring the stars.

She has bookshelves lining the wall and a desk to the side. It's clean, minimal, but I have a feeling my beloved has only ever had minimal possessions.

No more.

She'll desire and have everything.

"Towels are in there too. I'll be right back." She sprints out of the bedroom as if she can't get away from me fast enough.

I frown, lifting my arm again to sniff and I want to run away from myself. "Remind me never to get bit by a werewolf again," I mumble, hoping to never be in a coma for the rest of my days.

Wanting nothing more than to look around her room and get to know my mate, the urge to bathe wins out the impulse. I head to the bathroom and undress. My boots are rotted, my pants so thin, I'm surprised they haven't torn from my body, and my shirt but a string covering my torso.

I take everything off and leave it in a heap on the floor, then stare at my reflection. For 191 years old, I don't look too shabby. I need a shave and a good haircut. I rub my hands over the scar on my side and flinch, the screams of death still echoing in my head.

It's hard to fathom so many years have passed when I'm standing in front of a mirror seeing the dirt on my skin, the dried blood, and the wounds. It's as if it all happened today.

But the truth wins in the end, bittering my mood.

With a sneer, I step into the shower stall and turn on the water, uncaring that it's cold. It isn't long before the hot waterfall drenches me, seeping into my tight aching muscles that haven't felt peace for years.

The glass fogs from the steam and I hang my head, letting the water flow down my body. I watch as the water swirls down the drain, tinted red and brown. My hair hangs in my face, a curtain to hide the pain.

Their screams.
Atreyu's shouts.
The growls, the tearing of flesh.
Blood.
So much blood.
Maven.

I rub my hand down my face and over my head, flipping the gnarly strands of hair back.

The heat feels wonderous against my naturally cooler skin and after standing there for too long, I quickly scrub my entire body five times and wash my hair until the water runs clear. I use some of her peach scented shaving cream and slather it on my face, stealing her pink razor for a quick shave.

I inspect the feminine razor, so different than the one I used so long ago. I shrug a shoulder, there isn't another option. The pink contraption will have to work. It takes a few tries for me to get the hang of it and chunks of my hair fall to the bottom of the shower stall, the man in me being set free as the past swirls down the drain.

Next, I find a toothbrush in a cart attached to the wall and I steal it, promising myself I'll buy her another. I use half the bottle of toothpaste to scrub away the years. When I'm done, I turn off the water and open the shower door to find Maven standing there with a towel in hand.

Her mouth opens.

I can only imagine what she sees now. I'm about to ask if she likes what she sees, but the scent of her blood gives her feelings away.

Her heart pumps faster as she looks her fill.

The steam swirls around us, giving us a faint amount of privacy. Her eyes roam down my body, stopping at my cock, then up to my face.

Then down.

Up.

Down.

I rub my fingers over my shaved jaw, smirking.

She doesn't know where to look.

"Look all you want, beloved. I'm yours."

I'm hard, the heavy girth weighed down by the blood and sheer size of the muscle between my legs.

My vision flips as my lust becomes uncontrolled.

Before she can utter a word, I have her on her back in the bed, my naked body aligned with hers.

The towel is clutched tight in her hands, and I tug it free, dropping it on the floor.

"We can't," she moans quietly as I inch my hand under her shirt to toy with her nipples.

"We have to," I whisper into her ear. "We're only half mated. I can't wait any longer." I rip her shirt off, the material useless and unable to be worn again. I do the same with her leggings, needing her skin-to-skin with me before I go insane.

"Half mated?" she asks, confused. "But we're marked."

"On the outside." I tease the tips of my talons over her skin, watching irritated lines appear. I grip a hold of her hips, locking them in place so if she moves, my nails will pierce her skin.

I hope she does.

I want to lick the wounds.

I bend down and moan in delight as I take her soft breast into my mouth, my tongue swirling around the sweet candy. My fangs unsheathe and I scrape one along her nipples, loving how her body begins to wiggle under me.

"But inside? You're not marked." I snag her leg and lift it over my hip, pressing my thick crown to her core. My eyes drift to the door and notice it's locked.

She wanted this to happen.

This won't be gentle or kind. Foreplay can happen later. The need for her is too strong, I feel the agony for my mate in my muscles, in my fucking bones, and in my blood.

God, I can't wait another fucking minute.

Her body was made for the taking.

And I'm going to take.

And fucking take.

Until forever comes.

Then take some more.

Bending down, I kiss her for the first time since waking, groaning down her throat as I become possessed. With one hand on her leg, the other wrapped around her throat, I control every inch of her.

I'm unable to mystify her like other humans.

I'm unable to read her thoughts.

I'm unable to love another woman.

My beloved is my eternity. There are no others. She'll always leave me guessing. She'll be the only one I feed from for the rest of our lives. She's my life. My heart. My reason to live.

Maven will never have to worry about not having enough blood after we fully mate. Her blood will replenish for me and only me.

Our tongues collide and hers flicks over one fang, caressing it as if she's sucking on my cock.

I almost lose control.

She begins to take deep breaths, having to stop kissing me to try to get her bearings back, but I attack her mouth again, her lips reminding me of clouds, assuming they would be giving like her.

Reaching between us, I rub two fingers down her slit, her honey coating me. I suck my fingers into my mouth, the ecstasy her taste brings has me breaking. She's a drug, consuming the molecules in my blood.

Now, I need more.

I'm addicted.

I couldn't taste every bit of sweetness when I crossed the veil.

I'm incapable of stopping myself from loving her. I was created to give her my life.

I slide down her body, just a quick taste, nothing more. I don't have the control to wait much longer. I skim my fangs down the sensitive skin of her belly, loving the tremble in her muscles.

My tongue flattens along the dip of her hips. She tries to tighten her legs around my neck, but I yank her thighs apart, her clit engorged and swollen.

She needs me.

Her petals are slick with dew, and I lick down her flower, gathering the nectar for pure selfish reasons.

"Lex." Her fingers slide through my wet hair as my name pours from her lips.

My lips kiss and suck onto her bud, her legs trembling from the overstimulation. The harder I suck, the more she grinds herself onto my face.

Where I am, between the valleys of surrender, I hear the race of her blood pumping through her femoral artery. I slide my attention from her tits, her pink nipples tight and pointed to the ceiling, and lock my sights on the side of her thigh.

I growl as I eat her pussy, my need for her blood stronger every second that passes. It won't be a mating mark, but a mark it will be, nevertheless.

Shoving two fingers inside her hole, I pump into her hard and fast while skimming my nose along her thigh, inhaling.

Savoring.

Sucking a purple mark onto her milky flesh, I gently pierce her skin, my teeth sinking into the vein without issue.

She erupts, clamping on my fingers as she comes. Her blood becomes sweeter in her orgasm, her pleasure coursing through me with every swallow. The taste of her orgasm triggers my own. I snarl into her leg as I feast, her essence dripping from the corners of my mouth as I grind my cock into the mattress.

Gently, I retract my fangs and lick the pinpricks, taking care of her like she cares for me.

Which is what she chooses to give every time she lets me drink.

I inch up her body, hovering over her looking crazed. Blood is smeared on my mouth, my hair hangs wildly in my face, and my eyes are that of the devil.

Her eyes fall to my stained lips, and I drop my mouth on hers, delving my tongue inside. She tastes herself, licking and humming from the flavor as I settle between her legs.

The fat crown of my cock slips slightly into her hole and another savage sound escapes me, slipping down her throat.

I've waited 121 years; I'm not waiting a second longer.

Thrusting my hips forward, I don't take her virginity gently.

I own it.

I possess it like I want to possess her.

She cries out, clamping around me from the pain I've caused. The hint of her virgin scent fills the air and my mouth waters. I bring my lips to her ear, "In order for us to fully mate, I have to pour every ounce of my come inside you," I end, nipping my fang along the shell of her ear.

The pain and lust comes off her in waves, her nails digging into my shoulder, and the sting is so much better than the veil experience together. To take her mind off the agony, I lick and nip along her neck where my mating mark is.

She sighs, the tender caress of my tongue against where I feed easing her.

The lights darken in her room and her roses spread along the floor, up the walls, and cover the door until we are submerged in a botanical garden.

Her green eyes finally open, her red lashes blinking at me innocently yet full of mischief all at once. Her nails turn from a harsh pinch to a tickle causing goosebumps along my skin.

I shiver.

She has the power to send me to my knees.

I begin to move, a rumble erupting from my throat as her scorching velvet walls grip me like a vise.

Her pulse races against my fingers and my vision zeroes in on the vein. I'm an animal for blood, after all.

I tighten my grip around her neck and with a sneer, I flip her onto her stomach. I almost hate how much I want her, yet at the same time, I fucking love it.

I crave it.

This feeling of how much I want to tear her apart and put her back together boils my blood and throbs my cock.

Her back arches and her ass presses against me, the globes thick and round as I peer down. "You're so fucking beautiful." I tease my talons down her spine, watching as I ease back, seeing the blood of her innocence coating me. "Fuck." I curl over her and pull her back by her neck. "You have no idea how much I want to ruin you knowing I'm your first, your only, your last."

She turns her head and her arms spread out, gripping the edges of the mattress.

It's a good thing crosses have no effect on vampires, or the way she's laid out, her legs between mine and her arms across, I'd be the one burnt at the stake.

But damn it, the one thing I am going to do is prey on her body.

"Yours," she whimpers. "I was made to be yours."

"Words I will never be tired of hearing." I lick down her spine, relishing in the taste of her sweat, of my beloved.

My awakening.

I press my chest against her back and slip my fingers through hers. The veil doesn't stop us this time. Her fingers lock with mine and her mouth parts as I sink inside her, again and again.

Manhandling her once more, I flip to my back, wanting to see her body above mine. Her hair tumbles down her shoulders, hiding her breasts.

We can't have that.

I gather the strands and hold onto them, revealing the curves of her perky tits. Maven's hands land on my chest and my eyes drift to where she is grinding against me, and I can't tear my attention off her ruby hair trimmed above her decadent center.

I close my eyes when they begin to hue red, the monster is clawing at my chest, begging to be released.

"Don't hide from me," the words drift over my lips in a whisper. Her palm lands on my cheek.

I open my eyes as she wishes. Her fingers glide over my fangs and I tremble while an unhinged moan leaves me. "Oh, you like that," she teases, but then that unsure expression pinches her face.

"What is it, beloved?" I manage to say through strangled breaths.

"Am I..." she rocks back and forth, gasping. "Am I doing it right?"

"Fucking perfect, beloved," I grit, trying to make sure I don't finish before she has a chance to begin. I help her move faster by clutching her hips. Her clit rubs against me which causes her to stutter and her lips to part.

What a beautiful sight.

A privilege.

To be in a coma for so long and to wake up to her, what a fucking gift.

To feel this, to feel us, to be alive for all eternity and have her by my side, it's all a vampire could ever want.

I flip us so she's on her back again and I sink in as deep as I can all while raking my nails down her shoulders and arms.

She cries out and I'm about to throw myself on to a bed of silver when I see the wounds I've inflicted, but she orgasms around me, clenching me tight.

I hurry to clean up my mess, flattening my tongue across her chest as a river of blood begins to spill over the ridges of her ribs.

"Mmm," I moan, her flesh stitching together under me as I lick her clean. I take my time with each scratch. "I'm sorry. I should have warned you," I murmur, continuing my journey over the destruction I've caused. "I couldn't control myself. I needed..." my voice deepens an octave. "I needed to mark you." Pale pink lines remain from my scratches, but I know when our mating is complete, they will disappear entirely.

"Use me for all your needs," she slurs lustfully, giving me permission to rip her to ragged bits.

I lift her up, wrap my arms around her, her breasts pressing against my chest, and I balance her on my thighs. We kiss, we bite, we groan in unison as I slam into her harder with every stroke.

I swallow her cries of pleasure and the way she touches me, submits to me, it has me pulling back on my self-constraint and I let my instincts take over. My ability to think clearly is submerged under my vampire nature.

All that matters is what I want.

Nothing else.

"Oh, fuck!" she yells as I begin to move at a blurring rate, unable to subdue myself.

For me, it's normal.

For her, it has orgasm after orgasm exploding through her.

Before I can truly think, I have us against the wall, cushioned by her thornless roses. When I feel her legs shake and see her offer her neck to me, I strike. My fangs pierce her skin, giving like butter from the sharp edges of my teeth.

Her blood flows into my mouth, sweet and smooth, my favorite drink. I growl at the thought of her never being mine, sinking my sharp cuspids in further.

Mine.

Mine.

Mine.

For all eternity and universes this world can change into in every future.

Fucking *mine.*

She comes around me one last time, milking the orgasm out of me.

I explode, throwing my head back as I don't contain my roar. If other vampires were around, they would know I'd just claimed my beloved.

With every spasm, I try to sink in deeper, and I latch onto the other side of her neck, making sure each mating mark gets attention.

We slow our movements, our skin slicking together, our breaths mingling, and the area in my chest stings again. I glance down to see her making her mark on the other side. Loving that she likes her claim on me just as much as I like mine on her. I grip her chin, slowly meshing our mouths together, the taste of sweat reminding me of the ocean in summer.

The roses begin to disappear, the vines sinking into the ground, disappearing as if they didn't just take over the room. The scars down her shoulders I inflicted earlier vanish, but her mating marks remain.

I tumble backward and sit down on the bed, holding my beloved close. I kiss her mark again. If anyone ever tries to take her from me, I'll kill them.

She's forever in my blood.

I begin to kiss every inch of skin I can see, our breaths a mixture of bliss while we regain control of our bodies. She doesn't know this, but in a few hours, we will need to do this again. We'll go into a beloved mating heat. It will last for days. We have to be together at all times.

Being apart would torture us, sending us into a slow, agonizing, insane death.

She kisses my cheek and whimpers when she slides off my semi-hard cock. I grumble in displeasure when my come spills from her, dribbling down her thighs.

A waste.

Even the sight has the heat taking over me and my cock begins to harden.

"If that's what I have to look forward to forever, I'll die happy."

I grin. "It will only get better with time, beloved."

"Better?" she scoffs in disbelief, disappearing into the bathroom. She comes out with a rag and before she can say her next words, I have her on the bed, face up, snatching the damp rag from her. "It... doesn't get better," the heat glazes her eyes.

We really need to get out of here. I feel bad— okay, I don't feel bad— for claiming her in her grandpa's house, but I do *not* want to do it again.

"I take care of you," I state, cleaning my come from her skin in a huff. The predator inside me is unhappy. She should always smell of me.

I gently rub the cloth over her swollen pussy, wiping away blood and come. Unable to stop myself, I bend down and shove my tongue inside, needing a taste of what I've claimed.

My eyes roll as another orgasm flows through me. I catch my come with my hand, four, five jets into my palm before I'm pulling my tongue free. I clean off my hand and my mouth, but not my cock.

I want her staining my flesh. If other paranormals scent me, they will scent her.

I lift her up, toss the rag into the laundry bin, then wrap my arms around her, kissing her tenderly, the way I love her.

Vampires fall for their beloveds immediately. Love has no time limit, no rules, it lives when it's meant to.

And we are meant to.

"Oh my god." She cups her hands over her mouth, staring at me in horror. "What if Pa heard us?"

"We can hope he won't stab me with silver," I joke, but I am slightly worried. I would deserve it.

She inhales a jumbled breath, rushing to get dressed. "That's not funny." She slips on a new pair of panties, red lace, and I tease my fangs with my tongue as I watch her dress.

I'll be ripping those off later.

Maven slips into another pair of comfortable leggings, which I love because they are so easy to take off. I'll buy her all of the leggings. Next, a plain purple shirt that enhances the red in her hair.

Before she can close the drawer, I'm dressed.

"Unfair. Cheater," she teases me, throwing her hair in a messy bun.

My eyes drop to the mark on her neck, and I close my eyes, the heat engulfing me. I will myself to calm down, taking deep breaths which worsens my need because I fill my lungs full of *her*.

She's going to want to show off her mark, knowingly and unknowingly, it's a way to let others know she is mated.

It pleases me.

"Well, I suppose we should go face the music." She swings the door open and for the second time in my life, I'm a little scared.

The war between my coven and werewolves was the first time.

Now?

Facing her protective warlock grandfather.

If all else fails, I'll mystify him.

As in, if my life is on the line for fucking his granddaughter under his roof, nothing a quick mental erase can't fix.

Chapter Eleven

MAVEN

Oh god.

Oh my god.

I just had sex with a vampire in my room with my grandpa downstairs. I can only hope he didn't hear anything.

Anything being *me*.

My throat is still sore from shouting.

I fuss with my hair, not that it matters, because my cheeks are burning and there is no way he won't be able to notice what we were up to.

As I walk down the hall, the roses and vines take over the walls, the black petals slowly wilting as if they have been there without water and sunlight.

They are gorgeous, but I don't know why they won't recede like they did in the bedroom.

Just thinking about the bedroom and the aching between my legs makes me want a replay of what happened. I don't think I could, not today.

I'm already sore.

"I can still smell your lust, beloved." Lex's whisper sends my skin in a frenzy, giving me goosebumps. "It's making me crazy. We're in a mating heat. You better behave."

I spin around, my hair slashing through the air when I hear his words. "Ah, what?"

He pins me against the wall, shoves his knee between my legs and presses it against my overstimulated clit.

My eyes roll to the back of my head as my mouth falls open. Lex's hand muffles my moan by lying it over my lips while bracing the other hand against the soft vines curling along the wall.

"A mating heat." His teeth snap together, and his eyes flick back and forth from red to blue, as if he can't control himself. His fangs lengthen and I want his bite again. My mating mark tingles with need and my heart pumps harder, readying my blood for him. "Because we are just mated, our bodies are in overdrive with need as we adapt to those changes." He closes his eyes and tilts his head back, the curve of his neck showing tendons and muscles. He inhales, growling as he scents me. "Anytime of the day, any time of night, you're going to want me to fill you just as I need to." His chin drops to his chest and the sharp points protruding from his gums make me want to dare him to prove their carnality.

"We need to hurry because I can't take you again in this house." He drops to his knees and buries his face between my legs, groaning as if he is high. "You have no idea how delicious you smell. Your virgin blood, your come, my come, all mingled together to create a gourmet concoction that has my fangs aching."

I whimper, forgetting where we are. My restraint is gone. He can take me. Right here. Right now. I don't care.

"But good things have to be savored, so I'll wait." He stands, his hand grasping the side of my neck and tugs me forward, his lips meeting mine in a harsh pace. His tongue flicks and his fangs nick my bottom lip.

I barely have time to register the pain before his tongue lashes over it, healing the small prick immediately.

"So delicious," he says satisfied. "Come. We have explaining to do, don't we?"

Oh, I'll come alright...

I take a deep breath and nod, taking his hand in mine as we walk down the stairs. The house is quiet. The only sounds are the creaking of the steps as we descend. The roses continue to wilt, and the vines shrivel.

Something doesn't feel right.

When we get to the main floor, I pause, glancing around the room to see what is off. Everything is where it should be. The couch is still crappy with sagging cushions, the remote is on the arm of the recliner, and the lamp is on.

"What's wrong, Maven?" Lex's voice is on edge.

"I don't know. Something feels different." I watch the vines along the floor and crane my neck back to see them across the ceiling, petals drifting from above us as they turn to ash mid-air.

His hand lands on my lower back and I gasp, my body coming to life under his touch as I walk along the vines veining across the floor. "Maybe you shouldn't touch me while we are here." I swallow, hating the words as soon as they leave my mouth. "I don't think I can take it."

An expression that can only be described as desire etches across his face and his vampire shines through his blue pools. "I'll try, but I might fail." His talons lengthen and he curls his fists, pressing them into his palms until blood drips freely.

"Lex!" I reach for him, but he pulls away from my touch.

"Pain reminds me to be in control." He releases a breath. "I can't be in control with your hands on me."

Arousal zips down my spine. We need to get out of this house.

He uncurls his fists to show me he is healed. I have this odd urge to bend down and lick his blood, to drink it like he drinks mine.

Where does that urge come from?

Is that part of the mating heat?

"Pa?" I distract myself with the matter at hand. "Pa, are you here? We need to talk." I head into the kitchen, confused when I see dinner on the table, but Pa isn't sitting there.

He's by the sink.

And he isn't moving.

I run to him, the roses crunching under my feet. "Pa? Pa, can you hear me? Pa!" I shake his shoulders, but his eyes are trained out the window, a slight smile on his face. Tears gather in my eyes. Oh god, he is dead, isn't he? "Pa?"

my voice falls to a crackling sound. I press my ear against his chest and hear the steady beat of his heart thrumming inside.

I slump, relieved. "Thank god." I press my hand against my forehead, willing myself to calm down.

"Is he okay?" Lex asks, standing on Pa's other side.

"He's fine. He is frozen, though." I wave my hand in front of his face. "I don't understand." I follow his line of sight and notice the leaves in the air, usually swirling and flipping as they fall to the ground, paused mid-fall. "Lex." I point and his brows arch, surprised, but then his eyes travel beyond them.

"What?" I question, not liking the look on his face.

"The sun is coming up. See?" He points.

Now that I'm not focused on Pa and the leaves, I do notice the orange and pinks painting the sky just above the treeline. The dark is receding, replaced by the morning rays.

"That's impossible. It's morning?" I rush to the living room and turn on the TV, needing to see the date since my phone is dead.

The remote falls from my hand, clattering to the ground when I see the numbers staring back at me. Lex is at my side in an instant.

"What?" He nearly barks, concerned that I've hurt myself. "What is it?"

"It's been two days since we've come here. Two days, Lex. We were in my bedroom for that long, how?"

He gives me a look that tells he knows how. "It has to be the mating heat. I don't know specifics. Maybe the answers are in a book back at the estate. Perhaps, you slowed down time, Beloved. You're new to your power. You aren't in control of them yet."

"I didn't just slow it down, Lex! I made it stop. Pa is frozen!" I shout, panicked. "I don't know how to undo this." I rub a hand down my face and shake my head. "I don't know what to do," I yell.

"I bet it was a protective instinct. We wanted to be alone. It was a big moment for us. I should have waited until we were at the estate. I'm so sorry, My Sweet. Forgive me?"

He truly seems pained, taking the responsibility for my actions.

"It isn't your fault." How could it be? He can't help that he made me feel so good that all I thought about was that moment, us in bed, lasting forever.

"What?" he questions curiously when he sees my face light up.

"I thought about... you know when we were—"

"—Fucking," he rumbles, his chest vibrating with power.

I tilt my head down and my eyes lock on the growing bulge behind the sweatpants I gave him, courtesy of Pa's closet.

I nod, my face hot with being caught. "I wanted it to last forever. That's all I thought about."

"And to achieve that, you must have frozen everything around you."

"How could two days pass? It doesn't feel like it." Oh damn, I bet I missed the calls from Dottie and definitely the security guard turned construction worker who was supposed to drop off the materials for the house.

"We got lost in love. There are worse ways to pass time." He brushes his lips across my cheek. "Perhaps, if you think you want time to move forward, you just need to think about it," he suggests. "And please do it soon," he groans, eyeing my throat. "I can't wait much longer to take you again."

I melt under his words, my body becoming pliant and free for him to do whatever he wants.

"I want to bend you over my knee, spank your ass until it's red, then sink my fangs in the hot flesh. Your blood will be right at the surface for me. You'll take it won't you? You'll be a good girl for me."

"Yes, I'll be a good girl," I half moan on a lost breath.

This is not helping the situation I need to fix.

With more willpower than I seem to have, he steps back, but the heat in my body stays.

"Pa, and then I'll take you home and fuck you until you feel me tomorrow."

"I already feel you," I admit as I press my thighs together.

His irises morph into twin flames. "Go tend to your Pa, Maven, before I do something to set us back fifty years," he warns.

Nearly tripping over myself, I back away, my eyes lock on the expanse of his broad chest and muscular arms. His breathing is fast and like the predator he is, his eyes never leave me. If I move too fast, he might attack.

Those black talons gleam and promise wicked torment, the flash of him tearing up my skin slamming against my mind.

It didn't even hurt.

And what's odd is that I want it to happen again.

The inky black tendrils fall across his face, hiding the animal that lurks.

I keep slowly backing away until I find myself in the kitchen. Letting out a gust of air, I stand next to Pa, refocusing my attention to where it is needed most.

"Pa, I'm so sorry," I say to him, brushing his white hair from his eyes. I think about wanting to have dinner with him now, wanting to remodel the home now, everything needs to happen right this moment, but nothing changes.

The vines are still on the floor, dying.

As are the roses.

Why are they there? What can I do?

I snap my fingers in front of his eyes, but like a statue, he remains still.

Stomping my foot against one of the roses, I scream. "Just put everything the way it was. I don't know what else to do!" Harmonic sounds echo in my tone, the glass on the counters tremble and the vines finally begin to trickle away, the roses dissipating into ash. A blizzard of dead roses fall until the last flake hits the ground.

It all melts away as if it was never there.

Pa begins to wash the dishes as if he hasn't been frozen for the last two days.

I'm not sure how I'm going to explain that.

He whistles and I throw my arms around his neck. Bubbles from the soap fly in the air as I knock him off his feet.

Pa grunts. "Goodness. I didn't see you there," he chuckles. "Did you get Mr. Monreaux settled?"

Yeah... I did.

"I'm so glad you're okay," I say into his shoulder.

"I'm fine, Fireball. I'm just fine." He pats my back, forgetting his hand is wet. "Oh, sorry."

I know Lex is behind me because I can feel him. I can feel the pull of my heart dying to be close to him.

"She has been very... accommodating, Mr. Wildes."

I narrow my eyes at Lex because his words have a double meaning.

"Pa, I accidentally froze you for two days because Alexander is my mate or I'm his beloved and I'm so sorry. I didn't mean to." I blurt it out, leaving out the details.

He needs to be spared some truth.

"You froze time?" he gawks, dropping the plate in the sink.

"Only you and I assume Whiskey. I can't tell." I turn to see Whiskey still asleep near the stove.

"And the leaves outside," Lex adds. "And who knows what else."

"And I assume, in order for this to happen, you were in a state of mind that you weren't able to control?"

I open my mouth to answer, but Pa continues. "Your powers are so strong, Maven. I wish I had books on it, but I don't. I'm afraid I won't be much help. I can only do the simple things. My power, since I didn't have a coven to protect, has weakened over time. Eventually, it will stop existing. It's why so many of us witches and warlocks are rare these days. You stopped time," he repeats to himself. "How?"

"I don't know," I say honestly. "I wasn't sure I could bring it back, but I just got so upset and yelled? I guess I projected. I don't know."

"I have all of Sarah Wildes books at the estate. Since she was the last true coven witch, I'm sure they have valuable information we all need to know."

"What I do know, is a witch is at her strongest with a coven. We draw power from vampires. They enhance us when we are theirs and they are ours," Pa explains. "You might not have a large coven, but you have Alex. Your bond is a rare one, which is stronger than any strength a coven can provide. You two are the coven now." He grabs our hands and locks them, unknowingly heightening my arousal when Pa causes me and Lex to touch.

Lex tenses and a quiet, strangled hiss escapes him.

My blood begins to heat, sweat adorns above my brows and at the base of my neck.

Unsteadily, I say, "Why is that? Why are witches and vampires linked?"

"I don't know," Pa shakes his head. "I only have what was told to me, which was passed down from generation to generation." He snags a glass and fills it with water before waving us over to the kitchen table, where the food has gone cold. He pulls out a chair and he is about to do the same to mine like he always does, but Lex beats him to it.

There's a moment where his eyes crinkle and his mouth frowns, breaking my heart, but his sadness is replaced by a smile just as quick.

"I apologize, Mr. Wildes. I didn't mean to overstep." Lex takes the seat next to me, our hands no longer touching, but I can tell by how uncomfortably hot I am that he feels the same. There's a glistening of sweat on his arm and I imagine the dew covering his entire body.

"No, no, nonsense. I'm so used to doing it for her, but I'm so glad she'd found herself a proper gentleman. I'm so thirsty but that may be because I haven't had anything to drink in two days," he teases, taking a long swallow of cold water.

I avert my eyes down, embarrassed, hoping he doesn't ask why.

"Witches have been around longer than vampires. It is said, now, I don't know if this is true, it's just a story.

Stories change with every mouth that tells them, keep that in mind."

I nod, wanting to listen.

"It's said that witches created vampires to help split the power and to also have a companionship unlike any other. People burned witches at the stake, so the witches made it to where vampires didn't burn in the sunlight. Silver was used for cursed magic, so vampires repel silver. A witch sacrificed her blood, her power, and the vampire was born. From that moment on, we couldn't live without one another, and I guess we didn't. Until now. You two need to be careful." He suddenly leans forward and takes my hand. "Promise me, Maven. You're a new witch, but the power doesn't just appear and disappear. Paranormals live. Everywhere. In hiding. Your awakening could be a beacon. This could change everything. Another war might happen before long because there is always someone who wants the power more than any life he or she would have to sacrifice. The longer you spend with Mr. Monreaux, the stronger you will become. You feed off one another, but in order to… join your powers, to lock the connection of the coven, it isn't just your blood he must drink. You have to drink his too. If not, your magic will be out of control without another powerful force to anchor it. Witches and Vampires are cut from the same cloth. We exist for them as they exist for us. You have seen what has happened, Mr. Monreaux, when a coven doesn't have a witch. They get…"

"Obliterated," Lex says, agony and sorrow dripping from every syllable. "We're strong, but not strong enough. I remember the war. It felt like something was missing. The wolves were just too much. I wish I knew why we were so weak against their venom. I hate them having an upper hand," he snarls.

"Every creature has a weakness, Mr. Monreaux. You just need to find theirs. They were created too. No one is perfect, no one can be strong against everything." The house phone rings, interrupting us at a perfect time.

Pa stands and tiredly walks to the landline. "Yellow?" he answers, then grins. "Hi, Dottie. Yes, she's here. She's fine.

You'll have to ask her. She has all those answers. She'll call you. Okay? I know." Pa rolls his eyes and huffs. "Yes, I took my vitamins." He gives me the side-eye before turning his back and whispering in the phone. "Yes, I've eaten. Stop fussing over me like I'm an old man." He hangs up the phone before Dottie can say another word.

I snicker. That sounds like Dottie. I catch Lex's eye and his jaw twitches as he clenches his teeth together. This isn't passion.

This is anger.

"What?" I ask him, keeping my voice low.

"Nothing," he smiles, but I can tell he is hiding something from me.

"I suggest you—"

Lex hisses and pushes away from the table, clutching his arm.

I stand just as fast. "What? What is it?" I rush to him and take his arm. It's red and irritated, the flesh healing faster than I can piece together what happened.

"I don't know," he admits, confused.

"Maybe you got bit by a bug. Mosquitos like blood too." Pa cackles at his own joke and Lex's mouth tilts to the left. "I still got jokes."

"Don't let it get to your head," Lex teases. "It didn't feel like a bug bite. It felt..." he tries to find the word and I can tell when it dawns on him.

"What?" I push, getting impatient.

He reaches toward the sunlight. "It's like I got burned." His fingers breach the rays piercing through the window and smoke begins to lift from him, his skin reminding me of embers burning in wood.

He screams and blurs away into a corner where it is the darkest, the smell of burnt flesh lingering in the air.

"Lex!" I cry for him and dash to his side, holding his arm as the burns heal much slower this time. I give him my wrist, uncaring that Pa is there, and Lex bites down, sucking in long drafts of blood.

I can see when he gets enough. The burns vanish as if they never happened and he lets go, licking the two wounds shut.

I didn't get overheated with lust.

I guess nature knows when survival instincts need to be more important.

"What the fuck?" He sneers on a broken breath. "I've never been able to not be in the sun. Ever. Vampires have always been able to go into the sunlight, Mr. Wildes. Can you explain this?"

I've never seen him so desperate for answers, so frantic. He seems like a lost child right now, his eyes darting around hoping to find answers.

"Does this mean I can never feel the sun again? Why?"

The words are laced with fear and they break in two when emotion grabs hold.

I take his face in my hands, sliding my fingers across his shaved cheek. His skin is cold, but there is sweat beading at the top. He seems sick, like he might throw up.

"I cannot go through my new life without feeling the warmth of the sun. I can't. Warmth is made to be felt. I don't want to live in the dark."

I tilt his head down by gripping his chin. His eyes meet mine, the red gone and replaced with so much uncertainty. The blue irises are expanded, a light grey filled with exhaustion.

It's a new weakness for him. A weakness that can easily take him from me and I won't allow that to happen.

"I don't care what I have to do, my love. I will make sure you are able to walk in the sun again. I will fix this. I will find the answers."

Even if it means I sell my magic to the highest bidder in order for him to live in the day, I will.

This changes everything. We will have to remodel the house at night now. He won't be able to go back. The home has too many holes for the sun to peek through. I think back to the times we have seen each other, but in his ghost form, he couldn't feel the sun and every moment after that when he woke up, we've been together at sundown.

"You can stay here. I'll get some blackout curtains for the guest room. You'll be safer here," Pa says, taking the words right from my mind.

"I can't leave my brother. I'll stay in the catacombs during the day."

"That's no way to live," I say.

"I won't leave him." His tone is stern and unrelenting. "He wouldn't leave me." He grips the back of my neck, placing his forehead on mine. "I wouldn't be a good man if I kept a woman like you in the dark."

"If it means that's where you are, then that is where I want to be."

"Crazy witch," he mutters with a smile.

"Stubborn vampire," I tease in return.

He kisses me. It's fast and I barely have time to savor it.

"Things are already changing, you two. We need those books," Pa's words bring me out of my head.

I hold my hand over Lex's heart, the beating not as fast as it was, but I know this news will haunt him until we figure out what is causing this.

"I'll vampire proof the house." Pa slaps Lex on his shoulder. "Don't worry, son. You're safe."

I wouldn't think Lex was 191 years old with how he softens from Pa's words. He no longer has his family, so I'm sure Pa saying that means a lot.

Stepping away, I hold out my hands at my sides. "I bet I can do it. No need to waste sheets." I hope I can. I don't say anything, I just imagine. I imagine keeping Lex safe with no sun allowed inside.

I hear a gasp, but keep working, my mind bringing up every nook and cranny in this house I can think of.

"Fireball, I think you did it."

I open my eyes one at a time just as Pa lights a candle.

"Black roses and kudzu intertwined together and block the windows. I never thought I'd live to the see the day," Pa states, brushing his hands over the plants. "You can manipulate the elements. You have no idea what power you hold, Fireball. Amazing," he whispers.

"How long will they last?" I ask, afraid they will die and the sun will send Lex up in flames.

"As long as they are connected with you, for as long as you need, as far as I know."

Lex plops down in a seat and holds his head in his hands.

This is a temporary fix to his problem, but I swear I'll find a permanent solution.

Even if it means sacrificing everything I've come to be.

Chapter Twelve
ALEXANDER

Two weeks have gone by and still I'm the myth ringing true. I live at night.

I've experienced misery before. When I got bit and had to lie in a tomb, that was miserable.

But so is this.

Darkness can't come soon enough. I'm tired of being inside. I don't like that I can't be with my beloved during the day, to protect her, to be near her. It's too early in our mating for us to be apart like this.

My bones ache.

We've barely had anytime to give into the mating heat and I can feel the effects. I haven't had enough of her for my body to be used to this new life.

My fangs throb.

I need her blood.

My cock pulsates for her.

I need to claim her, to feel her body tighten and to hear her moans as she releases.

But Pa is always with us, and he doesn't know about the mating heat. It's difficult to fuck the way I want to fuck my beloved while we are here. I hate it. I hate I feel less than what she deserves.

I feel weak.

She's been trying to prepare the estate for me so we can work on it together. She could hole up every window like she did here with her magic, but then how could we work when plants are in the way?

And it isn't like we can get much work done now anyway.

That fucking guy dropping off his wood hasn't called her back.

I snort. "Yeah, I just bet he'd be dropping off *his* wood." The thought has my cuspids lengthening over my lips. I'm going to drain him fucking dry.

"Woah, who has got your fangs in a twist?" Pa laughs at his own joke.

I smile. "I apologize." I try not to drop fang in his home but I find it difficult. He doesn't care, but I want to be respectful. "I was just thinking of something and got upset." I inhale to calm down and the rotten smell of death ruins my attempt to relax.

Instead, I worry about Pa. We've gotten to know one another over the last few weeks, pouring over the books we've brought from the estate to try and figure out her magic and why I can no longer be in the sun.

We haven't found anything, but there are hundreds of books to go through.

"Are you ever going to tell her?" I ask, pouring myself a cup of coffee and add a splash of milk. It calms me. Coffee doesn't give us energy like it does with humans. It has the opposite effect. My nerves stop firing so fast and my breathing slows.

I've gone through a few containers of coffee in this house, but I make sure to pay my dues. Luckily, I'm very well off considering I'm the only living heir of the Monreauxs.

I'm a billionaire.

And I'm only buying coffee.

Pathetic.

I need to buy my beloved something. A new car, diamonds, dresses, anything she wants she shall have.

A quiet purr of content builds in my chest at the thought of taking care of her.

"Tell her?" He sips on his own drink, bourbon, while giving Whiskey some too.

Never seen a dog like liquor but times have changed.

His heart rate skips a beat being caught in his lie, and the putrid smell becomes stronger the more nervous he becomes.

"You're dying," I say simply, throwing it out there so we both know what is going on. I tap my nose. "Vampire senses. I can smell the death in your blood, Mr. Wildes."

He sighs, then leans his hands against the counter while hanging his head. "You can't tell her."

"I cannot lie to my beloved. If she asks, I won't keep it from her."

He doesn't do or say anything for a minute before nodding. "I can respect that. Too much is going on. I can't tell her. Not yet. It will destroy her."

"So will the lies you weave to keep her safe," I state. "She deserves to know. What is it? Cancer?"

He shakes his head, letting out a sarcastic chuckle. "No. Witches and Warlocks don't get human illnesses. I would have lived much longer if I would have had a coven, but since I didn't, I lived a normal human life." He turns to me, picking up his white mug that's chipped along the rim and brings it to his lips. He sips carefully so he doesn't burn himself. "My magic is killing me."

I almost drop my coffee. "What? How does that make sense? Magic is your protection. It's a part of you."

"Right, it is a *part* of me. I haven't been able to use it the way it was meant to be used. Like other things that don't get used, say milk, it spoils over time. My magic is turning my blood sour."

"Can't you use it now? I'm here. You're a part of our coven. I know there is only me and Maven, but there is room for you. Always."

His eyes brighten and the way his mouth grins, closed and not showing teeth, tells me my offer isn't possible. "I am not your coven witch and I do not have a beloved. I'm afraid my magic is unable to be used. I can still do small useless things, like flip pages in a book or stir the sugar in my coffee. Remember what I said, we need vampires to help us take some of our magic, to control it, I haven't had that. All my life, this force inside me has had nowhere to go, so now—" He shrugs a shoulder.

"Now it's killing you," I finish for him. "How much time do you have?"

"Oh, plenty. A year before the side effects really show. Right now, it's a cough I get every now and then. A fever too. Like a cold."

"Will this happen to Maven?" The thought of her dying burns my heart the way the sun burned my skin.

It is so painful.

"No, not only is she your coven witch but she is your beloved. She will live as long as you do. And I'm so happy for that. Truly. I've wanted more for her than this life, the one her mother left and wanted nothing to do with."

"Is her mother alive?"

"I don't know."

I can see the sadness in his eyes of not knowing, the memories that he has with his daughter playing in his mind.

"Anyway, it's better as it is. She hated that she was pregnant, and she didn't want to be a mom. She didn't want to be here with me, so she handed over Maven and that was the end of it."

My fangs drop at the thought of seeing her again.

Pa chuckles.

"I'm sorry. Anything that hurts Maven makes me upset and it's hard to control my impulse."

"Don't be sorry for your nature and don't be sorry for loving my Maven. I won't hear of it," he huffs and waves his hand through the air. "That's the past. Maven is all who matters now."

I hear a car pull up the driveway and the brakes squeak while it comes to a stop.

It isn't Maven's truck. I know that sound like I know her own heartbeat.

I glance at the clock, making sure the sun has set, but I still have ten more minutes. I slam my fist on the counter and snap the edge off. It falls, slamming onto the floor.

"I'll fix that," I grumble, hating I have to live my life by the hands of time.

"I'll see who it is. It is probably Dottie. She won't stay away. She isn't the type and Maven has fooled her long enough. She's too smart for that nonsense."

I grab his hand to stop him before he begins to walk. "Be careful."

He cocks a brow at me. "It's Dottie. The only thing that hurts is her temper."

"Something is different about her. I felt it when I was a ghost. She isn't fully human."

"I know," he says, patting my hand. "But I don't think she knows, so it's best if we keep that information to ourselves."

"How do you know?" I ask, a bit impressed he was able to find out.

"Witches can see energy. Auras, if you will. Paranormals have the same one, they vary from red to orange. Hers is slight, but it is there. The color gets brighter the older she gets. I don't know what she is though, and she might not be enough of it to ever know. She's kind, strong, and loyal to Maven. She's good people. Trust me."

I'll still wonder, but having his word calms me. I give a curt nod and release his arm, watching as he walks to the front door.

I hear the squeaking frame of Maven's truck flying down the driveway.

And I know something is wrong.

I run to follow Pa, but I have another seven minutes before I can step outside.

Running my fingers through my shaggy hair, I tug the strands, debating if I want to pull them out from frustration.

I'd burn for her if her life were at stake. I'd send my soul to ash and dust if it meant keeping her safe.

That isn't the case right now.

She's fine.

And if I stepped outside this instant, she'd wrap me up in vines and pin me to the wall.

My arousal that's been weighed down by the stress of recent events slams against me and I lose my breath. The mating heat is still strong in my blood and until it is sated, it will get worse.

Tonight, she's mine.

Tonight, I'll claim.

We only have the stars now and I'm going to own her under them.

"Maven, you little witch!" Dottie's voice yanks me out of my filthy thoughts.

I grin, knowing Dottie means that in every insulting way as possible while also, literally, stating truths.

Maven *is* an actual witch.

"Dottie—" the truck door closes "—I haven't been ignoring you."

I glance at the clock.

Three more minutes.

"My god, I swear a century passed quicker than waiting for the sun to set," I grumble to myself.

"You haven't just been ignoring me. You've been lying to me. You know I don't like that. Just be honest with me, Maven. You know I don't care you're a witch. I mean, I am the one that told you it wasn't a bad thing, so why won't you talk to me?"

I place my hand against the wall, using it to perch while I listen. There's emotion choking her words, tears maybe.

She's hurt and it's real.

One minute left.

"It's hard to explain," Maven states weakly. "Come inside and I'll show you why. I didn't know how you'd react. And so much is happening, but I swear, I'll tell you. I'm so sorry, Dottie. I didn't mean to keep you in the dark. I should give you more credit than to think you'll run screaming."

"Damn right, you should have."

Time is up.

Racing to the front door, I grip the knob and turn, swinging it open so fast it slams against the wall. Next, I push the screen door open, the hinges creaking. It crashes shut behind me and my boots pound on the porch which causes heads to turn.

"Beloved," I say on a breathless whisper as I head down the steps. I go to her faster than anyone can form a word and bring her into my arms. "I missed you." I can't hold onto her long without my body reacting, so I pull away.

Dottie looks me up and down, arms crossed as she clicks her tongue. "So this is why you've been ignoring me? You find a piece of tall, dark, and handsome and didn't even tell me! What the fuck, Maven? I thought we were closer than that. You know I would have been happy for you. I don't know how he ran to your side so fast, but I'm sure he's just a great runner or I'm tired."

Maven coughs. "Something like that."

"I'm Alexander Monreaux." I hold out my hand, staring at the hue surrounding her. It's faint orange. Pa is right. I didn't notice before because I wasn't focused on it.

"Like the Monreaux Estate?" her mouth falls open. "Damn Maven. You really landed a good one. I'm Dottie. The one and only best friend." She smiles and grabs my hand, the strength firm in her grip. "Wait a minute..." she lets go of my hand. "Alexander Monreaux, that's one of the names on the will that was found when we were at the auction. Great grandpa?" she asks.

"No. I'm Alexander Monreaux. The one from the will," I decide to be upfront and honest.

She blinks at me for a few seconds before tossing her head back and laughing. "Oh, Maven. He is funny too. That's not possible."

"I was in a coma for 121 years because I got bit by a werewolf and vampires can't heal from werewolf bites. The only way to wake up from that is for my beloved to find me, the one I'm meant to spend eternity with. When Maven came to the estate, she woke up my ghost, but not my body, not until she found me. When the house shook, and you heard a roar of sorts when you left that day from ripping the porch out? That was me. You couldn't see me, but I was next to Maven. She's related to Sarah Wildes, our old coven witch. Maven's powers became present when she met me because she's my coven witch. I'm a vampire and now I can't go out into the sun for some reason which is what she's been trying to find out, on top of getting the estate sun-proofed for me. We'll be over there tonight. Does that cover it?" I ask Maven, knowing our story sounds like fiction.

People love the idea of finding love in fiction.

Until they are confronted with it.

"Nope, that about covers it." Maven twists hers fingers together and rocks on her feet.

I wait for the typical response from Dottie.

The, "I'm crazy and need help" or some bullshit like that.

Dottie looks me up and down, uncrosses her arms and drops her hands to her hips. "Prove it," she says.

"Prove it?" I echo.

"Yep. Prove you're a vampire and all can be forgiven."

"You don't have to," Maven whispers, her hand landing on my arm.

"No need to hide from your best friend since she's going to be around a lot."

"Damn straight," Dottie agrees. "So let's see it. Come on. Show me your fangs." I can tell she doesn't believe me.

I could mystify her, but I find that very rude to do. It's a breach of privacy and should only be used in emergencies.

I turn to Dottie and lift one hand, causing my talons to lengthen at the same time my fangs show. My eyes turn a flaming red, nearly the same color as Maven's hair.

Dottie's mouth falls open before she steps closer and cocks her head, lifting a finger to touch my fangs.

I'm about to wrap my hand around her wrist to stop her. My fangs are only for Maven to touch, but Maven beats me to it.

"Ow," Dottie says on half a laugh.

"Sorry, but please don't touch him or his fangs. They are mine and I'm territorial right now because we haven't been able to complete our... mating," she whispers so Pa can't hear.

I love that she got territorial. I want to whisk her away to the estate and lock her up, tie her to the bed, and have my way with her.

Fuck, if we even have a bed.

We will by the end of the night.

I pull her closer and drop my lips to her ear, growling how she likes, and her breath catches in her sweet throat, the one I can't wait to fuck later so I can see her lips stretch wide while taking me.

"Oh," Dottie doesn't get it at first but then the light clicks. "Oh! You need... time... sexy time. Meow." She pretends to extend claws. "Well, say no more best friend." She leans in and gives Maven a hug before turning to me and holding out her hand, respecting Maven's wishes.

I like that.

Maybe Dottie isn't so dangerous after all.

"Okay, then. It's nice to meet you. Your secret is safe with me. I'm assuming it's a secret? Anyway, love ya." She blows us a kiss before getting into her car and speeding away.

She honks, waving with a big smile on her face before she's out of sight.

"Odd woman," I say.

"But the best. All she cares about is the truth."

"The truth is all that's necessary for people to accept what is around them. I'm glad you have a friend like her. And I'm glad she's so accepting. Not everyone is. I was afraid I'd have to mystify her."

Maven shakes her head. "Dottie is off limits with that. Please. Never."

I can't make that promise. If it means protecting Maven and my brother, I'll do what I have to do, but since Dottie won't need to be mystified, I agree. "Okay, beloved."

"You two should get out of here," Pa shouts from the porch. "While it's still dark out."

I don't bother with the truck. I'm quicker.

I lift her into my arms and hold her to my chest. "You don't have to tell me twice, Mr. Wildes." The wind rushes against us and her head tucks into my chest to protect her face from the chilled air. Trees become one. The road becomes a tunnel from my vision narrowing.

The iron gate to the estate is closed, but I jump over it without issue, landing on my feet seamlessly. I slow to a normal pace and brush her hair from her cheek. "We're home." I stroll down the driveway, fingers of the moss dragging along the ground, the fog beginning to come in and swirl around the trunk of the trees. A violent memory surfaces, but I push it down so I can replace it with this one.

Solar lights line the driveway and stop when we get to the house. There are concrete blocks for steps that lead up to the door since the porch isn't there, but there is a new door.

It's painted red.

Just like I remember.

"You painted the door red." I stare down into her twinkling green eyes as she looks up at me.

God, how lucky of a man am I to have her staring up at me as if I'm everything she's ever wanted?

"I want this house to be everything it used to be before it got taken from you," she answers, and I fall in love with her even more. "The steps are iffy..." she winces as I begin to walk up them and one shakes under me.

Opening the door, everything looks the same, except the piles of ash are gone. She must have seen my expression because she hurries to explain.

"I put the ashes in small vases. They are in another room. I hope you don't mind. I didn't want them to get lost or blown away when we started the heavy renovating." She nestles her face against my throat, her plush lips heated.

That's when the last two weeks of built-up mating heat rears its head. Her lips brushing against me has me kicking the door shut.

"Go to your old bedroom," she tells me, placing open mouth kisses along my jaw.

I moan, barely able to move my feet, but warmth boils my entire body, the worries of everything diminishing and the stress becoming nonexistent. Now instincts take over, nature takes its course, the protective boundary is gone, and lust encompasses the air.

I bypass the stairs and jump to the balcony, not wanting to risk falling through the weak steps. I throw her over my shoulder, and she yelps, giggling while smacking my ass.

When I get to my old bedroom, I notice that this door is replaced too. It's heavy, black, steel maybe.

Expensive.

Curious, I push it open and the curtains hanging from the window are parted, showing the stars dancing around the crescent moon. The ceiling is lined with her roses and a few hang down, the edges of the petals glowing.

Candles are placed around the room, varying in size and shape. The flames flicker, the shadows swaying along the wall.

There's a bed in the middle of the expansive space. Just a mattress and a box spring with big fluffy pillows and a comforter we could get lost in.

"You did this without me? Is that why you've kept me away?"

"I wanted to surprise you. We've been holding back what we have needed to do for too long, and I wanted the moment to be perfect."

I toss her on the bed, her body bouncing as I begin to unbutton my shirt. "It's going to be far from perfect, beloved. It's been too long and while I've been a gentleman for your sake at Pa's, here, in this house, I'm a monster, a beast, and I've been caged." I whip off my belt and stalk forward, pinning her hands above her head and loop the belt around her wrists. I tighten it almost too tight. Her hands turn a light shade of pink from the constriction, the blood roaring just under the skin.

"What are you doing?" She licks her lips and tugs against the leather, the flesh pulling.

"Keep them there." I would tie her to the bed frame, but we don't have one yet and I have to accommodate. "Be a good girl." I run my hands down her chest and groan when her nipples press against her shirt. Gripping the material, I rip it from her body, showcasing another lace brassiere, this one a mint green.

I want her too much.

I'll buy her a new one.

With one talon, I slice the straps, then the middle, the dainty lace parting. Her nipples tighten when they touch the cool air and I tilt my head back as my fangs make their appearance. I can hear her heart racing and the sound causes my mouth to water.

Skimming my talons down her stomach, I watch her muscles quiver from my touch. The outline of her ribs show under her skin every time she takes a deep breath in. I smirk before righting my face into a serious expression.

I love how she reacts to me.

An eternity won't be long enough to experience it.

I rake my nails across her ribs, enticing a soft moan from her pink impatient lips. She reaches for me and with speed she can't match, I pin them above her head again, flashing my fangs in warning.

"I said keep them there."

She licks her lips, wetting them as her eyes drop to my mouth.

Maven's becoming feverish, I can scent it. Her entire body is flushed and there is a sheen of sweat canvasing her body.

"Oh god, please, touch me," she whimpers, lifting her head to reach my lips. "It hurts."

There's no time to play.

Next time.

Even if that's what I said last time.

I didn't expect us not to be able to give into the mating heat. And now it's all bubbling to the surface. She's right. We can't wait anymore.

It does fucking hurt.

I kick off my pants and line her body up to my cock, her center warm and wet. With a satisfied groan, I sink into her and both of us cry out in ecstasy. My eyes turn redder, my nails become longer, and my fangs become bigger.

God, to know there is no barrier, no give, that I'm plunging inside her because I am the one that took her virginity almost has me spilling inside her too soon.

Because she's mine.

Her heart, her soul, her body, it's all fucking mine.

I slam into her harder, loving that it's only me she'll ever feel like this with.

She stares at me with large round eyes, the moonlight dancing upon her skin, her beauty outshining the lunar glow.

I lift her legs and place them on my shoulders, pressing my cheek against her left calf as I slide out just to plunge back in.

Her arms lift and she reaches out to me, her bound hands flattening against my stomach. With no warning, I drop her legs, and hover over her face. I don't move. I keep a rough grip on her wrists and pin them above her head again.

"I think my beloved has issues listening," I hiss through tight teeth. Her tits bounce with every hard thrust I give, her cunt clamping around me, rubbing against the sensitive length as she sucks me in.

I speed up, faster than a regular man, but not as fast as I can give, and her mouth drops open.

"Lex, I can't. Oh god," she keens, trying to break free from the hold I have on her.

"You will." My voice rough and deep. "You'll take every fucking inch I give you. You'll take it all, won't you, beloved? You'll take anything I give you." I grip one of her hips, then release her wrists to pin her to the bed by her throat. "Say it." I'm a fingerbreadth away as my lips become millimeters away from her lips. "Say you'll take it all. Say you're mine." I tighten my grip, her jugular pulsating wildly from constriction.

She remains quiet, rebellion shining through those emerald gems.

"I said tell me!" I roar, my voice taking on the power I hold within, shaking the flames flickering the candlewicks.

I thought it would scare her, but instead, her muscles give and flex around me. She screams as an orgasm rips through her, gripping my cock to the point I lose control.

With no ease, no gentle caress, I roughly take her lips in a mad, barbaric kiss as I come, burying myself to the hilt with every jet that leaves me.

It does nothing to relieve the burning in my body. If anything, the heat gets stronger.

"I'll take it all," she slurs, delirious. Her eyes are glazed over and there are beads of sweat gathering in the middle of her sternum. "I'll take anything you give me. Everything."

"Oh, beloved. You have no idea what you're agreeing to," I say, sinking my fangs into her neck. I don't drink. I pull free and make my way down her body, piercing the skin above her breast.

She whimpers from the sting, but I can smell the lust permeating the air. She likes this. She likes to be bit.

Good.

Because I'm a biter.

Chapter Thirteen

MAVEN

He bites every inch of exposed skin he can on my front, leaving two pinpricks behind. Small droplets of blood roll down the natural curves of my body, and then he is there, licking me clean.

I moan when he bites my calve and when I look down, I should be horrified with what I see, but I don't. If anything, I'm more aroused.

His marks are everywhere. I look like I've been attacked.

I guess in a way, I have.

He settles on his knees and looks down on me, his eyes roaming across his artwork. His nostrils flare and the florid in his irises bleed into the blue.

A tremor rushes through my body knowing I'm bound to such danger, but knowing he'd never hurt me.

"Look how beautiful you look with my marks all over you." He rubs his callused palm down my leg, each bite pulses with pain and pleasure.

His come leaks from me, slicking the space between my legs. I try to pinch my thighs together, but he isn't having it. He pushes my legs apart and hums in delight. His finger rubs along my clit while another scoops his seed and pushes it inside.

My eyes roll to the back of my head and the lights flicker in the house, from me.

"Someone needs to learn more control," he chuckles darkly while pinching my clit reciting a sharp gasp from me. "My beloved is so gorgeous. You were made for me."

"Please," I beg, my pussy throbbing with desire for him. It hurts.

"Please? Mmmm, beloved. I don't think you know what that does to me. I love to hear you beg." He flips me over suddenly and unhooks the belt from my wrists.

My hands tingle as the blood rushes back to them.

I turn my head just to see him press a kiss to my shoulder. He gives me a crooked smile before taking another bite out of me. He trails kisses leaving adoration in the trails his lips create and licks every wound, taking his time as he tortures me in the best way.

He pauses at my ass and grips the globes with his hands, the sharp points of the talons biting my skin.

"Perfection. Flawless." He kisses each cheek, and the caress feels so good, the softness of his touch. He rubs his cheek against me, the rough stubble marking my skin.

But the tenderness is short lived when he bites my left cheek, sinking his fangs into the meaty muscle. I expect him to release me quick like he did with all the other bites, but he hooks his arm around my waist and yanks me back, pressing my weight against him as he drinks.

If it's possible, I blush harder, my cheeks becoming hotter than the heat that's taken over our bodies. It's oddly more intimate than him drinking from my neck. I curl my fist into the blanket and bite the pillow when his finger breaches me again. Then another, and another, until he is finger fucking me in tandem with the long drafts he is taking from me. With how hard he is sucking, I wonder if he is getting anything to drink at all.

My lower belly begins to burn with an orgasm as it brews. As he brings me to the brink, he removes his fangs and licks the wound closed before moving to the next side, a primal predatory sound building in his chest before he attacks.

I can't hold back.

I shatter. "Lex, oh, fuck, yes," I moan into the mattress.

He doesn't give me time to recover. His fingers slip free of me, and the blunt head of his cock pushes inside before he impales me on his girth without warning. My breath is stolen as he fucks me hard and relentlessly. My cheek rubs against the mattress, and he pushes my legs together, pressing me against the bed. It changes the angle and the grip as he pounds into me.

He yanks my head back by gripping my hair, bending me into an uncomfortable position all while his cock deliciously hones in on every spot that makes me come. "You like this, don't you? Being used and fucked hard. Your pussy is so fucking tight taking me like this. I wish you could see what I see. Your come slick along my cock making it shine as I bury it to the hilt over and over again. Your ass shakes with every thrust. You have no idea what I want to do to you. All the wicked and bad things."

"Do them," I say without thinking.

He brings me to my knees and the pain in my back disappears since I'm able to lean my head against his shoulder now.

My hair sticks to his skin, and he slows his brutal pace. I press against him, wanting him to continue.

In and out, he takes his time, pressing kisses to my neck before his claws threaten my throat.

"Such a good girl. My good little beloved," he croons and the way he says it makes my body melt.

I'll carve my beating heart out of my chest to give him the last of my blood if it means he never stops touching me.

With slow, strong, and forceful strokes, he rams into me, breathing harshly into my ear. The warm breath ghosts over the back of my neck.

"Fuck, Maven. You feel fucking amazing," he says it as if he hates it, fucking me harder, wrapping his arms around my body to hold me close.

I lift my arms and wrap them around his neck and his fingers lazily trail up my stomach before his palms cup my breasts. I moan as he pinches and twists my nipples.

Before I can blink, he blurs us until we are outside, the blanket beneath us in the middle of a field. The house is to the left and I stare up at Alexander in disbelief, wondering how he is real— how any of this is real.

I trace his sculpted face, my index finger grazing along the edges of his jaw. He has high cheekbones and a straight nose, blue eyes when they aren't possessed by red. Alexander looks unkept with his shaggy raven hair hanging in his face.

A force to be reckoned with.

"You're so handsome," I whisper, watching the blush creep up his cheeks. He looks away, biting his lip.

I keep saying it, but I don't think he believes me.

That's okay.

I'll say it everyday until he does.

He sits on his knees and pulls me onto his lap, his hard cock buried still. I lie my arms on top of his shoulders and he skates his fingers down my back, his eyes still wandering over my bite marks.

"You're the beautiful one. Your beauty is unparallel in the sun, but under the moonlight, beneath the stars—" he thrusts his hips up and a whimper is forced from me, echoing across the field "—you're ethereal, beyond anything I've ever seen. And you're mine."

"Yours," I gasp, rocking against him.

Our groans and grunts mix together and his forehead presses against the middle of my chest as we slide against each other. His cock fills me, stretches me to the brink, illuminating pleasures a woman could only ever dream about.

"Maven," he chokes in wonder, his eyes casting to every corner around us.

Sunflowers.

Everywhere.

They become too tall, we get lost in their shadows and the bright yellow petals glow in the middle of the night.

"I'll always bring the sun to you," I tell him unsteadily as I ride him faster.

His hands grip my ass, holding me tight.

"You are the sun," he says before kissing down my chest.

He wraps his lips around one breast and sucks, letting it go with a pop before moving to the other.

My gums begin to tingle, and I touch my fingers to my teeth, a shocked expression crossing my face.

He drags my hand down and lifts my chin, a feral lust emanating from him telling me to run.

Maybe running would be fun.

"Look at your tiny fangs, beloved. So gorgeous," he strokes them, and I moan loudly, as if his touch against the cuspid is a straight shot to my clit. "Your body is adapting. What do you want?"

I run my tongue across my new teeth, the shock leaving quickly as I think about him.

His blood.

I bury my nose in his neck and his scent overwhelms me. I fuck him harder, faster, taking it all like he told me too. "I want you." I let instinct take over and bite him, his blood rushing into my mouth and I hold his head against me while I drink.

He tastes like the sweetest Moscato, and I'll never be able to get enough.

He moans before sinking his teeth into me next, and we drink each other.

All while we fuck like animals.

We orgasm together and bright colors that remind me of the northern lights surround us before seeping into our chests.

Memories of him run through my mind, from the time he was born, to the death of his family. I feel his fear, his loneliness, his need to survive.

His eyes swirl a light purple before fading into the icy blue I love.

"You'll never be alone again." He tightens his arms around me, holding me so tight I can feel his heartbeat.

I run my fingers through his hair, sitting conjoined while we both realize loneliness has been our home for far too long.

"What was that?" I whisper, just as the breeze rustles the sunflowers.

"Our souls combining."

"I drank your blood. I have fangs," I giggle in disbelief, reaching up with my hand to touch my new canines. They aren't as long or as sharp as his, but they get the job done.

He grumbles and his cock becomes hard again. "And they are the best thing I've ever felt."

"The best?" I tease, rolling my hips.

He curls the top of his lip, his hands falling to my waist to push me against his cock. "Second best."

I'm not ready to stop. I need him more than I did earlier. This heat is driving me mad. I kiss him, biting his lip before sliding off his lap. The emptiness I feel has me rolling my lips together to swallow a pornographic sound. His heavy cock slaps against his thigh, wet from our combined orgasms.

Long and thick, a bulging vein pumps it full. His sack is large, round, pulled tight to his body, and there are so many things I want to do.

But first, I stand.

He quirks a brow, his eyes roaming over my body. "Where do you think you're going?" The baritone of his voice causes shivers to drift over my skin.

He slowly gets to his feet, towering over me as his muscles flex in the seductive moonlight.

I take a step back.

And another.

"Be a good girl, beloved," he tsks as he sees the playfulness in my eyes. "You know you won't get far. Come here." He strokes his cock, a milky drop oozing from the slit. "I want those lips wrapped around me."

I take another step away and wiggle my fingers toward the ground. Vines snake and wrap around his legs, then arms, and then for fun, I wrap one around his beautiful cock, tightening it to the point he hisses and flashes fangs.

He loves it.

"I need a head start," I say before darting through the sunflower field I created. I take a peek over my shoulder, and I can see the violent rage of red reflecting in his eyes.

It turns me on.

I pick up the pace, the sunflower stalks whipping against my body. The air is crisp and cool all around me. I feel invigorated in my freedom here at the estate, relishing in the dream I always wanted for myself.

The pull I felt, the force, it wasn't to the property. It was Alexander I yearned for.

I stop running, gasping for breath as I stand in the middle of the field, the sunflowers shielding me as I listen.

It's quiet. There are crickets singing in the woods a few yards away and I take a step into the thick of the flowers to shield me from the vampire I provoked.

I wait.

My heart pumps.

My nerves get the best of me. I survey my surroundings, but I don't hear a thing. I cross my arms and the cold begins to get the best of me. The sweet perfume from the sunflowers drifts in the air. Everything is still.

The stars twinkle above me.

The moon full and round.

And in the distance, I think I hear a wolf howl, which is impossible.

An uncomfortable silent stretch lasts longer than what I'm comfortable with. Maybe I should surrender.

Right as I take a step forward, arms wrap around me and the yellow petals blur together as Lex speeds through the night. The breath is knocked out of my lungs as I'm forced against a tree. The bark scratches my skin, teasing my oversensitive nipples. Something like that shouldn't feel so good.

But I want more.

Alexander's front is against my back and his cock is trapped between my cheeks. Precome dribbles onto my lower back and I push against him.

His hand holds my head down and his wicked lips have plenty to say, "You think you can take from me after what you did?" He rocks, the silky flesh of his shaft rocking against me. "You can never beat me, Maven." He kisses my throat. "I'll always find you. You're in my blood now. Wherever you go, I follow, whether you like it or not." He strikes, those unforgiving points penetrating me at the same time he shoves my legs apart and embeds his cock where it belongs.

He drinks me, fucks me, claims me, right here against the tree. My skin rubs against the rough bark, scratching the surface of my skin, and it hurts but he feels so good.

That familiar purr building in his chest vibrates against my back.

He licks my neck, sealing the wound, and continues to mouth my mating mark which creates a quake in my body.

There isn't a worry that he'll hurt me as he takes me the way he wants me. Hard, rough, and a bit careless. I'll have bruises from his grip, and I know I'll feel the soreness between my legs tomorrow.

Having him inside me is like a scorching hot iron rod, burning me from the inside out, only I can take the pain, the burn, and the consequences loving a dangerous weapon brings.

I come again, my knees giving out and he holds me up, the sounds of our skin slapping reverberates through the woods.

"Take it all, beloved, fucking take it," he snarls, pressing to the hilt as he fills me with his seed. He lazily slides in and out, slowing his pace and sinks his come into my depths. "Mmm, good girl taking every drop." He kisses my shoulder. "Maybe next time you'll think twice about doing something like that. Next time, I'll bend you over my knee."

I hide my mischievous smirk, already planning on the next time.

Because there *will* be a next time.

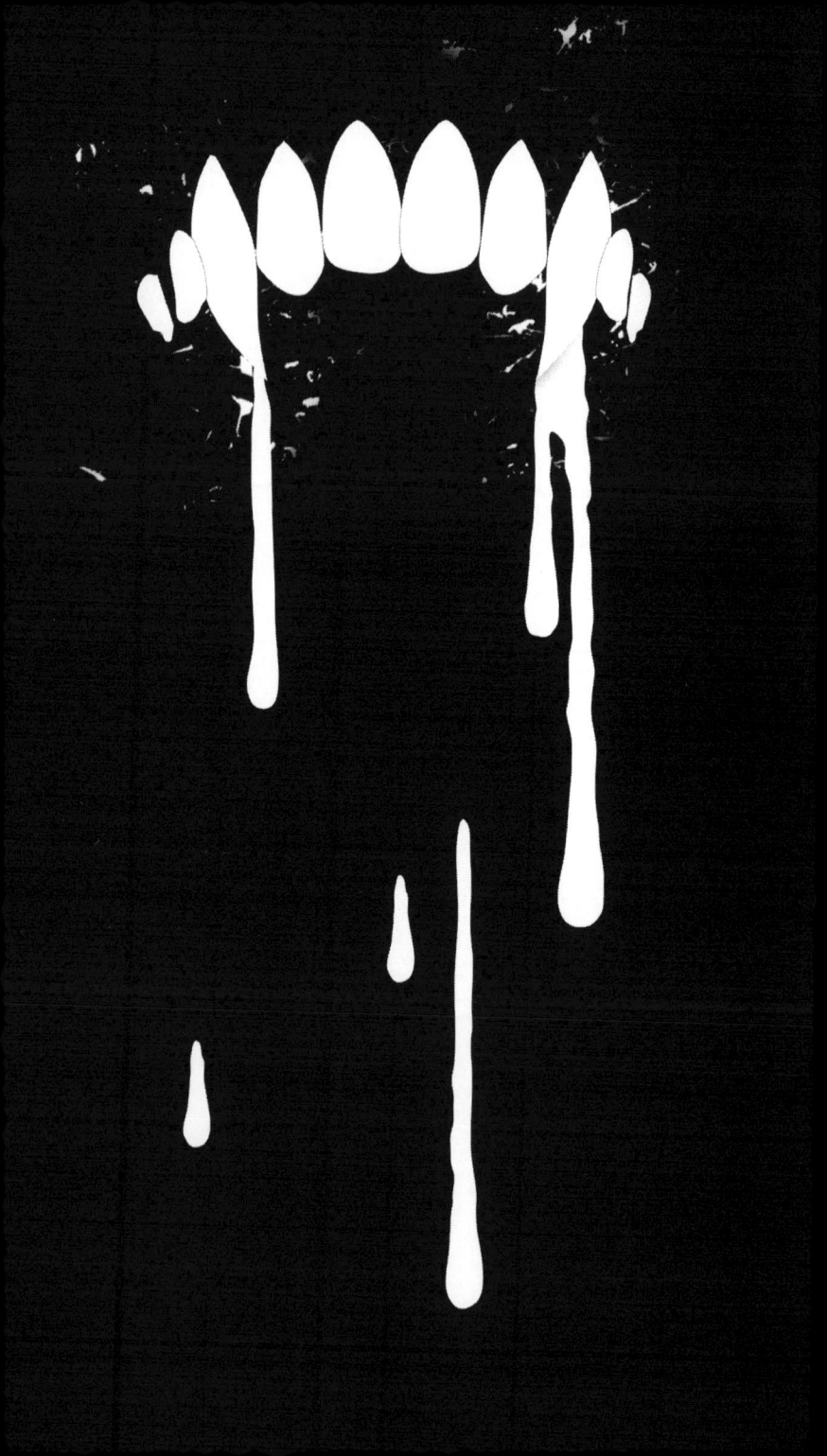

Chapter Fourteen
ALEXANDER

The mating heat has lasted an entire week. She proofed my— our— bedroom like she did her Pa's house, covering every inch with vines, roses, and kudzu. I was safe. I lost track of the hours and minutes I stayed inside her. We couldn't get enough of each other. My body roared with the spice lingering in her magic.

I feel powerful.

I understand now why witches need a coven and vice versa. We're stronger together.

I only have a sliver of her magic, but if it means it doesn't eat her alive, then I'll take as much as nature is willing to give me.

I feel grounded, reborn, stronger than I ever have, and it's all thanks to my mate. I turn to my side and brush her claret hair out of her face, sadness pierces me knowing the heat is over. We learned each other's bodies, our sounds, we shared memories, and pleasure. We are closer than anyone else ever gets to experience.

The bite marks I left on her body are gone now and my fangs itch to do it again. I want to mark her, so every other creature realizes she is mine.

Smelling of me isn't enough, having my mating mark isn't enough, I need more. I kiss her shoulder and she buries her face in the pillow, clearly not ready to get up. I'm sure she's not.

I bite my lip thinking of the ways she'll be sore and my cock stirs.

Let her rest.

I swing my legs over the edge of the mattress, hating that we seem to live in a shack. Now that our schedules have officially changed to night and this room is prepared to keep me safe from the sun, I can help.

And I can help quicker than that fucking wood guy could.

Where is he anyway? He dropped off the face of the earth all too soon and it leaves me suspicious.

Standing, I stretch, and slip on my sweatpants. Taking one last look at my beloved, I head downstairs. I jump off the balcony to skip the steps and my leg punches through the floorboards when I land.

I'll need to fix that.

I could probably cut down a few trees and make enough lumber myself to rebuild, then it can be a surprise for Maven.

Looking around my childhood home, I breathe in, wanting any sort of memory, but nothing happens. All I smell is dust. The only memories I have are the ones that have stuck with me. I rub my chest when I remember father giving me the long speech of how I'll be the coven master one day. It was the same speech all heirs get when they turn fifty.

I stood right where I'm standing now.

He gave me the Monreaux ring that last fateful night, the one passed down from father to son. I twist it along my middle finger, tracing the M, and hating it's the last thing I ever got from my father.

Instead of a peaceful goodbye filled with love, it was filled with fear and mystery.

Staring down at the onyx gem, I sigh, feeling the weight of the world on my shoulders. I want to make father proud.

I didn't expect to be the Master so soon in my life, but here I am.

A mate, but not master.

And I miss the connection fiercely.

Before I can rethink what I'm doing, I'm in front of the door that hid me for 121 years. The strong emotion I felt must have carried me down here without me realizing. I prick my finger and the blood travels through the nooks and crannies of the enchanted door before it opens.

A flashback of my brother carrying me through the halls and to this room play right before me.

I slowly stroll to his tomb and press my hand against the door, swiping blood on it. The red stains the white marble and I notice the old brownish color under it.

His blood from all those years ago.

The door opens and a concrete coffin, protected by Sarah Wildes magic lies in the middle of the room.

I fall to my knees and rest my hands against the lid. He gave his life for me and the guilt that eats away at my heart, knowing I didn't deserve to wake first, nearly knocks the breath out of me.

He deserves his beloved.

And now he only has nine more years like this before he turns to dust.

"Brother," the word breaks in my throat as my eyes water. "I fucking miss you. I wish you were here. It's not as lonely because of my beloved, but the connection with another vampire is missing. It's like a hole in my chest." I pound the space right above my heart.

Thud. Thud. Thud.

"There's no one else, Atreyu. It's just me. So many things have changed. This world isn't as we left it and I can no longer feel the sun upon my skin. Maven, my beloved, is a descendant of Sarah Wildes, she's our coven witch, so she's trying to find a solution for me in the library of books we have. I'm going to bring every woman to you in hopes you'll wake because if nine years come and you die..." I shake my head as a tear rolls down my cheek. I wipe it away, then smash my fist against the floor, cracking the marble. "I'll die. I'll do anything for you to be here. Come back," I plead, pressing my forehead against the lid of the coffin. "Come back," my whisper breaks and the memories of us running through the woods to get to the estate in time are fresh. I can still smell the blood, hear the leaves crunch under our boots, and the howls of the wolves as they hunt us.

I can taste the iron of the hunter I killed and feel the fear as the wolf latched onto Atreyu.

Our lives changing forever in one single night.

I sob, digging my talons in the concrete of his tomb and the urge to kill pumps through me.

Wherever those fucking wolves are, I'm going to kill them.

"I swear," I promise my brother. "Forever in my blood. I'll eradicate all of them like they did to us. I'll do it for you. In your name. In mother's, in Rarity's," I hang my head. "In everyone's."

"Lex?"

I wish Atreyu was awake. He'd correct her and say my name is Lexy.

I hide my face from Maven so she can't see my pearlescent face. Vampires aren't very pleasant looking when they cry.

"Lex," she whispers my name, coming closer.

I feel her near me, her heat, her scent, and I inhale while closing my eyes, letting my beloved take over every sense I have. Her hand lands on my shoulder, then caresses across my chest as she walks around me.

I tilt my head down, but it's too late. She's kneeling in front of me, and her fingers slide under my chin.

"Don't hide from me, my love. Let me see you," her voice sweet just as the scent of the sunflowers in the once dead field.

I lift my head and lifting my swollen puffy eyes, letting her see the side of me no one else will ever see.

"I've seen you like this before, remember? When you woke up from your coma?" She brushes her fingers through my tears, and I lean into her touch.

I forgot about that. I'm ashamed with how I acted. I yelled and cried, attacked her and drank her blood without asking.

"I don't care about your tears. I hate that you're bleeding." She presses her hand against my heart, and I hold my hand over hers. She doesn't mean the blood seeping from my hand, but the pain I feel.

"I miss him," I say honestly. "He's my best friend."

"I know." She brings me into her arms and holds me like a child. "We'll come visit him every day and read while we search the books?"

I lean away. "You'd do that?"

"I'd do anything to make you feel peace, Lex."

"He'd love you, you know. He's grumpy and a real ass sometimes, but he'd like you. I hope you get to meet him one day."

"I will. I believe that. I know it, Lex. I feel it."

That brings relief. Witches who have that feeling are usually always right.

The sound of gravel crunching in the distance has me turning my head. I listen, narrowing my eyes as I try to place the car.

I don't recognize it.

I wipe my face and cradle Maven in my arms before rushing out of the catacombs, leaving an important piece of me behind.

"Someone is here." I gently set her on her feet in the living room. I open the door and a Hall's Construction truck shines its headlights in my eyes. There's a ton of lumber in his trailer.

Being newly mated, any man I don't know around Maven makes me want to kill and I already don't like the guy.

He gets out of the truck, and I cock my head, noticing the aura surrounding him. It isn't red or orange, but a crackling black and it makes my insides want to turn out. He's bad news.

Maven slips from beside me and heads down the makeshift steps she created. I hurry after her, wrapping an arm around her waist to stake my claim.

Not that I need to. He's paranormal, he can see the marks on her neck.

"Brenden, this is a surprise," Maven begins, holding out her hand for him to shake.

He shakes it with a smile, their aura's colliding like oil and water, not mixing. "I hope it's a good one."

A growl of disapproval rumbles in my chest. He doesn't give a fuck she's mated.

"Um, now isn't a good time. I've already made arrangements for new lumber. We didn't hear from you after that storm, so I didn't know what happened." She sounds genuinely sorry, my sweet and innocent beloved. We have to work on her abilities so she can tell when she's speaking with another paranormal.

The wicked ones will take advantage of her naivety.

He takes off his hat and his hair falls as he regretfully runs his fingers through it. He blows out breath. "Yeah, the storm soaked all the wood since it was onset and unexpected, I had no time to cover the lumber. It was already loaded in the truck. I'm sorry. I had to order more. And after that, I had some family issues to take care of, so I fell off the grid. I should have been more communicative. I apologize, it was unprofessional of me."

I narrow my eyes and his gaze flickers from her to me and for a split second, I see right through him. He lets his guard drop, and the bad intentions cloak him. I squeeze her hip to maintain control.

Why do I feel like I've seen this guy before?

"Who is this?" He turns his body in my direction.

"This is my... husband. Alexander Monreaux."

She doesn't know she can say the word mate but hearing husband inflates my ego. I might puff out my chest and broaden my shoulders to appear larger than he is. I am by a few inches anyway, but I wish I towered over this asshole. I want to make him feel small and insignificant.

"Alexander Monreaux? Your family owned this property then?" Brenden asks, his snake eyes assessing me. His eyes are soulless windows. Nothing lives behind them.

"Something like that," I mumble, not wanting to give answers to something I bet he already knows.

"Nice to meet you. Hell of a piece of property you have here." He holds out his hand and I take it, squeezing it harder than necessary and I don't miss the confirmation he needs. His eyes narrow and a slight lift of his smug smirk tells me he has a plan brewing.

He knows I'm a vampire.

And I know he is up to no good. I scent the toxin of evil in his blood and no way in hell am I ever letting him near Maven after this. And we are not using that lumber. I don't trust him to use his materials to build our home.

What is he?

"I'll leave the trailer here and call me when you need me to pick it up. I didn't know you were married. Congratulations. I'll leave you alone."

I can hear how much he wants to say, 'for now' and holds back.

I roll my lips to hide my fangs, breathing in and out not to rip his throat out.

He unlatches the trailer and then hops in his brand-new truck. He gives her a friendly wave and slightly curls his lip at me. The tires crunch as he heads down the driveway, red taillights gleaming in the new night.

"We aren't using that wood."

"Lex, there's no reason to be jealous. It's perfectly good wo—"

"—He isn't human, Maven. We need to strengthen that ability in your power so you can protect yourself. The feeling I got from him, his aura, it wasn't good. He has bad intentions, okay? Trust me. We are burning that lumber. I'll build everything myself and I'll get it done in half the time."

"He wasn't human?" She stares off into the distance, watching the truck get smaller the further away it gets. "How do you know?"

"I smelled it, felt it, saw his aura. He also took silver supplements. No doubt he knows who I am and what I am. Whatever he wants, we haven't seen the last of him and I hate I don't have a coven to protect you."

And I can't be in the sunlight.

My ways of protecting her diminish every day.

"Hey, it's going to be okay." She wraps her arms around my waist and tilts her head back to look up at me.

I clench my jaw and inhale, his scent ruining the scent of fresh flowers always coming from Maven.

"How about you go to the store and pick out anything you want for the house? Call Dottie. You should have a few hours before closing and by the time you get back, I'll be nearly done with the house."

She snorts and begins to laugh. "You can't be serious? It's months away from being done, Lex."

"You want to bet?" I lift a brow, daring her to challenge me.

She nibbles on her lip and nods. "I do."

I blur us to a nearby tree and pin her against it. "That's dangerous, are you sure you want to do that?"

"How bad can it be?" she says breathlessly as our lips hover over one another.

I twist her red hair around my finger and smirk. "If I have it built, the first thing you're going to do is suck my cock." I keep my touch light, my fingertips drifting down her arm, and Brenden long forgotten. "You're going to bend over my lap next and I'm going to spank you until your pale flesh turns red and the blood rushes just below your skin. I want to see my handprint marking you. I want you to feel the burn, the slight edge of pain, but the explosion of pleasure."

Her heartbeat thumps in wild rhythm and her lust overcomes the stench Brenden left behind. "And if I win?" She struggles to say, her body arching into mine as I skim my lips across her cheek.

"Is my offer really losing? Is it really so bad to think about my cock down your throat?"

The wind begins to pick up and lightning flashes in the sky.

I'm making her lose control.

Me.

"You want that, don't you?" I cup her wicked addicting cunt through her pants, and she moans, thunder rolling above us as rain begins to fall softly. "You want to please me because you're a good girl. My good, sweet beloved. Isn't that, right?" I threaten to bite her neck, teasing my fangs along her mating mark.

But I take a step back, not hiding my erection. "I guess I better get to work before it pours." Lightning cracks at the same time crimson floods my sights.

I know she sees a monster in the dark right now, but the last thing I'd ever do is hurt her.

"If I win, you let me tie you up and have my way with you," she counters, pulling out her cellphone with a smirk and pink cheeks as she smiles.

"Oh, Maven. Maybe I'll take my time then," I wink, rushing away before I throw her over my shoulder and take her against a damn tree again.

She needs to rest. She's sore, I can tell by how she walks.

I set up the night lights and unsheathe my talons. I don't need a saw. I have everything I need right here.

The truck protests as she starts it and I make a mental note to buy her a new one.

As she drives away, a few things are on my mind as I run through the woods and begin cutting down trees.

How fast or slow do I want to work?

Being tied up sounds awfully fun.

Chapter Fifteen
MAVEN

"He said for you to get anything?" Dottie asks, running her fingers over an expensive purple Victorian couch. It has a gothic appearance with a black frame and a modern velvet material. It's gorgeous.

I want it.

"He did and he gave me his card, but I have money too. I don't need to use his." I think about how upset he'd get if I didn't let him buy everything and what he'd do to me.

Maybe I'll 'forget' I had his card.

"To me it sounds like you have double the funds. What all do you need?"

"Have you seen the house? Everything." Hairs on the back of my neck stand while goosebumps trickle over my body. I turn my head over my shoulder and look around, not noticing anything suspicious. There's an old woman fumbling through her purse and a kid throwing a tantrum about not being able to use the gumdrop machine. I imagine the gum drops flooding the area, the glass breaking just to get him to quiet down.

The boy has a set of lungs on him.

Suddenly, the gumdrops fall down the swirling slide inside the machine one by one, until they ting out of the metal flap. The kid watches as it bounces on the floor away from him.

Was that me? Did I do that?

Then, the glass breaks and red, yellow, blue, white, and green gumballs fall everywhere. The kid giggles and stuffs as many as he can in his pocket while the mother screams at someone to clean up the mess while tugging her kid by the arm out the doors.

What all can I do?

Am I like my grandpa and can only do little things? Or can I do more?

"Yeah, we will take one of everything in this set and in every color. Do you have beds to match?" Dottie asks the salesperson. "Money isn't in question. I need kitchen supplies too. Black everything with pops of red." She turns to me and winks. "Get it? Red? Because, you know."

I roll my eyes at the bad joke when that feeling of being watched hits me again. I look around the store, nothing but sofas and cabinets in my view but my instincts are telling me to run.

"Oh and towels. The best, we need everything. Honestly, we are redoing a house, you know, the old Monreaux Estate, and it deserves all the expensive things, so why don't you just round up those items, throw them in a truck, and I'll go through it when everything is delivered. For every room." Dottie takes over the shopping trip, her decision to say 'the hell with it' and get everything is a relief.

I hate shopping. I find it stressful. There are so many options and decisions to make.

"Yes, rugs too, but not the ugly rugs with weird patterns. Stick with deep rich colors please. Oh, we need paint." She snaps her fingers and begins to tell the man all the colors she wants along with black metallic wallpaper. I don't know what the hell she has planned, but she can have at it.

I've never been a decorator. Maybe that's why Lex told me to come with Dottie. She's very assertive.

"Yes, chandeliers. Not the large tacky ones. No. We're better than that. Come on, Randall." She teases the man, bumping him with her elbow and his cheeks turn a bright shade of red. He smiles behind his fist as he coughs, clearly flustered.

I'm the witch but this woman holds all the power.

"I want the ones where we can adjust the light, let's stick with black and can we have one red one?" she continues and the more I focus on her, the more I see a hue surrounding her.

The more I focus, an outline of some sorts tries to take shape around her, but I can't tell what it is. The more I try to see it, the more it blurs. I scrub my eyes and blink, but then the aura is gone.

Am I imagining things?

"Fridge, all that, yes. The big restaurant kind. I have a feeling that house will be full," she says knowingly. "Big stove too."

I tune Dottie out when an icicle swims down my spine. Instead of looking around, I sit still, wishing I had a shield of some sorts and that's when I see a light purple energy project from me. I watch it spread, the diameter getting larger and a warmth takes over me instead.

In the distance, almost as if the voices are in the back of my mind far away, they whisper, "*Is that her? Do we wait? Will she take us?*"

I jump out of my seat and spin around.

"*She's the one. She's the answer.*"

"*Tell my sons I love them. I'm here. I'm right here.*"

Panic builds in my throat as the voices double, triple, and it gets to a point where I can't understand what they are saying.

I clutch the sides of my head and want to scream.

"Hey." Dottie touches my arm and the form surrounding her gets larger, but I still can't tell what it is. I want to ask, but Dottie is so honest and upfront, she might not know.

I bet my Grandpa does. I'll have to ask him.

"What's going on? You look pale." Dottie places her warm hand against my forehead. "You're freezing, Maven. Are you okay? What is it? Was someone bothering you? Where? You know I'll pluck their teeth out." She grips my shoulders and darts her eyes around the room.

"I'm fine. Really. I'm fine. Just suddenly not feeling well is all."

"Well, I bought everything we need. I put a rush delivery on it all too. I need his card though."

I hand it over without thinking, placing my hand against my stomach. "Go ahead, I don't care."

"Awesome. When they deliver, you can go through it then and see what you like. I figured you'd like that more."

"What would I do without you?"

"You'll never have to find out. Best friends for life," she says, squeezing my arm. "Okay, Randall, ring us up." She hands over the shiny new black card Alexander just got in the mail. It took him reinventing himself with forged papers and a new name. Alexander IV. I guess he'll continue to add roman numerals to his name.

I don't even want to know the total. I'll get buyers guilt and go to Big Lots, where I'm used to going, instead of this fancy furniture place.

"She's going to change everything. The future will be different."

I press my palms against my forehead and tell myself I'm going crazy. I'm hearing voices now.

"Maven?"

A familiar voice startles me, and I jump, holding a hand to my chest. I look up to see Brenden, a concerned look on his face.

What is he doing here?

"Are you okay? You look like you've just seen a ghost."

Psh.

I've seen a ghost and I still didn't feel like this.

"I'm fine just waiting for my friend," I say coolly, remembering Alexander's warning about Brenden. I focus on his aura. I don't see anything at first which makes me wonder if my powers are on the fritz.

He sits down next to me and that's when I feel it, that iciness that's been hanging in the air.

"You sure? You look like you aren't feeling well." He lifts his hand, and he brushes my hair over my shoulder.

A flash of him standing in front of an older version of Alexander pops in my head. It's my head playing tricks on me because Brenden doesn't look a day over thirty-five years old.

But these days, age doesn't seem to matter.

I hold my breath, watching as the air around him crackles with energy that makes me feel sick to my stomach. Is that why I'm like this? Because of Brenden? And why didn't I feel like this before? Why am I so aware now?

There needs to be a manual of witchy bullshit because I've already had enough of it.

"So beautiful," he mutters, more to himself than anything and I scoot over, uncomfortable.

"Please, don't touch me," I state, trying to sound brave with a backbone. "I think it's best if you leave. Alexander is here," I lie.

Brenden's laugh is dark, ominous, and evil. My fingertips itch to release power, but I can't do it in the middle of the store.

Brenden leans in, inhaling while I keep my spine straight and my hands in my lap. "He isn't here. He is at home. He left you all alone, Maven." He taps my mating mark, and my skin shocks him in retaliation. "Oh, someone is learning new tricks."

I grit my teeth together, not knowing how I did that, but thankful it happened.

"Let's get one thing straight, Maven—" his hand lands on my lap and the frigid temperatures of his power soaks into my bones and my teeth begin to clatter "—I'll let you be a whore. I'll let you fuck that vampire, so you can get that cunt ready for me, but make no mistake, you're mine. I've been waiting for you for a long time, and I won't let a blood sucker take that from me."

I dart my eyes to him. "Sorry, but he is my mate. I'm his beloved. I'll never be yours." I rest my hand on his thigh next, sending a jolt of lightning through his system. It would kill a normal man, but all it does is stun Brenden.

He removes his hand and stands. "Magic is stronger than fate, Maven. Remember that." He spins on his heel and vanishes, leaving me staring at the space he sat in.

The cushion is still indented.

Dottie is sashaying down the hall, the smile on her face falling when she sees me. The hue around her becomes vivid and bright and the form around her grows taller, bigger, but I still can't make it out.

"Maven? What happened?"

"I need Le—" the automatic doors open at the same time a loud crack sounds outside accompanied by a flash.

Lex is standing there, soaking wet, water dripping from his angular face. His hair is drenched, and his black shirt is sticking to his body like a second skin.

In the attempt it takes me to inhale, he is at my side, taking my face in his hands as he bores his blue irises into mine. "He was here," he sneers, displeased, his eyes flashing scarlet. "I smell him."

"Damn, you knew she needed you?" Dottie asks, her finger twirling a piece of her hair.

"I can feel when she's in trouble. I got here as quick as I could. Was it Brenden?"

"Sir, I'm sorry. You can't be in here soaking wet. You're getting water on our furniture."

"Oh, fuck your furniture." Alexander stomps toward the sales associate and grips his neck, staring right into Randall's eyes. "Did you see the man sitting next to my wife?" Lex says calmly.

Randall relaxes, slumping into Lex's hold as if he is warm and safe. "No. I saw no one. Just Dottie. She shopped."

"I'm going to look through your memories. It's going to feel like a tickle, okay?" Lex's voice is drenched in silk, it's so soft and relaxing, I almost forget my troubles.

Randall giggles and sighs, then blushes. "That's a dirty one."

Alexander releases him. "I didn't need to see that. That was..." Alexander shakes his head. "He didn't see anything. Brenden was smart."

"Hot security guard contractor guy? Oh, is he a bad guy? Do we not like him?" Dottie throws her hands on her hips and cocks her head, the anger causing her cheeks to burn cherry.

"No," Alexander bites. "We fucking hate him. Randall, you won't remember me. You'll sleep well tonight. You'll call your friend and have another fun time when you get home."

"Yes, fun," Randall says as if he is a robot, dazed.

"You'll be safe this time, Randall. Won't you?"

"I'll be safe." Randall nods.

"You'll tell me if you see anything suspicious."

"Yes. Anything. Everything."

"This is so cool," Dottie can't help but say. "And you felt her? I want a vampy for myself," she pouts.

Alexander clears his throat. "Randall, you're going to tell your boss you aren't feeling well and you're going to go home once you are done ringing her up, so you get the commission. Okay?"

"Okay," he sighs happily, and Alexander releases his neck.

"Go on, Randall. It's alright. You're great."

"I'm great." Randall grins, then spins on his heel and skips away. "I'm great!" he shouts.

"We need to get out of here. We don't know how many people Brenden has manipulated here."

"Um, I need to know what that was and how you did it?" Dottie asks.

"I mystified him. It's a vampire thing."

"He's a witch, isn't he?" I say when the realization hits me like a bag of bricks. "I felt it. His power. It made me feel funny, slow, sluggish, and cold when he touched me."

"He touched you?" Alexander prowls toward me. "Where? Tell me everything."

"Not here," I whisper glancing around to make sure no one is paying attention to us.

"Dottie, meet us back at the estate. I'm taking her home."

"In the rai—"

But Alexander doesn't give Dottie time to answer. He has me in his arms and he sprints into the chaos of the storm outside. The more I think about Brenden, the voices, the cold, the stronger the storm gets.

It's me. I'm causing this.

Dottie and I drove nearly an hour away to the best furniture store we knew of, so at vampire speed, we're home in about five minutes.

He sets me down under the Spanish oaks and I get out of his arms slowly, my feet barely keeping me standing as I stare at the manor in front of me.

It's done.

It's really done.

The porch wraps around and there are a few chairs strategically placed and a swing in the corner. The shutters are red and the outside smells of fresh paint since the house has a new coat of white brightening the siding.

"UV protected windows. The inside is bare and empty but renovated."

"Oh my god, Lex." I press my hands against my mouth and stare at my childhood dream home. "It's perfect. How? When? How?" I repeat, slowly walking up the steps.

"Who better than me to renovate? I'm quicker with my abilities and I knew the layout of this house like the back of my hand. Everything is the way it was plus a few upgrades, but I don't want to talk about that right now." He leads me to the new swing, and we sit. He pushes us and the view I have is wild.

The storm wreaks havoc. The dark clouds bloom and roll, lightning flashes through them. The insidious darkness the storm holds shines. Rain comes down in heavy sheets, casting sideways. The sunflowers whip back and forth, drowning in water and assaulted by wind.

Lex takes my hand and I remember to breathe, but the storm doesn't stop.

"What happened at the store?"

I lock my eyes onto the clouds. "I felt someone watching me. I thought it was all in my head, but then I swore I heard voices. They sounded distant like they could see me, but I couldn't see them. Then I saw Dottie's aura, which I knew nothing about, but I'm starting to piece everything together since no one tells me anything," I say bitterly. "She has something protecting her. It's huge, but I can't tell what it is. And then Brenden sat down, said I didn't look well." I touch the spot where he touched my hair, running my fingers through the soaked strands. "He touched my hair and moved it over my shoulder," I say in a hypnotized state. "He called me beautiful, but then I said you were at the store. He knew I was lying, and he said he'd let me fuck a vampire if it meant…" I swallow the truth.

"If it meant what?" he growls.

I turn my head to see his fangs, the reflection of the sharp white points shining in every jolt of lightning. "If it meant getting my cunt ready for him. That I was his. Magic was stronger than fate and then he was gone." Tears blur my eyes.

Alexander's chest heaves as he takes deep breaths. He stands, gripping the railing so hard I hear the wood crack.

"What does that mean? What does he mean magic is stronger than fate?" I ask.

"I don't know. Nothing is stronger than fate, you hear me?" He cups my jaw and brushes my tears away. "I'll kill him, Beloved. He's signed his death warrant for fucking with my heart," he states, leaving no room for argument.

"I need to know everything. I'm going into this blind, Lex. He is a witch, isn't he? I felt it. I saw his aura and it was black. Why? What else can I do? Why does he want me? Why am I so important? Why am I hearing voices?" I shout question after question, the thunder rolling with every word from my desperation, a plea to understand.

"I'll tell you what I know, beloved, but you're different than any of your kind I've ever met, and he wasn't a witch. He's a warlock. A bad one with evil intentions. I don't know what he wants with you."

"And the voices?"

"I don't know," he admits, regret in his tone. His thick black brows furrow. "I wish I knew, but I don't."

I take a deep breath and nod, cross my arms, then head inside. I need space to think. As soon as I walk through the door, flames ignite in the fireplace and I'm too angry to appreciate the beauty of our new home.

I have too much on my mind.

I head straight for the library, looking for any kind of answers as to why I am the way I am.

And why I went from no one wanting anything to do with me, to being the wanted witch of the east.

I flip the light on out of habit, expecting it not to work, but it does. It flickers, but after a few seconds, it becomes steady. I throw my hair into a wet bun and grab a book, but my tears blur my vision. I scream, throwing the ancient book across the room and it slams into the shelf, knocking a few to the floor.

They fall onto the floor and one opens, the pages aged, yellow, and fragile. Wiping my cheeks, I sit down and grab the book, the binding glowing when it touches my palms. I gasp, the feeling of home entering my bones.

Flipping the book over, I notice the same engraving from the mausoleum etched in the leather of the book, the W in the middle.

I sniffle, flipping it open to the first page.

The name on it says Sarah Wildes in bold black ink.

"What did you find?" Lex comes from behind me, his hands massaging my neck.

"I don't know." My eyes round when I watch Sarah's name fade and mine replaces it. "Lex? Lex, look! It's changing."

He bends down and we watch as the book begins to write within itself.

The Wildes Grimoire.
Only a Wildes can read it.
This book is protected by:
Maven Wildes.
Coven Witch to the Monreauxs.
The beloved to Alexander Monreaux.

"I always wondered why I'd flip the pages of that book and it was blank. All my father ever said was that no one was to write in it. It was important. That one day, this book would be the reason we lived again. I thought he was crazy, but he was right."

I flip the pages and laugh, happy tears rolling down my face. "It tells me about auras on the first page," I chuckle.

Excited, I keep flipping, bypassing spells and warnings.

I stop when a page labeled "Black Magic and it's bindings."

"Seems like we have about a thousand pages to read."

"You don't know how relieved I am, but maybe we should invite Pa over? He deserves to see it. He should be able to read it too."

"I wonder if that book holds any answers for werewolf bites," he sadly jokes.

But the book listens, flipping pages as if a huge gust of wind blew. It stops abruptly and the page on the right has the drawing of a werewolf and on the left a vampire.

I clear my throat and proudly hold the book out in front of me. "Werewolf venom is toxic to vampires, but does not kill," I read and Lex scoots closer, listening intently. "It sends our vampire family into a coma and only a beloved can wake them up," I read, slightly bored because we know that. I skim the page, bypassing how rare it is.

Until I reach the next paragraph. "When a beloved wakes a vampire from a coma, the werewolf venom mutates the vampire. The vampire will be immune to werewolf bites but sacrifices the abilities to feel the sun. To fix that, please see page 576."

Holy shit. He'll be able to feel the sun again?

"Immune?" Lex runs his fingers through his hair. "I wonder if you're immune too? Our children? Will anyone that agrees to be a part of this coven be immune?"

His question has mine long forgotten.

The book stops me from flipping to page 576, listening to my beloved's questions by flipping to another page. It's toward the back, 894. "A beloved will be immune to the werewolf venom, their children, and anyone that pledges to their master by taking his or her blood. Immunity can't be transferred to a changeling when it's forced. The change has to happen willingly and be needed," I read. "Wow, this book knows everything. Too bad it doesn't know why I'm so important."

The book slips from my hand and shakes on the floor, rumbling the shelf behind it as the pages flick at an alarming rate. The lights flicker and rain beats against the window.

When it stops, the edges of the paper burn and I smack the embers a few times to put them out.

"Maven,

You'll change everything. You'll open the door to the paranormal world again, but it isn't you that causes the ripple in dimensions. It's the child you're carrying. Half vampire of the original vampire lineage, half pure elemental witch, your child will be the most powerful and the most feared. People and creatures around will want you dead to make sure that child is not born.

But they must be.

Everything will change, Maven.

Have Alexander take you to the cove. He'll know why.

Count on your familiar, she'll protect you at all costs.

Listen to yourself and you'll change the world.

I never met you, but I love you. Be the witch you were always born to be.

-Sarah Wildes. Previous Coven Witch to the Monreauxs.

And as soon as I read it, the page goes up in flames, vanishing from the book forever.

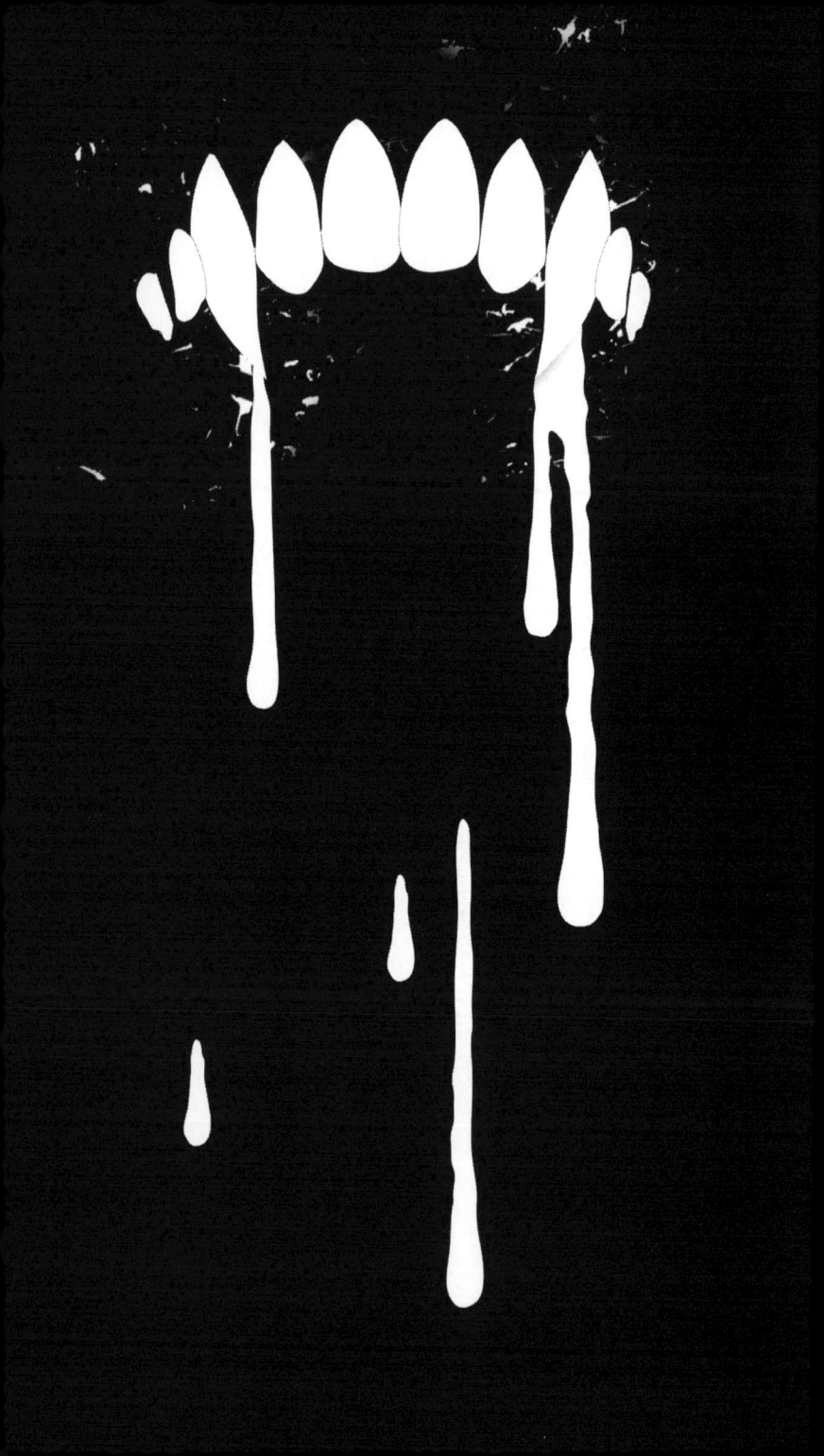

Chapter Sixteen

ALEXANDER

"Pregnant? I'm not pregnant," she scoffs, slamming the book closed, then leaving it in her lap. "I'm not. I'm due for my period…" she trails off trying to remember the date.

Frantic, I bury my nose into her neck and inhale as deep as I can, searching for the different scent, but I don't smell a thing. My father could tell when my mother was pregnant. He knew immediately. I wonder if I can't because Maven is a witch and not a vampire. I prick her skin with a fang, and she gasps from the slight pain. The blood beads and I flick my tongue across it and focus on the memory the blood carries.

My eyes snap open and morph as pleasure, possession, and joy fill me. I see two embryos, just shy of two weeks, maybe less. Nothing but a bundle of cells at this point, but since I know they are there, they are *mine*.

I fall to my knees and press my palm against her lower abdomen, wondering how I didn't know earlier. I wasn't focused on the memory of her blood and what it carries.

"It's true. You're pregnant. It's early," I smile fondly. "Maybe two weeks. Twins."

She inhales a sharp breath and presses her hand against mine. "Twins? Oh my god, are they okay? Can you communicate with them?"

"No, nothing like that. Vampires can usually scent when their mates are pregnant, but I wasn't paying attention. You're so early they don't have heartbeats yet. I had to focus on your blood, pry the memories out of the cells, and that's how I saw them."

"I'm pregnant," she grins with watery eyes, but the smile fades, the happiness gone as rain turns to hail, pounding against the roof like baseballs. "They aren't safe. The letter. Sarah said—"

"—I will die before anything happens to you. You understand? I'll risk everything to make sure you and our children are safe. You're mine. Do you understand?" I push her onto her back and lift her damp shirt over her head.

The need to claim her rushes through me, knowing she's carrying my children, mine, fucking has the bloodlust inside me roaring.

In a rush, I tug her leggings down to her ankles and fumble with my pants just enough to free myself.

"You're fucking mine." I thrust to the hilt and she tosses her head back as she is filled to the brink. "Your body is mine." I thrust hard, her pussy soaking wet for me. "Your soul is mine." I thrust again and she groans, slapping her arms against the new floorboards.

I press my palm against her stomach, fucking her hard and fast. This is going to be quick.

I let my fangs show, my eyes burn a shade of flame, and my talons drag along the wood. I want her to witness my lack of control. I curl over her, moaning my own pleasure in her ear. Nothing compares to the feel of her around me.

"Fucking all mine," I mumble, high off desire.

"Yours," she gasps on a strangled breath. "I'm yours."

I grasp her hips, slamming harder and harder into her, touching her occupied womb with the tip of my cock. I growl deeper, more dangerous and lethal than I've ever sounded.

"Oh god," she shouts just as lightning clashes outside at the same time her pussy tightens around me.

I sink my fangs into her throat, my orgasm taking me by surprise. My eyes roll as I drink her nectar, the taste so different now that I know she's pregnant. She's sweeter. I pump my come into her, stream after stream wishing she could get pregnant all over again.

We live forever and I feel like with her being pregnant now, we will have a thousand kids.

She comes, her muscles contracting along my flesh to pull my seed deeper where it belongs.

I don't pull away from her neck, I continue to drink, thirstier than I ever remember being.

She orgasms again, moaning as the shocks rush through her.

Her small canines slide into my vein and shock me. Making me coming again, overflowing her with my seed.

She pulls long drafts of my blood, feeding her need, satisfying the craving of blood she needs now that she's feeding two vampires.

I suck deeply before licking her mating mark and she shutters, dragging her fangs free as well. We kiss lazily, blood twisting along our tongues as they duel. We stay locked together, my hand roaming down her bare thigh.

The rain stops abusing Salem as Maven relaxes in my arms.

I lick her lips clean and stare into her green eyes. "We will be safe." And then I remember Sarah's words, to take Maven to the cove.

I've forgotten all about it.

Folklore and myths were born there, but no doubt they live. I remember my father telling me about it, how it used to be a portal. He always took my mother on walks through the fields, always going to the cove. It was their place.

I'm wondering if it could be ours too and if Maven is the secret to unlocking the portal.

Not tonight though.

Tonight, I need to continue to claim her, wash the memory of Brenden away, bathe the distress the spell book brought down the drain, and let us worry about the real world tomorrow.

Right now, I want to celebrate.

"I never thought I'd find you and now you're here." I slide my half hard cock out, my come spilling free. "The mother of my children." I could cry. I won't, but I could. This life was never supposed to be an option. And having kids? That wasn't even on my radar. I remember knowing I'd die in that tomb. I felt the hopelessness, the fear, the end. Meeting her wasn't a possibility. It wasn't an option, but a dream.

Maven is and will always be my dream come true.

My chance at life.

My reason for eternity.

And if no one thinks I'll drain them of their blood, even if silver burns me from the inside out to protect her, I will. They have no idea what's coming for them.

I kiss down her body, focusing on her flat stomach. My hands fall to her hips, gripping them gently while pressing my cheek against her.

"I love you," I say. "I've loved you for 191 years, Beloved."

"And I'll love you for 191 eternities," she replies, running her fingers through my hair.

I part her legs, run my nose down her pink petals, never smelling a more gorgeous flower. I run my tongue over her engorged clit, my cock turning to steel as I suck the rose bud in between my fangs.

"Lex, yes," she hisses my name, which makes me want to have her curse it. "More." She takes her hands and shoves my face between her legs, and I delve my tongue inside, licking our combined juices. I suck each lip into my mouth. I grip the inside of her thighs, force them apart, and bite into her femoral artery, the blood flowing so fast I can hardly swallow in time before it trickles out of the corner of my mouth.

Another orgasm shakes her core, her slit slick and ready for me again.

Using my enhanced speed, I sit in the chair and take her over my knee. Her ass is up, the round globes causing the skin of my palm to tingle. "I believe we made a deal, good girl. I want to collect."

"That would mean me sucking your cock first," she reminds me.

"I want that after." I'll be so worked up from seeing her ass red, that I won't be able to hold back.

I rub two fingers down her spine, licking my fangs as I pass the dimples above her ass, and then trace the crease of her cheeks. She whimpers when I continue on, pushing my fingers inside her tight core.

"Mmmm, I'd think you'd still be a virgin if I didn't take it and taste it myself." I pump my fingers slowly, loving how soft and tight she is on the inside.

"Lex," she squirms, arching her back which causes her ass to perch higher in the air.

I wrap my hand around her throat while yanking my fingers free, leaving her empty. The vibrations of her pleasurable sounds cry from her throat against my hand. Turning her head, I make her watch me, fangs and all, letting my nature come out to play as I suck the honey from my digits. Her flavor rolls around across my taste buds, my blood singing.

"You taste so good." I plunge my fingers inside again before pulling them free. I force her head to the side. "Find out for yourself." I shove my fingers between her lips and her tongue circles, sucking me clean.

I can't wait to feel those lips wrapped around my cock.

"Enough," I growl a warning when she begins to bob her head.

I can only handle so much before I blow.

My cock pokes against her stomach as she lies across my thighs, smearing precome like paint as if she is a blank canvas.

Yet she's already a masterpiece.

She's pregnant.

How will I keep my sanity for nine months?

I lift my hand and slap my palm against her left cheek. Maven moans loudly in pain and pleasure.

I do it again and again.

The loud *smack* causes my full orbs to pull tight to my body. My orgasm looms as I hear her get louder. I inhale to catch my breath but drown myself in her lust. I glance between her legs, noticing the sheen glistening against her thighs.

She's dripping for me.

I spank her harder, the blood rushing just below the skin, my handprint glowing.

"So fucking pretty," I marvel, running my hands over the heated cheeks. Her puckered star winks at me as I lift her closer to my face. I bite just as I promise, the angry blood trickling into my mouth.

The liquor comes out much slower from the bottom since the muscle and fat is thicker here than the rest of her body.

And fucking perfect.

When I'm done, I push her onto her knees and gather her hair so it's out of the way. "Suck," I order harshly.

She blinks up at me, the innocence fading as she grips my cock with one hand and my sack with the other. She teases the slit with her tongue, flicking and circling, tasting the precome she milks from me constantly.

I tilt my head back against my shoulders when she sucks the head into her mouth, hollows her cheeks, and takes me to the back of her throat.

"Such a good girl," I praise, unable to take my eyes off the way she bobs so eagerly.

She flicks her attention to my face, relief shining back at me from her blown pupils.

She *wants* to be good for me.

Maven squeezes the base, twisting while sucking me to the point she gags. Her lips are stretched wide, her jaw must be aching, but she doesn't stop. Her nose presses against the trimmed black hair surrounding my cock before she gags, lifting off me a bit to suck in more air.

Sweat breaks out over my entire body as she ignites a fire between us. A drum beats against my chest as I hold back a keen of delight.

I thrust my hips, unable to stop myself and she chokes.

I fucking love that sound.

"That's it, my little witch. Choke on your mate's dick." I do it again and her throat constricts around me. Her hand disappears between her legs and a magical moan hums through my cock.

"Fuck, fuck!" I shout as my orgasm approaches. A tingle warns me at the base of my spine. I yank her off me so fast, she doesn't even have time to wipe the spit from her lips as I lift her up high enough to pull her down on my length. I shout and snarl, spilling inside her just in time. My eyes close as stream after stream leaves me.

Her nails dig into my chest which has my eyes snapping open, her orgasm hitting her sudden and quick.

Violently, I yank her close to my face by tugging her neck with my talons. "My come belongs in that sweet pussy because it's mine," I tell her, almost angry with how much I mean it. I flex my hips, burying my cock a few more inches to get my point across.

She bites her lip, forgetting her little fangs and nicks the plump cloud. I dive in, sucking her lip into my mouth, battering it with my tongue.

I pull away, gasping for breath, my own mating marks burning and tingling from what we just shared. She must sense it because she kisses them gently.

Holding her close, we sit tangled in each other's arms as we catch our breath. I'm so consumed by her, the taste of her lingering on my tongue, and knowing she's pregnant, I don't hear the car approach.

A loud banging sounds on the door and I'm dressed before Maven can yawn with exhaustion. I wrap her in a blanket. "Stay here," I command, and she nods, settling in the chair with wide eyes. I slip on my sweatpants but hide my hardened cock in the waistband.

I hate interruptions.

Rushing to the door, I let out a breath when I see a soaked Dottie, her mascara running down her cheeks.

"This is ninety-dollar mascara." She shoves by me and sniffs the air. "Whewie," she waves her hand. "Smells like sex and a good time." She twists her hair like a rag, letting the water out.

"Dottie?" Maven pokes her head out from the library and steps out into the living room, keeping the blanket tight around her body.

"Did I interrupt?" Dottie questions.

"Yes."

"No."

Maven and I clearly think differently on what is considered an interruption.

"So, who wants to catch me up?" Dottie clasps her hands. "Can I stay here? Do you have food? I'm thirsty."

I notice the hue around her again, this time a bright sparkling ruby, and the image that Maven talked about struggles to form. It's big, protective, but I can't make it out either.

Seems the more time she spends with us, the stronger her aura becomes.

"Do you hear that?" Maven asks, tiptoeing through the living room, stopping right in front of me, peering over my shoulder toward the front door.

I turn to see if someone is behind me, only seeing the wet footprints on the floor from Dottie entering our home.

"Hear what, beloved?" the taste of her teasing the tip of my tongue as she's still on my lips.

"The voices."

Fear replaces the happiness I felt moments ago and I'm worried Pa might not have known everything about magic.

What if her power is killing her but is affecting her mind first? My eyes drop to her stomach and dread sweeps through me. If anything happens to my family— again, in this life— I'll step into the sun myself.

What is life without my heartbeat?

Chapter Seventeen
MAVEN

I'm not crazy.

I swear I'm not. I hear them. There are so many, I can't decipher what they are saying. White noise blinds me, static popping in the neurons in my mind. My hands holding the blanket around me loosen their grip and slide along the side of my head. An inhuman noise leaves me, something along the lines of a crackled screech and my temples throb.

My fingers tug on my hair and the blanket falls, draping around my feet, my knees bucking like a pissed off bronco.

"Maven!" Lex's arms circle around my waist, catching me before I hit the floor.

"God, Maven. What the hell?" Dottie runs out of the kitchen, a cloth in her hand. She is inches taller than me, but she never towers over my height to gain respect. She's more motherly than that, even if she doesn't want to admit she has a sweet bone in her body.

She dabs the cloth under my nose and when she pulls it away, the material is stained red. "What did you do?"

"Me?" Lex nearly yells his innocence. "I didn't do anything. Maven, what is it?" His eyes are on me, assessing me, his hands pushing my hair out of my face as we sit down on the floor. "Talk to me, sweetheart. Talk to me," he begs, lying me over his lap. He's holding me as if I am a child.

"So many," I choke, my eyes rolling to the back of my head as flashes of the past creep into my mind. "So many voices." My back bends as one voice that's stronger than all the others takes control of my being.

I fall slack, watching through a fog as another entity possesses me.

"Maven?" Lex whispers, holding the back of my head up.

My vision hazes, a cloud of white coloring what I see. I try to take control, but whatever is inside me, is stronger. I can sense it won't be for long. However they are doing this, they aren't strong enough.

"Tell Alexander to take you to the cove. The cove. Go. We're here."

"We're here!" The words are torn from me in violent rampage as the entity who used me to relay his message, vanishes. The words are so loud, they use all the air I have in my lungs. I roll from Alexander's lap, my palm slapping against the new black hardwood floors.

Lovely.

"Christ, Maven." Lex rubs my back as I try to catch my breath.

I wipe my mouth and lick my lips, copper rolling on my taste buds.

He covers my naked body back up with the blanket and tugs me close. "It's okay, Beloved. It's alright. We will figure it out. I got you. Always."

I wrap my arms around his neck and hold on tight, trying to make sense of what happened, but I can't.

Who am I kidding? It's magic.

Maybe if I do as the voice says, they will stop.

And I'll give anything to make them stop.

"Your eyes turned white, Maven. Are you sure you're okay? I'm going to go get you some water." Dottie touches my arm and a warmth, protection and love soak through me. Powerful and strong. I gasp when sparks dance between her fingers across my skin.

She yanks her hand away as if I burned her. "What the hell was that?"

Your familiar will protect you.

I remember the words of the letter Sarah left me. I had no idea what they meant, but Sarah recognized my familiar as a woman.

It would make sense it would be Dottie. We've always been friends and she's never cared what people said or whispered about me.

Was she always meant to be by my side?

"This is getting weird. Don't get me wrong, I don't mind the hocus pocus, creepy crawly, fang, blood-sucking, witchy stuff. I don't know why it doesn't bother me, but I'm a bit freaked out, so if someone could please shed some light—"

I cast a light over her head, wanting to ease the tension and her shoulders slump while she deadpans me with a hard look.

"Funny. I'm glad your humor remains intact after…" she waves her hands in the air… "That."

I sit up and groan, feeling like I got hit by a bus. Lex zips to the kitchen and when he comes back, he doesn't have water, but something a little stronger.

Whiskey. Actual whiskey, not the dog.

I give him a gentle smile, placing my hand on my stomach as a quick reminder of why alcohol isn't a good choice.

His lips part and his eyes round in horror as if he can't believe what he just did. He tosses the amber liquid back himself, disappointed with himself. He doesn't say a word and dashes to the kitchen again, coming back with a bottle of water.

His crooked smile is the sight I need. "Sorry, I guess we should go grocery shopping. The pizza and leftover Chinese food with tap water isn't cutting it."

"That's what you're feeding her? Are you kidding me? You're both rich and you don't have your own cook? Unreal," Dottie bitches, shaking her head. "Good thing I'm upgrading your kitchen or you'd both die of heart disease."

"We haven't needed anything," Lex mumbles under his breath.

I blush thinking about what else has satisfied us. I can feel his blood roaring inside me, my gums tingling for another bite of him.

I'm not a vampire, but it seems I am when it only comes to him.

I stare at Dottie a bit longer, the aura around her brighter than ever. It's taller than she is, a bit wider, arms of neon scarlet engulfing her own body, moving as she moves. I don't feel fear. I know she'll protect me.

But *what* is she?

"And what's this cove?" Dottie asks, cleaning the blood off the floor that dripped from my nose. "You wouldn't stop shouting it."

Lex steps in front of me and takes a defensive stance, broadening his shoulders and tightening his fist. "How do you know about the cove?"

Dottie scoffs and points the dirty rag at me. "She was just yelling about it."

"No, she wasn't. She didn't say a word. She sounded like she was choking, but she never spoke."

Dottie's eyes turn to saucers and her sight falls on me. "Maven?" Her voice quiet and meek.

"I didn't say anything, but the voices in my head yelled it. They wouldn't stop."

"Why did I hear it?" The words shake from her throat.

Lex sighs and relaxes his hands, his veins bulging in his arms still. "You're paranormal, Dottie."

She shakes her head. "No. I'm a teacher. I teach. I can't..." she sucks her bottom lip into her mouth, nibbling the flesh.

"You're a paranormal. I can see it in your aura. Pa knew. He said your aura was faint, but it got stronger over the years. Whatever you are, she isn't ready to come out yet, but she wants to give her service. You're Maven's familiar. Do you know what that means?"

I appreciate his tone, how soft and gentle he's being while he speaks to her about something she has no idea about.

"Familiar? No. I don't understand."

"Witches have familiars. When they first come into their power, the familiar reveals him or herself. They can be anything, whatever form that will help the witch the most."

"I can't see what your form is. It's big though. Tall. Powerful," I explain to her. "I wasn't able to see your aura until the other day, but the more you're around us, the stronger she becomes. I think it's why we've always been friends. We've been drawn to one another, always." I reach for her hand, but she steps away from me, thick droplets spilling down her cheeks.

"And you didn't tell me?" Her mouth opens as she tries to calm her breathing, the heels of her palms pressing against her eyes for a moment to stop the tears. "You didn't tell me? After everything, after me believing you and that you're in love with a vampire, who, might I add was a fucking ghost, and *you* didn't think to tell me the truth?"

I scurry to my feet, swaying and Lex wraps his large hand around my forearm to keep me steady. "I didn't know how. I didn't know what to say. I barely understood it myself."

"Pa said he didn't want to scare you. He figured whatever you are, when she was ready to come out, then you'd be ready for the truth."

"He was wrong," she says between gritted teeth, her face pinching from rage. "I should have known from the beginning. I should have known!" She screams. "This isn't just about you. It's about me. I don't know what... I am."

"If I knew I'd tell you. I swear." I'm desperate for her to believe me.

"You didn't at first, but you did know. You did and I hung around like an idiot, not understanding why I have this need to always fucking be there for you. Always."

"I'm sorry. I'm learning too. I should have been honest with you from the beginning."

"Yes, you should have." Her shoulder meets mine as she strides by me. Before she gets too far, she pauses, turning her head slightly to speak, "Is this how a witch treats her familiar? With dishonesty? If so, I want nothing to do with it." She swings the door open, slamming it against the wall.

The image around her grows, almost as if the bigger she becomes the more Dottie is protected. The mysterious creature's head tilts and her arms spread before folding in, hugging her.

Dottie stops walking when she's able to feel the connection with her animal and holds a hand to her heart.

I run out the door and stop just above the steps, the wetness still hangs in the air after the storm. "Dottie! Please, don't go. Please." My pleas end when a bolt of lightning strikes just in front of me, but I don't jump, I absorb the energy.

And as Dottie ignores me, the storm brews again, fallen leaves carry over the ground.

"Dottie!" I cry out once more.

She stands by her open driver's side door and stares at me, letting the rain fall and soak her for the second time tonight. Her animal looms over her, staring at me too. With a pinched mouth and dark soaked hair, she gets in the car and slams the door. Tires spin against the driveway, gravel flinging and clanking along the underside of her car.

The tail lights glow as she leaves and the pain of losing my best friend has the rain pouring harder, a sheet that can't be pierced.

Lex's hand lands on my shoulder and squeezes. "She'll be back. She just needs time. It's a lot to accept when you aren't raised with knowing this."

"How do you know she'll be back? I don't want her to come back because she feels like she has to or because she's my familiar."

"No, beloved. She'll come back because she's your friend. Friendship like yours doesn't end. Love doesn't break easily. Cracks can be mended."

"But mended things are never the same after."

His lips press against my mating mark. "Sometimes. Sometimes they are stronger once they are put back together. The weakness, what makes them fragile is gone."

I lean my head back and rest it against his chest, hoping time can fix what magic cannot. Spinning around, I brush my fingertips along his shoulders, admiring the ridges of his collarbones and the smooth skin of his chest. He has sparse hair along his pecs that trail down his stomach.

So masculine.

Every inch of him.

"Take me to the cove."

And maybe all this madness can be over.

Chapter Eighteen

ALEXANDER

I push away from her and rub a hand over my face. "It's a puddle now. Nothing more, nothing less, nothing but a place where my parents went to escape us. It's nothing."

"What if it's everything?" she asks, closing the distance between us. The hope on her face nearly has me succumbing to her need. "What if it is the answer to everything? What if it tells me what I need to know? What if it stops the voices? The letter said to go to the cove. If anything, I should listen to Sarah."

"It's nothing special," I tell her, leaning my shoulder against the doorframe.

"Why are you so adamant of that? How are you so sure?"

I close my eyes and think back to the day I lost everyone I ever loved. My heart begins to beat faster, my palms begin to sweat, and there is a drum of fear still living in the back of my mind. "It was the last place they were headed. My family. Mother, Father, Greyson, and Uncle Luca." I swallow when I think of Rarity. "And my baby sister. She was just a day old."

Maven's light footsteps brush across the porch. She places her hand in the middle of my back, dragging it up to my shoulder and down my arm. "Is that why you never talk about them?"

"Do I not?" I repeat, thinking of the times her and I have spent together, the moments we have shared.

And I haven't. Not really. I talk about Atreyu because in a sense he is still with me.

I rub my chest and grunt. "I guess I don't. Thinking about that day is painful."

"Why do you think they went there?"

"I don't know, Maven. Maybe to die where they loved?"

"Tell me about them. Tell me about your family."

I smile, my memories jumbled together. I take Maven's hand in mine and bring it to my lips, then drag her down the steps. Then I remember she's just in a blanket. I run up to the closet, grab a nightgown and a robe, then come back down, dressing her before she can protest.

I toss the blanket on the porch. "Come on. Let's take a walk through the woods." I'll take her to the cove like she wants. I hope it helps her. I know it won't help me.

"I like it when you go all vampy speed on me."

I quirk a brow and roam my eyes down her body, her breasts sitting snug in the tight royal blue silk of her gown. "I'll have to keep that in mind."

We don't say anything for a few minutes. We walk the path, the dirt, leaves, and twigs crunching under our feet. The ground is wet from the rain and there is a chill in the air promising winter. We should be better dressed. Again, we don't have everything we need.

Another way I'm failing her as a mate.

That will change tomorrow.

"My mother's name was Esmeralda and my father's was Severide."

"Esmeralda is a beautiful name. I never heard of the name Severide. I like it. It's different like your brother's."

"Mother loved unique names. When my sister was born, November 7th, 1900, she had white hair and violet eyes. Vampires don't have features like that. It just doesn't happen. My mother named her Rarity."

"Oh, I love that." She drops her hand to her flat stomach. "I guess I'll have to keep the tradition."

I yank her toward me and kiss her deeply, thrusting my tongue between her lips. It almost hurts how much I love her, and I try to show it through the passion of fusing us together. "I'd like that." I press my forehead against hers for a second before pushing away.

"What were we talking about?" She laughs and loops her arm through mine.

"Forgetful?"

"Only because you kiss-stified me."

I toss my head back, a throaty boisterous laugh reverberating off the trees. "Oh yeah? It's my fault?"

"Yep. I blame you. You should come with a warning label," she says as-a-matter-of-factly.

"I do." I flash my fangs and a typical person would be shocked to see them, even after a few times, but my witch of a beloved rolls her eyes.

She isn't fazed.

"Anyway, my big bad vampire, you were saying?"

She tilts her head on my shoulder and I retract my fangs, loving the simplicity of this moment. There's no drama, no stress, no tension. It's us doing something normal for a change.

"Right. My family. You nosey little witch." I bop her nose and she play bites me, pretending to snatch it. "Did you know there were things called matching ceremonies? They were for unmated vampires. Since finding a beloved rarely happened, it was a way for vampires to meet someone who sang to their blood. Still nothing or no one sings to the blood like a beloved, but it was the next best thing."

"Sounds so… business-like."

"It was. In a way. Well, that's how my father met my mother. He went to a ceremony, but the ceremony was for my mother's sister. One look at Esmeralda and he knew he wanted her and no one else."

"That's so devious. Your father crashed the party."

I grin thinking about my father's mischievous side. "He did. They started their life together that night."

"So fast?"

"Vampires aren't like humans. We live a long time, and we want partners for it. An unmated vampire can live up to two hundred years. Mated but without their beloved, a thousand. With a beloved?" I spin her around, dancing to no music except the crickets chirping. I yank her back to me with enthusiasm.

I'm a man that's been deprived of happiness for far too long.

And I have it right in front of me.

I plan on never letting it go.

"Eternity," she answers my question, eyes locked on my lips.

"Eternity," I echo, continuing to dance.

She steps on my foot and stumbles. "Sorry. I'm a horrible dancer. Two left feet."

"That's alright. I'll be all the feet you need." I swing her into my arms, like a bride waiting to be carried over the threshold. I rock back and forth, lazily making a circle.

We're quiet like that, just enjoying each other's peace and solitude. After a while, I break the silence. "So for female vampires, there are two days a month where they are fertile. Well, they wasted no time. That night mom was pregnant. Vampires can tell right away but with you I didn't know. I don't know why. Maybe because in some ways I'm still a young vampire. I've been missing out on a lot."

"I guess we aren't that different. I bet I was pregnant on our first night too," she states.

A growl of delight escapes me, and I think about pushing her against the tree, lifting her nightie, and sliding into her from the back. "Damn right you were. Mine." I play bite her neck.

She giggles and leans away. "Don't get me distracted. I want to know more."

I let out a dramatic, theatrical sigh. "Fine." We've been dancing for some time now, so I change course and head to the cove. "My Uncle Luca is great. My father's brother. He's spirited, happy, positive, and he's always been there for us. Actually, him and Greyson, my father's head of security, saved my mother's life."

"No way. Tell me, tell me," she begs so prettily, curling her fingers into my chest. Her almond-shaped green eyes beam up at me with excitement. Oh, my girl likes a little gossipy drama.

Good to know.

"Well, back then, we didn't have paranormal doctors. Rumor had it they got stuck in the portal but no one ever truly knew. After the burning of Sarah Wildes, finding a witch to help us was difficult. Healers, doctors, nurses, usually came from mages, witches, or fae. Someone who could use magic and the earth to heal. We had no one, so my parents didn't know they were having not one, but two children. The birth was hard on my mother. My fault. I wasn't headfirst. My foot was. Father had to cut her open himself. He bit, tore, and clawed for us. It was a memory I didn't mean to see, but I did. Greyson and Uncle Luca fed my mother their blood. It's... frowned upon for unmated vampires to do that with one another. It can be sexual. You can have new desires, sexual fantasies, and even love start to form. He had to risk it or mother would have died. His blood wasn't enough. To his surprise, they didn't lust after his mate. They did form a close bond, like brother and sister. That's it. Greyson was... strong, like what you'd imagine a statue would do if it came to life. That was him." I take a deep breath, then let it out, immersing myself in the pain for a minute. "I miss them."

"I know." She rubs my chest, kissing where my heart pounds. "I'll take care of you for them. I promise."

I set her down gently and kiss her forehead. "You take the best care of me." I push her shoulders to turn her around and point to the cove. "Here we are. See? Puddle of water."

She runs forward and smiles, her eyes flickering with... something. Gold?

"It's gorgeous. I bet it's beautiful in the winter when the snow falls and the pond freezes over."

I squat down and touch the ground, focusing on the dirt as I rub it between my fingers. I inhale next, trying to find memories, and there is.

There's one.

It's faint.

I hear my parents laughing, my mother's smile bright as she stares at father.

And then I taste blood, feel the rivers of it gliding over my fingers. I yank my hand away and stand, trying to shake the feeling that something horrible happened here. I could find out more if I really focused every ounce of memory channeling I have, but I don't want to.

Wiping my hands on my sweatpants, I clear my throat, then lift my head to see what my curious witch is doing. She's on her knees, peering into the growing abyss of the water as the banks that receded over the years begin to refill. It must be because of Maven. This cove, maybe it is a portal and it is drawn to her magic. I bet the key was found when the puddle was dried up or maybe the portal spit it out.

I don't know. There are too many questions that have no answers for me to fully believe this cove leads to other worlds.

The pond appears to be deep with an inky darkness beneath its surface, but you can walk across it. It's shallow.

A fucking big puddle.

So how in the hell could someone sink into it and travel?

"Find what you're looking for?" I sit down next to her, intruding on a frog. He jumps and croaks, hopping across the cove to get away from me.

"I'm not sure," she says in a trance, staring down at her reflection. "The voices are quiet, like they are holding their breath." She gives the water the slightest touch, her fingertip causing ripples across the slate.

I never believed in this portal. It was just another fairytale that liked to be told in the middle of the night when everyone was bored.

Then again, my beloved is a fairytale, isn't she? And she surpassed my wildest hopes, dreams, and expectations.

Maven's hair tumbles down her shoulders, the tips taking a dip in the water as she examines it for the answers she's looking for. She shuts her eyes and exhales, her hand on the surface of the water.

For the first time, I notice the water is clear. I can see her hand under the surface.

How in the world does the cove remain so black? Why can't I see to the bottom?

Magic.

I glance up when the trees begin to rustle, the branches bending to kiss one another. The crickets become louder and the frogs croak one after the other, as if we are surrounded by hundreds.

"Maven? What's going on?"

When she opens her eyes, they are ridden with lightning bolts and sparks. She presses her hand under the water and a shimmery golden hue glitters across the top. She flicks her wrist, spinning the water until the entire cove changes momentum. The water circles like a tornado downward. The cove becomes larger, the hole becomes bigger as the water twists with the electricity of her magic.

"Maven?" I call out to her, but she can't hear me, she's in a trance. Her veins begin to glow, her hair turning a deeper shade of red.

What's she sacrificing to allow this to happen?

I tackle her to the ground, breaking the focus she has on the cove.

"What are you doing?" I shout over the growling wind.

"I'm bringing them back." She stands onto her feet with determination, shoving both hands into the cove.

"Who? You can't bring back the dead!" I try uprooting her again, but she's planted her feet, tree roots binding her to the ground.

"Not the dead," she says, her words laced with a magical, faraway component.

"Then, who? Don't do this. Please." There's a strip of gold, sparkling like fairy dust that replaces a chunk where red used to be. It's pretty.

Pretty sometimes means vile.

Depends on the magic being used.

"Maven? Damn it, answer me!" I shout over the tropical storm force winds.

Her eyes meet mine, the sparks flying into the air like fireworks on the fourth of July.

"Your family."

Chapter Nineteen
MAVEN

It all makes sense.

The story of the cove, hearing the voices, it wasn't all a myth or a story. It's real. All this portal needs is a little bit of magic.

But not any magic.

A Wildes magic.

I'm starting to learn my abilities and bloodline are very powerful.

"*It won't be enough, Maven.*"

I gasp, staring across the cove to see a woman in a tattered cotton dress. She's pretty. She has long red hair like me.

"Sarah?" I try not to be apprehensive about who I am seeing, but it's hard not to be when a witch I've known to be dead seems to be standing in front of me.

"Sarah? No one else is here, Maven. You're worrying me. Stop. Let this go." Lex grabs my wrists and I imagine a barrier between us to block him.

Tree roots shoot from the ground, boxing me in where he can't reach me. He begins to tear apart the barrier, ripping the root from its place and I do something I'll never forgive myself for.

I lace everything with silver. The metal veins through the vines and roots, the hissing sound of his skin burning causes my heart to faulter.

"Fucking damn it, Maven!"

"Everything will be different, but everything will be worth it." Sarah promises, disappearing into a mist of sparks.

"Maven, I can smell your blood. You're bleeding. This is too much for you. Stop!"

He's right. Blood is dripping from my nose and down my lip, slipping into my mouth.

"I can't hold it!" I scream as the power is ripped from my veins. The winds whip around us, leaves blinding my vision and slapping against my face. The orange and gold sparks of the cove become brighter; the hole larger with every swirl until it bursts. I fly backwards, slamming against a tree.

The wind stops.

The ground is still.

The water of the cove doesn't ripple.

It's just how we found it.

I failed.

I try to get up and cry out, my leg giving out from under me. Lex is there, his arms wrapping around me as I fall limp. His skin is healed from the burns, a bit red and irritated on his arms, but healed.

"I'm so sorry," I choke, trying to hold back the swell of regret. "I hurt you. I thought... I thought I could bring them back."

He carries me through the woods, running to the house until I find myself lying in bed. "I love you for trying, but never do that again. Ever. I can't ever lose you." He cups my face, his blue eyes full of concern. "But what's lost is lost, my sweet little witch. They cannot come back, no matter how much I wish they could be found." He bites into his wrist and places it over my mouth. "Drink, so you can heal. You broke your leg when you hit the tree. You'll heal on your own in an hour but drinking from me will heal you now.

I suck greedily, the ambrosia of wine giving me life.

He moans, pressing the heel of his hand against his cock tenting his grey sweatpants. "Fuck, that feels good." A wet spot forms on the material and the harder I suck, the louder the sounds are coming from him. "Beloved, you're in no shape to tease me right now. Behave."

I want to make him feel good even if my body is broken. I'm already feeling better, my body and bones aligning together once more. I feel brand new. I suck harder on his wrist, and he snarls, tossing his head back as an animalistic pant is the only way he can breathe.

"Maven," he seethes my name as a curse and a warning. "That's enough. Stop. You've been through too much tonight."

I have, but now that I'm safe in bed, healed, my power restored, I want more. My leg is sore, yes, so I'm not ready to move.

But I don't have to.

I bite his wrist, abusing the skin so I can have more access to his blood.

"Goddamnit, Maven!" He roars and with the next drag I take from him, his thighs straddle my head.

My eyes nearly cross as I look down to see the outline of his cock. I love grey sweatpants. They leave nothing to the imagination. The thick ridge around his blunt, wide head is the most noticeable pressing against the material.

Liquid heat pools between my legs and his nostrils flare as if he can smell my desire. I don't know why I'm feeling like this. It should be the last thing I want after what just happened, but I feel like it's a process to recharge and Lex is a part of that process.

"Is this what you want?" He shoves the front of his pants down, his magnificent cock bobbing free. It's heavy and weighed down. A bead of precome fills his slit and I rip my mouth from his wrist and suck the tip into my mouth, moaning over his salty flavor. "Fucking hell, Maven." His hands fall on the wall behind us, and he tilts his head down, the carmine pigment illuminating his irises glow in the darkness.

His fangs lengthen and if I didn't know him better, I'd think I was looking at a demon.

Not that I'd mind being dragged to hell by him. He's the burn people warn you about before getting too close to the fire.

He's far from evil though, far from damnation yet he is sinister all at the same time. His hands move to my head, his fingers tightening in the strands. My scalp screams and my eyes water when he thrust his hips, using my throat as his own personal fuck toy.

I love it.

"I love seeing your lips all stretched out, struggling to take me but you always manage to."

I choke when he touches the back of my throat, gagging on the wide intruder.

"Fuck yes, I love that." He isn't gentle with me. He begins to fuck my face, unrelenting and without apologies. I flick my tongue across the tip every time he slides out, lodging the tip at the opening of my mouth before stuffing my throat. I cough and choke, spit dripping down my chin.

He reaches down, talons caressing my cheek before gripping my chin. "Look at you taking every inch," he praises and it makes me want to be better for him. I hollow my cheeks and his eyes flutter shut. "So good, beloved. So perfect for me." His heavy sack slaps against my chin as he gains more momentum. "You're going to make me come."

I hum in approval, a pulsating throb aching between my legs.

"Suck every drop and don't you dare let it go to waste," he threatens before planting himself as far as my throat will allow.

Warm cream hits my throat accompanied by a feral groan. Every spurt that leaves him, he flexes his hips, trying to pour himself deeper inside me. I do as he says, drinking him down, swallowing every drop.

Like the good little beloved I am.

And I clean the pale pink bulbous head, dipping my tongue in the small slit to gather every drop of liquid I can.

He hisses from the sensitivity and pulls his semi-hard cock free, dragging the wet head down my chin. My tongue traces the edges of my swollen lips, and he drops between my legs, smelling my desire.

"I want to fuck you but I know you need rest." He spreads the leg that isn't sore wider, giving him better access. "So wet. Is this all for me? Did sucking my dick turn you on? Did you like tasting my come?"

I whimper with a nod, gripping the sheets as his fingers slide between my folds.

"This will be quick, won't it? You're going to come all over my fingers and then lick them clean, aren't you?"

"Alexander," I moan his name, a sexual promise tugging from my chest.

I was born to please him.

He owns my body.

I'll do whatever he wants, whatever he says.

"Such a filthy girl," he grumbles in delight, pressing his thumb against my clit. Immediately my thighs shake, my muscles trembling from my nerves being fired upon.

I'm in a war with myself, my body the gun.

A trigger that Lex easily pulls.

He inserts two fingers inside my slick hole and with his other hand, he applies pressure against the bundle of nerves with the heel of his hand.

"Fuck. Oh fuck." I toss my head back and squeeze my eyes shut.

"So fucking tight. You have no idea what it does to me to know I've been the only man to touch you." He slips in a third finger, burying it to the knuckle. Lex increases his pace, finger fucking me like it's his cock filling me instead of those skilled digits.

The speed becomes inhumanely fast and hard all while keeping the circular motion on my clit.

My orgasm hits me fast and out of nowhere. My come drips down his fingers and a grumble of approval vibrates his chest.

"Yes, oh, yes. Lex. Oh, god." My orgasm doesn't seem to end. My toes curl, my fingertips tingle, and my lower belly burns.

He bends down, licking my seam before pulling his fingers free and stuffing them into my mouth. I lick myself off him, the tangy sweetness making me suck his fingers just like I sucked him.

His canines pierce my thigh, taking a few swallows of blood before pulling free. "God, I love how you taste after you come. Your blood is drugged with oxytocin. It makes me high for a few seconds." He licks the blood off his lips and it's the last thing I remember before closing my eyes and falling into the deepest sleep.

******

I wake with a start, my eyes blurry and my stomach rumbling with hunger. My head pounds as if I drank an entire bottle of liquor.

Did I?

The last thing I remember is the woods. The cove, but everything after that, it's blank. My body feels good, great actually. I stretch my arms above my head and groan. Then that's when I notice a few things different about the room.

There's furniture.

I smell fresh paint.

A long black Victorian dresser is to the left, perfume bottles line the counter with a few white candles in black gothic style holders.

I glance to my right and see a fluffy cotton robe on a purple chair in the corner. Confused, I get up, and slip myself into the soft material then tie the belt around my waist. It's a pale grey with plush white lapels. I run my hands down it, immediately feeling warm.

The bedframe is against the wall waiting to be put together. It's red with intricate designs of flowers and vines. I've never seen a red frame before, but I love it. I make my way down the stairs, pictures hanging on the walls and more furniture in place. The black chandelier is hanging in the foyer and there's a bench against the wall with a deep blue cushion. It's more for appeal than use.

I run my hand down the newly polished rail while taking my time assessing my new home. When I get to the bottom of the staircase, a purple rug almost takes up the entire floor, a gold antique mirror hanging to the right of the doorway into the living room.

Peeking my head around the corner, I see a fire roaring in the hearth, the purple couch Dottie picked out is in front of it with a circular matching ottoman.

Voices coming from the kitchen have me changing direction.

"She's been asleep for three days, Mr. Wildes. I feel like something is wrong."

"No," Pa scoffs. I can almost see him patting Lex's shoulder in comfort. "What you need to understand, using so much magic, so much energy, sometimes it drains a witch. I've studied it before. It's normal for her to sleep for days on end without waking once. She's recharging."

"It was unlike anything I had ever seen Mr. Wildes. She was so sure that portal would open. It was beautiful, yet dangerous."

"Mmm, bonding with you made her more powerful. It didn't work then? Awakening the portal?"

"No," he says on a sigh that sounds like a relief.

"You don't sound too upset," Pa chides, clicking his tongue in surprise.

I lean against the wall and eavesdrop.

"I'm not. I am, but I'm not. I would love to have my family return, but it isn't in the cards. They are dead. I'm at peace with that. I didn't hope for the portal to open so I'm not disappointed."

Whiskey barks and I think I've been found out.

"Oh, ya beast. Here." Pa must have tossed a piece of food in the air because I hear those loud jowls of Whiskey chewing.

"You sound disappointed. I can't be fooled, Alexander. A part of you is upset. You have every right to be. There was a little hope that your family would return. A little, but even the smallest of amount of hope can feel like the biggest of burdens."

"It's silly, right? A ridiculous dream to have the family I once had return to me."

I peek around the corner in time to see my Pa lie his age wrinkled hand over my vampire's. My heart catches in my throat when I see Alexander look down, perplexed.

"My dear boy, there is nothing ridiculous about that. You'll always want the love that was lost. I am only sorry the magic didn't work for you to have that again."

"Even magic has its limits, right?"

"I suppose." Pa didn't sound like he believes that. "Maven, Fireball, you can come out from hiding now."

I frown from being caught and slip into the kitchen, holding my breath when I see the fridge and stove, the pots hanging from the ceiling above the island. The counters are a rich, sleek black, reminding me of the cove. "When did all of this get here?" I can't help but to be in shock. The furniture delivery must have happened but how did I sleep through it all?

The dining room table is long with twelve chairs, the mahogany wood menacing and elegant at the same time. There are red place mats in front of every chair and black candles in silver candelabras vary in different sizes in the middle of the table.

"The truck came yesterday. You slept through all the noise. The house is complete. I have to say, it's very modern on the inside now compared to what it was. I like it," Lex explains.

"Did Dottie come? And what happened after the cove yesterday? I don't remember a thing."

His mouth presses into a flat line, answering my question. I take a deep inhale to relax the emotion pressing against my chest.

"I'm sorry, beloved." Then, he coughs. "But you don't remember... anything?" His cheeks pinken in embarrassment and I realize we must have done something naughty.

I gasp when a memory comes forward, him stuffing his fingers in my mouth and me moaning as if it's the best thing I've ever tasted.

Now it's my turn to blush.

"She will come back, Maven. You'll see. Familiars can't stay away," Pa reasons, not picking up on the sexual tension building in the kitchen. Thank God.

"I don't want her to come back for that," I say, my voice small.

"I know." He pats Whiskey on the head. "My familiar is this lazy thing. I suppose familiars reflect the magic their witches possess. Yours is supernatural, a powerful being. You should be proud."

"How can I be when I lied to her? I don't care about semantics or politics of whatever it is that should make me proud to have a strong familiar. I want my friend back."

"And she will come when she is ready."

"She's mad at you too, Pa. Pissed, actually."

"Yeah, well. She'll see it was for her own good. When she's ready to accept what she is, maybe then her creature can be released. Have you been able to see what it is?"

"No," I shake my head. "I try, but her aura is too blurry. It's big though, tall. Protects her. I saw it hold her when she was mad at me. It bent down and wrapped her in her arms."

"I imagine knowing the paranormal exists and knowing you are paranormal are two different things. She'll struggle, but she will come back when she's meant to."

I nod numbly, hoping he is right. Maybe I should go to her? Do I respect her space? I have no idea. I hiccup, then press my palm against my stomach as it turns.

"Let me." Lex kisses my cheek and pours me a cup of coffee. "Don't kill me. It's decaf."

I pout my lips, knowing I'm allowed to have a little caffeine, but I don't argue. I'm still too tired. "Does Pa know?" I whisper.

Lex shakes his head. "I thought you'd want to tell him."

A violent cough has me turning around swiftly. Pa is hunched over, face red as the wet cough turns abusive. Lex is quick to pour a glass of water for him and is at his side in a flash.

"I'm fine. I'm fine. Just a cold."

He's lying to me. His aura is fading. Something isn't right. I don't want to argue with him about it. He'll wave me away and while I'll get the truth one day, today, I want us to have a good day.

"Pa." I sit down, the steam from my coffee billowing high until it disappears into thin air.

He takes a swig of water, finally catching his breath. "Fireball," he says with a tired smile.

"You're going to be a great-grandpa," I whisper while holding my breath. I meet his gaze, water filling the cloudy irises and his cheeks puffing in and out.

He wipes the corners of his eyes and then covers his mouth, shoulders moving up and down. The wrinkles on his face become more pronounced, deeper, showing a lifetime of stories.

"Oh, Maven." He gathers me in his arms and holds me tight, as if I'm about to float away and be lost forever. He leans away and seeing the tears dripping down his face cause me to cry too. "I'm so happy. A grandbaby. I can't believe it."

"Two," Lex corrects. "Two grandbabies."

Pa's mouth is agape, his attention darting from me to Lex. He stands from his seat and fist pumps the air. "You hear that, Whiskey? I'm going to have two grandbabies. You're going to be a granddog!"

Whiskey barks, wagging his tail, and his big pink tongue flops out of his mouth. He jumps on his hind legs and Pa grabs his paws and they do a little dance. Whiskey barks and Alexander laughs, wrapping his arm around my shoulders.

There have been many ups and downs lately, but right now, the up is looking pretty damn good.

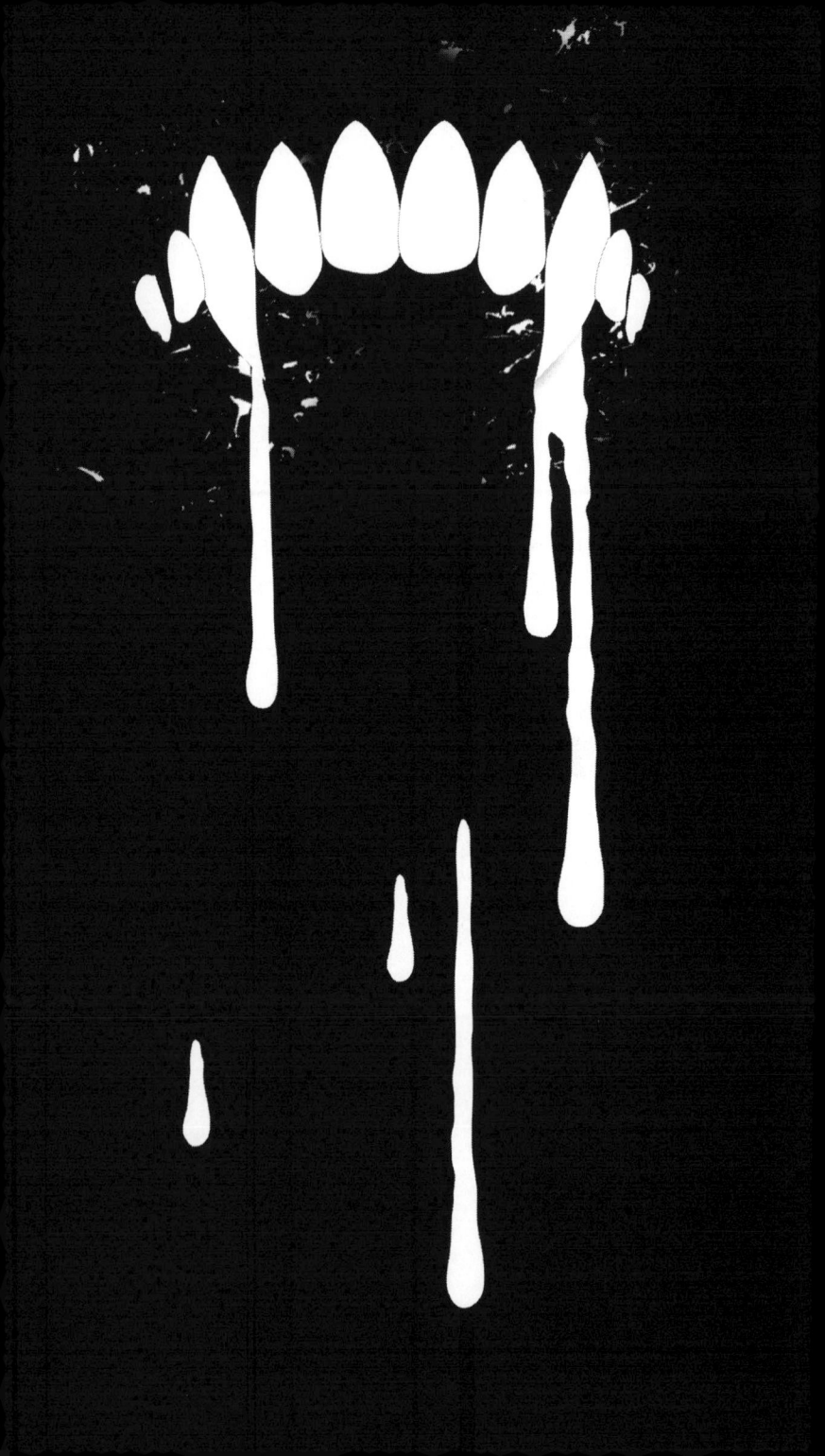

Chapter Twenty

ALEXANDER

I can't sleep.

I keep thinking it's because I know Pa won't likely live too long to see his grandchildren grow up or the guilt that chokes me every day because I know his magic is eating him alive. Maven still doesn't have a clue.

But no, that's not it.

I throw the comforter off me and turn to make sure Maven is still tucked in. Her angelic cheek is pressed against the pillow. Her red hair is splayed out and I twist the new golden strip around my finger, worry slithering in my chest. This should have never happened.

And she did it for me.

Kissing her shoulder, her lips curl at the edges, a smile caused by me in her sleep. My knuckles drift down her cheek. "Dream of me, Beloved."

She sighs in content and rolls over, her hair drifting down her back to reveal the mating mark on her neck. I can't help myself. I bend down and place a kiss, my cuspids lengthening on their own accord to pierce the flesh they have claimed.

Maven stretches her neck to the side, presenting her- self to me even in her sleep and moans.

As much as I'd like to, I know she needs her rest. I'm not fully convinced something didn't change within her. I can't help but be worried.

"I love you," I whisper before getting out of bed.

I tuck her in more, not wanting to leave just yet, but I need to figure out what's going on that's making me so restless.

The moonlight trickles in through the window, a glow spotlighting my beloved. Knowing she's safe, I head out of the bedroom, noticing it's nearly four in the morning. She only fell asleep an hour ago. Sometimes, she can stay up with me, others she can't. I try to sleep too but knowing I can't enjoy the sun changes everything. At least with the UV protected windows, I can walk freely in the house. So, it isn't horrible.

I'd give anything to walk in the sunflowers with my beloved in the daytime, to see her hair shimmer in the sun's warmth.

The loud snoring coming from the guest room yanks me out of my depressing thoughts. I chuckle to myself as I take my time going down the steps. Pa sounds like a freight train.

When I get to the kitchen, I pour a glass of scotch and sit down by the window overlooking the sunflower field. Those flowers shouldn't be possible in this weather, the chill should stop them from blooming until summer. Maven's magic makes it possible. I could think about her magic for days, about the bad things, but getting lost in the beauty of the good things is always better.

I bend one knee on the bench, keeping the other leg on the ground. I lean my back against the wall and take a sip of scotch, needing to feel something other than uncertainty. Taking in my new home, I should feel more thankful. It's beautiful with rich colors with a mixture of black.

But it doesn't feel like home. Not yet.

Not with my brother in a coma. Not with my family dead.

There will always be an empty space in this house.

Who's a coven master without a coven?

Just a lonely vampire.

I toss back my scotch and swallow, staring up at the full moon and bitterness fills me.

Where are those damn wolves? Where have they been? They were everywhere all those years ago and now I haven't scented one. They only hate us because they were a failed creation by the witches. They were supposed to be vampires, but the witches couldn't get it right at first. It took experimenting.

According to Maven's grimoire.

Placing my glass on my knee, I swirl it around, the small amount of liquid rolling at the bottom.

I perk up when I hear a car coming down the driveway. Dottie.

I rush outside, waiting for her at the corner of the driveway. When she pulls in, her eyes are red and puffy. Our attentions meet through the window, and she just shrugs.

Opening her door, the breath she lets out is a rush and her eyes start to well again. "Are you okay?" I ask softly. Maybe that's what I've been feeling, her. I don't know how. She isn't technically a part of the coven. She has a tie with Maven though, so maybe that's why.

"I couldn't stay away," she says with a sniffle. "I wanted to come back. I feel like… I feel like that maybe this is where I belong now. I needed to come home, but I'm scared, Alexander. I don't know what to make of this. Of me."

I hold out my hand for her to take and try to give her a reassuring smile. "Because you do belong here and it isn't because you're her familiar, but her friend, her sister at heart. And we will help you. I'll protect you and I know Maven will too. This is the safest place you can be." I stretch out my hand a little more, hoping she'll take it.

She alternates her shoulders to wipe her cheeks. "I know." She slides her hand in mine, and I help her out of the car. Her brown hair is a mess on top of her head and she's wearing pink sweatpants and a matching hoody.

"She's going to be so happy to see you. She's been off without you." Now that I think about it, I wonder if that's why she was so out of it at the cove. She didn't have Dottie by her side to keep her anchored.

"Me too. I didn't mean to get so angry, but I've always had a bad temper."

"Maybe that isn't you, maybe it's your other half," I hint.

She's stunned, then laughs in relief. "Why didn't I think of that?"

"Come inside. I'll pour you a drink and you can tell me about everything on your mind. Pa's here too. Hope that's okay."

"I love Pa. I'm angry he didn't tell me, but I'll never not love him. He's family," she explains, crossing her arms as we walk at a slow steady pace across the lawn and to the front door. "It's an adjustment."

"I understand." I open the door for her, and she stares inside, not moving. "So, do you have to be invited into homes? Did Maven have to say 'Yes, please, come in?'"

How did these ridiculous rumors get started? I'm almost humiliated. Almost. "No. The house is in her name now, but there are a lot of things that aren't true about vampires."

"I'd like to know them," she states and takes a step forward before falling back again. "Do you see it too? The thing surrounding me?" her voice is so quiet, if I were human, I wouldn't have heard. "I do, kind of. I've been focusing when I look in the mirror. It's huge whatever it is."

"I can't see it," I say and her shoulders slump. She wants answers and I'm afraid I can't give them to her. "You're right, she is big. Not *it*. She's a part of you and the more you think that way, about her being *you* instead of this separate entity, a 'thing', I have a feeling you'll learn quickly what she is." I let my vampire vision come out to play and I get a better glimpse of her aura. I look her up and down, tilting my head back to follow the garnet hue. "She's got to be close to seven-feet tall, but she won't make herself known. She's still blurry. She means no harm. I feel nothing but warmth coming from you. You know, when you were crying when you left the other day, Maven said she saw her hug you."

Dottie smiles to herself, holding a hand over her heart. "Is that what I felt? It was so warm and comforting."

"The creatures that live within us are one and the same."

I notice the way her creature stands up straighter and Dottie turns her head a second later after her other half does. Kind of like an actress speaking on TV but the sound lags. It seems the oddity Dottie struggles to come to terms with knows more about what's going on around her than Dottie does.

I follow her line of sight and listen, staring into the ominous shadows of the trees. It's still dark out. The same owl that always hoots flies from his tree and across the sky, away from us predators. I hear Maven tossing and turning upstairs, as if she's having a bad dream. I want to go up there, but my feet won't move. Pa is snoring and Whiskey is just as loud.

"What is it?" I ask Dottie, unable to hear anything that's a cause for concern.

"Nothing. I... I thought I heard something. That's all."

"Come on, let's go—" Something hot and painful smashes against my back, the flesh burning to the point I can smell it. "Run, Dottie!"

"Not a fucking chance," she bites out each word, taking a strong stance in front of me. Her creature becomes impossibly taller, wider, the red nearly blinding me. Another silver ball of energy shoots through the night and Dottie braces her arms together in an X, a force field surrounding her, crackling blues and whites. "Holy shit," she breathes, but her shock leaves her open and vulnerable to the next orb that hits her.

Dottie flies across the porch, smacking against the swing. The chain breaks and one side of the bench falls. She groans, holding her side.

The silver begins to eat away at me, the tissues and muscles disappearing the more it takes over my body.

Another ice-cold sphere is tossed in the air, and I try to move, but I can't get up. I brace myself for impact when Maven's scent fills the area around me. Sweat trickles in my eyes as I look up, watching her catch the malevolent spell before it can hit me.

Floating between her palms, the orb becomes brighter as she soaks her own magic inside it, replacing the ice with her fire. Dottie stands, limping over to her witch and stands next to her side and the power grows.

"Well, well. Look who came into their power like a good little witch."

Brenden.

I seethe. I grasp the handle of the door and force myself to my feet. If I don't get blood soon, this silver will kill me.

Maven doesn't answer. She's in her trance again. Her hair shines as if it has been dipped in glitter and painted fire engine red, the gold streak glistening like the sun. She throws the energy back at Brenden, stronger and faster, it slams into him, and he screams, the sweet sound scaring the birds from the trees.

"I'm going to be your worst nightmare, Brenden. You don't come here and fuck with me and my family."

His sardonic laugh has the hairs on the back of my neck standing up and my instinct to protect Maven pull at my soul.

But the silver has weakened my ability. I can't even feel my fangs. My knees buckle and Dottie is there, shoving a wrist into my mouth. I widen my eyes in surprise, but that's when I notice her eyes.

They aren't hers.

They are Maven's.

Maven has somehow channeled Dottie, giving me permission to feed. If I do this, it isn't a drop that will bind us as a Coven but it will bind me to Dottie like a brother. It's a million times stronger than a coven bond.

I can't. I don't know if Dottie knows, and I can't do that to her. I turn my head away and Pa is there, this time it's his wrist in my mouth except it's already bleeding. I taste the wilted magic in him, the rancid anger of his power unable to be used and I nearly can't stomach it. I know the blood won't hurt me, it will heal me, but nothing would work like Maven's.

She can't though. She's too busy saving the day.

That fucker must have had a cloaking spell. Somehow, I couldn't sense him.

But why could Dottie?

"I know I taste like ass, but it's your only option if you won't take Dottie's. Drink!" Pa demands, and I squeeze my eyes shut, swallowing the bitter blood. It tastes nothing like Maven's. Her's is sweet and spicey while his is sour and thick, like oil.

All a vampire needs is blood, granted, Maven's is grade-A, like Dom Perignon of blood. Her's gives me a high, a magical fluke, and I'm addicted.

So, Pa's blood will do in a pinch. When I get enough, I rip my mouth away. I don't want to be rude, but I hide my face. The blood climbs up my throat and I cover my lips, forcing myself to swallow.

God. I truly have never tasted anything so foul.

I do something I don't expect, and I throw it up. My body rejects it.

"Alexander!" Pa drags me inside away from the danger and I hiss, trying to roll on my side.

"I don't know what happened. I don't understand why I couldn't keep it down."

"You need Maven. You probably can't drink from another again or my blood is just shit."

"I don't know." My head begins to throb as the silver pumps through my veins. "Maven needs me." I crawl to the screen door and collapse, the cool hardwood pressing against my feverish cheek.

"Take care of my girl," Pa says before stepping outside and yanking Maven inside with me. "I'll hold him off. Feed him, Maven. He's dying."

Maven's eyes return to the beautiful green shade, and she begins to fumble, scooting herself near me. "Lex?" She begins to cry and places her neck by my mouth. "I'm so sorry. Take what you need."

I strike, unable to stop the moan that leaves me when her blood hits my tongue. My back begins to heal, and the silver pushes its way out through my skin, forming into small beads that clatter onto the floor.

With a flick of her wrist, they roll into the fireplace, bursting into smoke.

"Are you okay?" She takes my head into her hands, and I nod.

"I'm fine now."

"Ah, damn!" Pa staggers back, holding a hand against his shoulder. Whiskey is barking to be let out, but Pa doesn't open the door.

"Old man with weak magic. It's killing you. I could have so much fun with you."

I get to my feet and Maven bangs the door open. Whiskey runs out and begins to lick Pa's hand that's at his side.

"What do you mean? Killing him?"

"You don't know? Oh, goody," Brenden laughs. "Witches need covens, my darling."

I flash my fangs at the endearment and step in front of her, but Maven tugs me back, protecting me instead.

"Without a coven, the magic slowly eats away at the body. He's dying. Been dying for a while now." He sounds bored, puffing hot air against his nails before shining them on his shirt.

Maven spins to her Pa. "Please tell me he is wrong," her voice riddled with anger and sadness. "Please."

"I'm sorry, Fireball. I'm so sorry," he says, wincing as he tries to move. Blood coats his fingers.

"Lex can change you. He can—"

"—I'm too old to want to live forever, Maven."

"But—"

Brenden cuts her off. "Aw, yes. It's so sad." He snaps his fingers and werewolves stand by his side.

They look the same. Tall, grey, large canines, and a light coating of shaggy fur.

I growl when I see them, ready to attack. Memories of the pain they caused me surge in my heart and I remember the promise my father made to his.

To kill all the wolves for killing grandmother.

Finally. After all this time, I can fulfill a promise that should have never been passed down from generation to generation.

"Ah, you remember the last time. How did that work out?"

"How do you know about that?" I whisper, tilting my head.

"I'm the reason your little family is dead. Why you got bitten, why so many things happened."

"Why?" I shout to the point my throat is raw. "What did we do?"

"Your grandfather signed a contract with me. The first of his family to ever meet their beloved would have to sacrifice her and give her to me. I knew about you Maven, for a long time. I waited. I followed. I watched you grow into the powerful witch that you are. Wildes hold the most power and the Halls are—"

"—The dark ones. You're the outlaws," Pa coughs. "The holders of evil."

"That hurts my feelings," Brenden pouts, the wolves cackling the best they can in their wolf form. "More like, the most powerful of the damned. Think of me as Lucifer and the Wildes as God. If we joined, imagine the strength of our children. We could rule."

"I want nothing to do with you. I'm mated. I'm pregnant already."

"Nothing a spell can't fix." He throws a black smoky sphere next, and Dottie stands in front of Maven, blocking the poison from entering her. The smoke dissipates, hitting the shield Dottie created.

"Nothing can break a magical contract. Not even fate."

I roar so loud, the ground shakes and I charge, speeding to my enemy faster than a bullet.

The wolves attack next, and I jump over one, blurring to the point he can't see me. I wrap my hands around his neck, his fur tickling my skin, and I apply slow pressure. Each bone gives under me until he falls limp.

The other wolf locks his jaw around my side, the same place the one bit me so long ago, and sinks his teeth in. I laugh, gripping his jaws as my brother did and pull them apart, tearing his head from his body.

"Looks like history repeats itself," Brenden muses.

I reach out to snag him, but he vanishes before popping up in another area of the yard.

"Jokes on you," Maven states proudly, coming down the steps. "He is immune now since he survived the bite once."

"Impossible," Brenden spits, his gaze darting between us. I love seeing him afraid. If vampires are immune, we can rule anyone and anything.

I stand next to Maven and show my side, watching it heal right in front of me. A part of me was worried it wouldn't work.

"My grandfather would never sign a contract with you," I say, returning to the matter at hand.

He takes a step forward, an insidious cloak flowing around him. "Anyone will do anything for love. After wolves ripped his mate apart, he asked for her back. He didn't read the fine print of the contract. No magic can bring back the dead, but he could join her."

"You fucking cheat!" I go to charge him again and he shoots one of his little fucking orbs at me again. I dodge and duck, but this damn warlock knows my every move and eventually zaps me again. This time with enough electricity to send me to the ground, my entire body quaking.

"Not my fault he didn't read the contract fully." He steps over me and produces the scroll from 1900. "You're mine Maven. Come with me and I'll show you everything. You can't break this. I'll keep coming back. I'll kill everyone you love next time. Alexander can confirm. I've done it once already." His voice deepens. "I'll do it again."

I get to my hands and knees and spit on the ground before dragging my eyes from the dew clinging to the blades of grass to Maven. It looks like she's actually thinking about it.

"Maven, no." I can't believe she takes a step forward, but Pa grabs her hand to stop her.

"He's wrong, Maven. I love you so much. Okay? I love you." He turns to Brenden and spreads out his arms. "Death will. A willing member of the Wildes family, a guardian willing to die will break that fucking contract. No way in hell will my granddaughter be with you. Over my dead body." He peers over his shoulder and time slows as Maven screams.

He looks at her for long seconds, water filling his eyes. "I love you, Fireball."

Pa grips the scroll in his hands. "Immolare me," he chants over and over again. "Next time, read the fine print," he sneers with victory. The scroll is first to turn to ash, a ripple of a magical wave slamming against me. His body begins to drip with his blood before going up in flames. He doesn't scream. He doesn't cry.

He turns his head to stare at Maven, a singular tear falling down his cheek before the fire takes all of him, turning his body to dust and ember.

Maven falls to her knees, her heart wrenching scream becoming louder, shaking the world around us. Her hand falls to the ash and her veins turn purple soaking in his magic. I forgot about that. When the power of a witch has nowhere to go when the body is dead, it goes to the next of kin.

She doesn't seem to care. She fists a handful of ash and holds it to her chest. Lightning cracks across the sky and rolling black clouds take over. Thunder shakes but it isn't as potent as her wails of heartache.

Rain begins to pour, and Brenden snaps his finger again, wolves at his side once more.

"Kill them," he orders.

I refuse to fail this time. I somersault into the air, landing just behind the warlock. Reaching for him, he vanishes into the sheet of rain. Maven's cry vibrates the air, sound waves forming to roll into the distance.

Her pain the echoing song of heartbreak.

In my moment of concern, a wolf protects his master, raking his claws down my shoulder. Flashes of the past immobilize me and another painful gash slices across my chest in my moment of weakness.

It isn't the pain that brings me back to reality.

It's the force field protecting Maven as she claws at the dirt desperately to get the ashes of Pa.

She screeches again and the sound causes the energy field to burst, shooting me, the warlock, and the werewolves a few yards away. I roll across the sloshing wet ground and when I lift my head, a wolf hits a tree, snapping his spine in two.

He falls limp.

Three wolves remain and one circles Dottie. Her brown hair has electric streaks, like lightning hugging the strands. Her creature grows to a giant size, a snout forming for a moment before turning gold.

The wolves claws dig into the dirt, flipping chunks into the air with every step as he snarls and snaps. Drool drips from his teeth, his fangs slick with venom. I'm not sure what will happen if Dottie is bitten. She has to be careful. We can't help her if we don't know *what* she is.

Dottie lifts a hand into the air and a bolt of light streaks down from the sky, forming a dangerous glowing sword in her hand. She grips it tight, grinning and drives the natural born blade straight into the beast's heart. The weapon disappears into the werewolf's body, electrifying him to certify his death sentence.

I'm so caught up in Dottie, I forget about the real issue.

"I'll have her. I have too many plans. I've waited too many years." Brenden says, limping towards me from the sunflower fields.

"I have my plans too." He can't hear my words since I whisper them more to myself. My future has a plan and my life, my world, it all revolves around Maven.

My beloved.

Not fucking his.

My lips are wet from the rain and I lick them, watching Brenden's body come closer, the shadow of him turning into a man.

Two wolves are left and they are at his side, marching like trained soldiers.

Enough.

I'm done.

And death is too good for a man that constantly brings pain.

With as much speed as I can gather, I run. I run at a rate I never have before. Time slows to a crawl. The rain comes to view and each droplet is its own shape. I see the reflections of my growing coven in each drop, reminding me of what I am fighting for.

Dottie's entire being pulsates as if she is being charged, her eyes a bright yellow in this one second of time. Maven is on the ground, succumbing to the pain of losing her family.

Everything is changing in this moment□ time is paused for me, yet life still moves on and becomes worse, morphs, adapts, and tries to thrive in a world that would dare be so cruel.

With revenge, with vengeance, I stop behind Brenden and wrap my hand around the base of his neck. "The only plans you'll have of her are the ones you dream about, and you'll be dreaming forever." Before he can react, I bite into his neck and lock him to my body, driving my talons in his back. A mewl of discomfort and fear gurgle from him and he coughs, the blood flowing like a river down his torso.

He tastes of poison and hatred, curses and broken promises. I make sure not to sift through his memories because if I did, I don't think I'm mentally strong enough to survive what I see.

When his heartrate slows to the beat of a dying drum, I spin him around so he can see who is taking his life.

I spit out his blood, regurgitating the vile liquid. His rotten liquid a useless pool in the murky puddles under our feet, mixing with mud and dirt.

The life dims from his eyes.

"You can't die just yet." I pull his limp body against mine and whisper into his ear, "I have something better planned for you." I rip into my wrist and yank his head back, holding my arm over his face and watch as drops of my blood fall into his mouth.

Then I crack his neck, the sound in tandem with the storm above. In order for someone to turn to a vampire, they have to die.

His transition won't be long now.

I feel stronger than ever, Maven's magic pouring through me. Triumphant, I snag a beast by the thick of his neck and for some reason, he doesn't fight me. The beast is staring into space, locked in a trance.

I wait for the warlock to rise.

Anyone can be turned.

Vampire blood has that strength.

But when he returns, will he only return as a vampire?

A few minutes tick by when I see slight movement on the ground.

Brenden groans, rubbing his neck and I use my talons to force him to stand by forcing them into his shoulder. "Your damnation will last forever, warlock." The wolf's jaws are pliant since he is in limbo and I shove the venomous fangs into the crook of Brenden's neck. "You know what's great? I know for a fact my werewolf immunity won't work on you. Immunity can't be transferred to a changeling when it's forced. The change has to happen willingly." I remember hearing Maven say that while reading her spell book.

Brenden struggles to say something— anything— trying to form words but they come out as strangled whimpers. Thick rivers of saliva drip down a wide fang into the wounds on Brenden's neck.

I smile.

Victory is so sweet after centuries of waiting. I almost hate it is over.

"You made her hurt. I'll make you suffer like I suffered," I sneer into his ear before tossing the wolf across the yard when I'm done with him.

The other comes to his senses, the trance breaking at last. He backs away, the ominous black eyes confused when his Commander begins to weaken.

"You will never win," Brenden laughs. "I'll always be one step ahead."

"Maybe, but good luck having a beloved find you. You'll finally die instead of living off people's broken hearts and stolen lifespans."

He sardonically grins, his heart slowing, the venom working quicker than it did with me. His confidence faulters. With a final hushed and fervent breath, he bites out his last words, "I have something you'll never get but always want." With the remainder of his energy, his eyes lose their spark and his fingers snap, leaving me holding nothing but air and rain.

The wolves stagger. Their bones break and morph as they return to their human form, a sight I have never seen. They are huge men, stout and bulky, and clearly confused.

I want to kill them, but something tells me they were under the influence of a very powerful warlock.

They lift their hands, the black clearing from their eyes. "We don't want to hurt anyone," one says, voice trembling with fear. It's apparent he hasn't spoken in some time. His words are rasped, his throat dry, and he rubs the column on his neck with his hand.

"You've always hurt my kind," I sneer, unable to sheath my talons. "We've always had bad blood." Chest heaving, control dwindling, my skin itching to attack, I barely contain myself from launching at the beast and ripping him into pieces.

"We had nothing to do with that. I don't even remember how I got here. Please. This isn't even our home," the other explains, his voice so deep I can hardly understand what he says. "We beg you." He holds his hands up in defense. "What year is it? Where are we? Who are you?" Tears and desperation brim his eyes.

"You remember nothing?" I ask, not trusting a damn thing this dog has to say.

They shake their head. "You can look through our heads if you want."

I'm at his side before the bastard can bark and I grip his chin, staring into his pupils to see into his soul. "I'll do that," I say, not missing the cries still coming from Maven. I need to do this for us so nothing like this happens again. After my influence mystifies him, his pupils blow wide, letting me into the depths of his mind.

I shift through his memories.

A young teen, barely learning to shift forced under a spell, taken prisoner from his pack. I follow his journey, his mind a haze as if he has been drugged. I can sense him trying to fight the spell, but his mind is controlled, forcing him to be latent. The warlock made him and the other do things they never wanted to do.

What if there are packs of werewolves missing loved ones because they were taken prisoner and put under a spell? It changes everything I have known.

"Fuck," I curse, letting him go and turn to the other. "You, come here."

He steps forward without a fight and I siphon through his memories, hoping to find something that allows me to be vengeful.

Nothing.

He's the same.

"Goddamn it, you were used as weapons." I shove him back and lace my fingers over the top of my head. "Your names?"

"Anwyll," the younger one says before he kneels. "Master."

My eyes round at his submission.

"Aziel," the other answers, also falling to his knee.

Oh, fuck no.

I'm not about to be a Master to fucking werewolves.

Chapter Twenty-One
MAVEN

"Maven?"

"Maven?"

My name is being called but I can't focus on anything other than the ash in front of me. I can't feel anything but at the same time, I feel one thing immensely.

Devastation.

I bury my hands in the ash and hang my head, crying so hard the rain can't seem to catch up. "He's gone!" I yell, the air around me vibrating from the power laced in my voice. "He's gone," I whimper. "I can't." I shake my head. "I can't do this without him." My tears are riotous as they steal from my soul.

Falling forward, I shake my head, gripping the ash that's turned to mud now that it's rained. "No, no, no!" I pound my fist against the ground. "He's mine. He's mine. Come back. Come back." I grip the middle of my chest, trying to apply pressure to the wound of my bleeding heart.

The clouds twist above me, tunneling into a twister the longer I think about destroying everything around me.

I can't think.

I can't breathe.

How am I supposed to live without him? He was… everything. He was my everything.

I fall forward, splashing into the mud. I lie there. Numb. The memories of us together rolling through me like an old film.

"Maven?" It's Lex and he lies down on the ground next to me, cheek in the mud. His blue eyes pierce me in the dark, but they aren't enough to bring me out of it.

I ignore him, letting my pain take over me. The twister hovers above the sunflowers, waiting to cause the destruction that's just been placed on me.

"I know how much it hurts, Beloved. I know." He takes my hand, and the reminder of my mate has me blinking, his love seeping into me like hot water. "It's okay to hurt."

A sob bubbles in my throat. "I can't be in a world where he doesn't exist. I don't know how to live that way."

"You adjust. You adapt," he explains. "But the pain is always there, but I swear, I'm here to shoulder it with you."

"I don't know how to think," I croak. "My world revolved around him."

"I know."

"He was my father. I never had a dad. He was… he was everything," I weep, my shoulders shaking so hard, hail begins to fall.

I don't care if the weather takes me, I seem to bring it with me everywhere I go anyway.

"I know," he says again, pushing a wet piece of hair out of my face.

"I don't understand." I shake my head the best I can, wondering how Pa knew about sacrificing himself to save me. "I didn't get to say goodbye. I didn't get to tell him I loved him." I sob and Lex pulls me into his arms. We still lie on the muddy ground, unmoving, and he knows I have no plans to get up.

"He knew," Lex says with a ghost of a smile. "He knew how much you loved him. Your love kept him alive for as long as it did."

His words irk me. "You knew, didn't you?"

He sighs and nods. "I'm sorry I didn't tell you. I smelt it on him when I met him. He didn't want you to know."

"I should be mad at you for that, but it isn't on you. He should have told me, and he died anyway. I could have had years left with him. Years!" I scream, but my anger quickly fades. "I just want him back." I curl my fingers against

Lex's chest. "Give him back." I press my cheek against his shoulder, and he kisses the top of my head.

"I wish I could." He squeezes me tight. "I wish I could."

I let him hold me in the storm I've created and cry. I don't know how long we lie there, but eventually my howls of pain turn to whimpers.

The tornado disappears.

The rain finally stops.

The leaves drip water onto the ground.

And Lex continues to cradle me.

"I'm so sorry, Beloved. I know how much this hurts. I wish I could take your pain."

"Can't you make me forget?" I ask, hope blooming.

He pets me, drifting his fingers through my hair. "No. Remember, I can't mystify my beloved."

"Oh. Right." I fall deeper into the puddle with resignation. It's good I can feel this.

Feeling nothing means never feeling the good.

Sometimes, even the good hurts as much as the bad when it's taken from you.

Lex finally stands and holds me in his arms. I don't move. I lean my head against his chest and let him take over. I don't want to be in control anymore. I don't want power. I just want to be a woman mourning over her loved one's death.

"I got you, my beloved. I'll take care of you."

I don't say anything. I don't care. When I see Whiskey inside, he whines, and it only makes fresh tears spill. "I know, boy. I know. I miss him too."

Whiskey lies there and begins to cry, high-pitched whines that sound more devastating than a humans.

"Dottie is okay. She's taking care of our... guests."

I close my eyes and when I feel a burst of wind, I snap them back open, seeing that we are in the bathroom. The soaking tub is huge, big enough to sit three, with a curtain that draws shut around it for when you want to shower. The basin is a deep purple color, and the walls are gold leaf. Any other day, I'd appreciate the beauty, but today, I don't care.

He places me in the tub, and I shiver from being outside in the cold, drenched in mud and blood.

Pa's blood.

Pa's ashes.

Another fresh sob escapes me and Lex strips me of my dirty clothes, tossing them in the laundry hamper. He turns the knob of the faucet and waits for the water to become warm before turning on the shower.

He undresses next and steps in with me. No sexual expectations. His cock is impressive still, lying soft against his thigh. He squeezes a lavender shampoo into his palm, rubs his hands together to form suds, and begins to wash my hair. I turn around and look down, the tears never ending as I see the murky water tinted with blood and dust swirl down the drain.

"I have you," his hypnotic voice is gentle as he croons into my ear. "I'll always have you." He rinses my hair out and washes it again for good measure, massaging my scalp along the way.

He grabs a loofah next, pouring cucumber melon body wash onto it and then scrubs it to get it foamy. Next, he washes me, making sure to get every inch of my body. I can't help but blush when he parts my legs and cleans me there. It's a different kind of intimate.

He squeezes the loofah out and grabs his bottle of body wash, a mix of pepper and rosewood.

"Let me." I clear my throat when I hear how rough it sounds.

"You don't have to. I just want to take care of you."

"And I want to take care of you," I reply, drifting my fingers down his arms while never taking my eyes away from his. The loofah fills my hand and I take it from him, inhaling his scent. It grounds me, comforts me, and reminds me I'm not alone.

Pa is gone and it hurts, so bad, but Lex is here, in the present.

And I need to be here with him and not get lost in pain.

It's easy to do. The worse you feel, the easier it is to fall into the depression pain brings.

It's a killer, pain. It waits, letting you grieve and scream, shout and protest. Then, it digs its roots deeper and it turns into unbearable hollow sadness, a void a person can get lost in if they don't have someone to pull them free.

Wicked torture is a trap *pain* likes to set.

And when it gets you in the box, there isn't always a way out.

I scrub the mud off his body, taking my time like he did with me, so he sees that I'm appreciative. That I love him.

His cock comes to life as I wash him. It's hefty weight in my palm makes me wonder how it fits inside me, but it does, oh it really does, hitting me in all the right places.

"Hey," his fingers ghost over my shoulder. "None of that. No pressure. I don't plan on anything sexual. I can't help reacting to you touching me."

That's when I realize I've paused cleaning him. "I know," I tell him. "You always impress me, that's all." I dip between his legs, and he hisses, standing on his tiptoes from the shock of me behind his sack. He doesn't look away from me, but he feels the same vulnerability I did.

It's different.

Something has changed between us. In a good way. It isn't about bathing one another, but trust.

I trust him to take care of me.

I kiss his thigh before standing up and working suds over his broad chest, his hair clinging to the bubbles of the soap. His nipples are pink and hard, his pecs lean and defined with muscle.

It's his back that always gets me. Muscles flex in every divot of his body, dimples settling above his bubbled butt.

A work of art, yet a lethal weapon.

A vampire living and breathing right in front of me. I get to touch and kiss him, knowing he'll always protect me.

"You're perfection."

He turns around, shoving his fingers through his wet hair. His eyes a dark sapphire in this light. His lashes are wet, sticking together, yet somehow it causes his eyes to be brighter. He places one hand on my hip and the other in the crook of my neck. I lean into his touch and the love he has for me steals my breath. The air shakes in my lungs as I try to let it out.

My chin wobbles, and I shut my eyes so he can't see the tears build.

"It's you that's beautiful, beloved."

His kindness has me breaking. "I don't know what to do."

He wraps his arms around me to keep me upright. "Let me love you. That's all you need to do right now. Okay? Trust me."

"I trust you with my life."

He pecks a kiss to my lips and pulls me to his chest. We stay under the water for a long time, his hand drifting up and down my back. The water turns cold and Lex shuts it off. He snags a towel from the rod against the wall, drying me off first. He dries the space between my legs and his eyes flicker sanguine, nostrils flaring as his fingers drag between the trimmed hair of my pussy.

He looks away to gather himself before standing, his cock still hard. "I'm sorry. It's a reaction, I don't plan to act on it."

"Don't apologize for wanting me. The day you don't, is a day I'll need to worry." He is a primitive man, a predator, no matter what, his beast senses something is wrong and all he wants is to make me feel good.

He's a protector.

And everything about that is an aphrodisiac.

He grins and his thumb brushes the apple of my cheek. "How are you?" he asks, his tone serious yet looming.

"Broken," I answer honestly, his thumb catching a tear.

"I'll do my best to put you back together. Remember, sometimes things are stronger once they're mended," he says, reminding me of our previous conversation.

He holds out a hand and helps me out of the tub. Naked, we make our way to the bedroom. The morning sun spills into the windows and every time Lex walks through the rays, I hold my breath, even knowing they are UV proofed.

I yawn, exhaustion taking over me, mourning, and a deep ache weakening my muscles. Lying on the bed, I sigh as the soft comforter rubs against my nude body. Suddenly, there's a weight straddling me, warm oil pouring onto my skin before his strong hands begin to rub my back.

Groaning, I sink into the mattress. "You don't have to do this," I slur, half asleep as if I've drank too much.

"Like I said, I want to take care of you. Let me. It's been… a heavy day." His strong fingers dig into my shoulders and my eyes grow heavy. He massages my neck, turning me into a pile of mush before working his way down my back. A grumble sounds in the room, and I smirk as he takes my butt cheeks in his palms.

A moan falls from me. I didn't expect *that* to feel so good.

He bends down and presses a kiss in the middle of my back before swinging his leg to get off me. I stop him by gripping his wrist.

"Beloved?"

"Make me feel better."

"I don't want your muscles to be sore. You're already going to be in pain—"

"—No," I stop him. "Make me *feel* better." The yearning in my tone is too hard to miss. I flip over and crawl up his body, admiring his chest with my hands. His hair tickles my palms, and I gently tease his nipples.

He snags my hand, stopping me before I make my way lower. "Maven— I— this isn't a good idea. You're in pain. We should rest. You need rest."

"It's why I want this. You always take the pain away," I admit, touching his hips and wrapping my arms around his waist. "Please," I beg, the desperation in my voice pathetic. I kiss his neck and the Adam's apple that bobs in the middle of his throat. "Please, Lex. I need you." I drag my tongue along his collarbone, then find my way to my mating mark, sucking it into my mouth.

He bucks against me, cursing. "Maven… I… No! Damn it, you're making this impossible."

"Please." I lick my way to the other mark, loving that these are tattooed forever on him.

He pushes me down on the bed and lifts my head up, his eyes scorching mine, trying to read them to see if I truly want this. I spread my legs, inviting him in, wanting this more than I ever have.

Lex slams his lips on mine, sliding his tongue against mine passionately, kissing me so I can feel his want in my core. I return the heat, the desire, yet keep his pace. Slow and steady, wanting and desperate.

It's me.

I'm the desperate one.

His cock rubs between my folds pulling a whimper from me. I claw at his back, my body trembling every time his cockhead rubs over my clit.

I'm barely able to get a breath before his mouth is on me again, taking control of the kiss by gripping my jaw. He's bruising me with hard long strokes of his tongue. Lex continues to rock against me, coating his steel pipe with the juices he easily ignites from me.

He curls his hips, moaning every time I let out a sound for him. I don't care what anyone says, hearing a man like him fall apart and groan for me is all the pleasure I'll ever need.

His arms wrap around my body, pulling me harder against his chest, quickening his pace, piercing the swollen nerves.

"You're soaking me. Maven, fuck." He dips a hand below and pushes his fingers through my forbidden lips and teases my hole. "So fucking wet. All for me."

"Yes," I breathe. "All yours."

"You make me feel so good," he replies, burying his lips against my neck. "No one and nothing has ever felt as good as you." His mouth parts, brows drawn together. "Ah. Oh, God," he babbles from the pleasure. "You're my last everything and I love you."

The emotion burns behind my eyes and a weight lifts off my chest.

This. I needed this. I needed to be close to him. I needed to feel his love and he is giving it to me. He always gives me what I need.

He licks the tears off my face as they fall. "Do you like hearing how good you make me feel? I could come right now. I want to come on your body and rub it all over, marking you so every fucking paranormal can smell you're mine. The wolves, the warlocks, and whoever fucking else exists. You have no idea what you do to me. You unhinge me. I'm no longer damned because of you." He changes the angle and in the next stroke, he fills me, hitting every spot that causes my body to sing.

I'm already so close to euphoria.

He's slow and deliberate, lifting my leg over his hip as he slides in and out. He sucks his lip into his mouth, his canines pronounced and evident. His eyes flip from the color of the sea on a sunny day to spilt blood. Lex glances down watching himself saw in and out of me. His eyebrows pinch together. "You look so good taking me. I wish you could see your pretty pink cunt sucking me in, those lips spread wide as I stretch you open. I've never seen such a sight."

"Me either." I stare right at him, lifting my hand to rub his fangs the way he likes. His eyes flutter shut and his pace falters, hips stuttering as they lose their rhythm.

Me. I did that.

He falls over me, turning me to my side and lies next to me. Lex pushes my leg out of his way and inches his way in my body that he has claimed.

We moan in unison until he is settled. He presses soft, open mouth kisses down my neck, gripping my ass as he plunges in deep and hard. He keeps his thrusts slow, driving me crazy, keeping me on the edge as he makes love to me.

I realize that's what he is doing. He's making me feel *all* of him. Not just physically but emotionally.

Oh, I love you. You have no idea. You'll never know the depths my heart feels for you.

Without thinking, I answer him.

I love you too, Lex. With my entire soul, with all my power.

His hips stutter and my head is yanked back abruptly by him using my hair as reins. "What the fuck did you just say?"

Turning my head is painful and the pieces of my hair hold on tight to my scalp. "I answered you back."

"In your mind, Maven. We spoke to one another through our bond," he sounds like he's in awe, but that changes as quick as it came.

A tumultuous storm lurks in his eyes, a blooming copper threatening to overtake me.

Alexander wants to make me his catastrophe.

And I'm going to let him.

Even if it means it kills me.

"I don't think you understand how rare that is. Granted, I don't know much about beloveds since we are the first in a long time, but still," his last words end on a savage gravel. "This changes things." He keeps me locked to him, wrapping my hair around his wrist to hold me still. My back is arched to an agonizing stretch.

The only warning I have is the flash of his fangs before he buries them into my neck, squeezing me tight against him as he drinks and fucks me.

No longer is he easy and gentle, but brutal and fierce, as if our bond strengthening to telepathy drove him mad.

He's unrelenting and disrespectful ramming into me, his swaying sack slapping against my ass with every hard stroke.

Manhandling me, he snakes his hand around the back of my neck and flips me around to my hands and knees, his body still curled over me and his teeth still embedded.

My blood drips onto the comforter, rolling down my neck as he takes as much as wants.

"Lex, more. More. Give me more," I needily beg from him, fisting the sheets until my knuckles turn white.

"I'll give what I want to give you," he mutters against my neck, barely taking a breath before sinking those sharp points into my mating mark.

I love knowing I'm feeding him and it's a feeling that can't be explained in a lot of words. I'm taking care of him in a way no one else can and it sends me into a tumbling, earth shattering, body convulsing orgasm.

Muscles tightening around him, clenching his big cock with my rippling walls, I lose my strength falling headfirst into the bed.

He holds me down, hand shoving my head harder into the mattress as he picks up to a speed that no human could match. I'm sent into another spiral of a soul awakening orgasm, coming around, playing me like an instrument to get the sounds Lex wants from me.

"Fucking take it all, beloved. Take it all from me," he sounds mad, sneering as his nails scrape down my back.

The bite of pain shatters me. My legs give out and he shoves them together until I'm lying flat. He licks the wounds on my back before sitting up, grunting as he holds onto my ass for leverage.

"I want you to feel me tomorrow," he says into my mind.

"I'll feel you tomorrow and the next day, and the next," I reply, knowing the way he is battering me with his cock, it's impossible not to be sore.

"You're going to make me come, good girl. This pussy is so fucking good. I'm going to fill you up. And you're going to take every damn drop I give, aren't you?"

"Yes! Yes, give it to me. Come inside me."

He flips me onto my back, never pulling out, and slides his hand to the nook of my shoulder. Lifting me up, I'm dead weight, lying there as he uses me. The vein in my neck is occupied by him again as he eases his sharp teeth into the mating mark.

Lex pinches my clit and small tremors bring me back to life.

"One more."

I shake my head. "I can't."

"You'll come with me," he orders through his blood drenched fangs, the words muted against my neck.

His hips stutter and my own gums tingle as my canines' edges turn sharp. With the energy I have remaining, I bite, drinking him. Feeling his lust and love for me have me following his order. I come again as he plants himself once, twice, and finally buries himself to the hilt.

Lex tosses his head back and roars, a sound everyone in the house will hear. Blood drips from his chin, his teeth are stained red as his warm seed travels to my core.

I'm so tired, so out of it, drained of all my energy, the last thing I remember before sleep takes me is his hand protectively on my stomach.

Chapter Twenty-Two
ALEXANDER

"Jeez, you two really need to soundproof this house. So much for getting sleep," Dottie grumbles, dark bags under her eyes as she makes herself a three-tier sandwich.

How does such a little person eat so much?
I should be asleep, but after the worst night of my life and the best sex of my life, I cannot sleep. I have too much on my mind.

Like how distraught Maven will be when she wakes up tonight. It's a burden I can hardly bare, her heartache.

I snort and gather the coffee from the cabinet and scoop it into the maker. "Maybe don't listen," I sass, liking this new banter between me and Dottie.

"Maybe don't roar like a beast and I wouldn't. I can't help I can hear, Alexander," she rolls her eyes.

She pushes her tower of a sandwich to the side, grabs another plate, and begins to make another.

"Surely, you can't eat two three-tier sandwiches." I gape as she slathers it with mayo and mustard, pickles, lettuce and tomato with slices of chicken. When the first layer is done, she begins the next.

"Want to make a bet?"
I lift a brow, knowing I'm about to be fooled, but I want to witness this. "What's on the table?"

"I want to learn how to fight and use the library as research to figure out who I am."

My face softens, the humor fleeting for a moment. "Dottie, you don't need to bet to do that. This is your home."

"Then make me a part of the coven," she states, nearly dislocating her jaw to take a bite of her sandwich. "I want to be."

I take her wrist and force her hand in the air, flashing a fang. "You sure? Once this is done, it can't be undone."

"I'm sure. I want to be a part of this family."

I prick my finger, a bead of blood coming to the surface and then do the same to hers. She gasps. This isn't enough blood to bind us like what happened to my mother, but it will allow us to connect, to have that feeling of safety. I'll know if she's in danger and I'll be able to protect her.

"Repeat after me, then."

"Don't I need to finish my breakfast first?"

Two monster sandwiches for breakfast. What in the world does this girl eat in a day?

"No, no bet is necessary when I want you here, Dottie. I, Dottie..."

"Kitse," she finishes.

I've heard that name before. I've read it. I think. It tickles something in the back of my mind.

"Dottie Kitse, do you promise to pledge your life, your loyalty, and your blood to the Monreaux Coven? And do you swear your allegiance to me, your Master? In times of peril, in times of love, of sanctuary, do you give me this oath?" I can't believe I'm doing this over a chicken sandwich. If father were here, he'd be livid.

"Yes," she breathes, tears forming in her eyes.

I swipe my finger across her lip, then do the same with hers. Her blood settles in mine and that emptiness I felt about not having a coven slowly becomes smaller. She isn't vampire, but she's family now.

"Oh, wow," she says, her red hue becoming brighter, flickering like flames and her eyes glow a bright orange for a second before settling down. "It feels right," she whispers. "Thank you... Master Monreaux."

"Don't call me that unless others are around or we are in a meeting. It feels... well, honestly, it doesn't feel right.

I don't feel like a leader just yet. It's hard imagining I'm taking my father's place."

Dottie offers me half of her sandwich. "Eat. It will make you feel better."

I smirk, lifting the heavy concoction into my hands. "Thanks. Don't mind if I do." I'm so happy vampires can eat food. Granted, I need to be sated with blood in order to do so, which I am. I took so much from Maven this morning.

It would have killed a human.

It's a good thing she's mine and I can take as much as I want.

Suddenly, Dottie drops her sandwich and runs out the front door, the two wolves Anwyll and Aziel chase after her. I keep my pace lazy, eating the sandwich Dottie made which is delicious.

"Who are you?" Dottie shouts across the field.

No one is there, I can't see them.

But I hear them.

The ragged breaths.

The stumbling footsteps.

More than one.

There are several.

"Get inside," I bark at Dottie.

"No way in hell, Master."

Stubborn freaking woman.

The wolves flank her sides, and I keep a close eye on them, not trusting them at all, but I can't rip their throats out either.

I'm a vampire caught between a rock and a hard place.

"What's going on?" Maven's sleepy voice has me holding out an arm so she can't go outside.

"I don't know. They heard something and someone is here." I didn't hear it. I should have, but I wasn't focused on a new threat. I guess that's where I need to change. Things are different now. I have people here, a mate, children on the way. I need to be more astute to my surroundings.

I need to learn how to be a coven master and the only person that can teach me, is me.

Maven's eyes swirl that gorgeous gold that takes my breath away. Her brows pinch and cute wrinkles form between them. "They are afraid. I can see it." Maven's hand grips mine. "Don't harm them."

"I won't unless they change my mind." It's the only answer I can think of to say. I have to protect what is mine.

This estate, these people, Maven.

All mine.

And I have a feeling her magic and us being beloveds are going to bring new challenges we never thought we would have to face.

"Is it Brenden?" her voice trembles. I can hear herself holding back the urge to cry at the sound of his name.

"Impossible. He's in a coma by now. I don't know where he is." Now that I think of it, how was he able to vanish with magic?

What if I created a new monster by turning him?

"There has to be a way to find out." She runs through the living room and to the library and when she returns, she's flipping through the pages of her spell book. "A location spell... something. I can't rest until I know where he is."

"Master Monreaux," Anwyll calls me by my title to get my attention. He doesn't even seem annoyed he has to.

The irritation I feel about these werewolves grows by the second. Surely, they couldn't have been forced to commit genocide? To eradicate a species.

"They are here," Aziel finishes, and Maven walks out on the deck.

My brave little witch.

It's so fucking sexy when she shows how strong she is, but it's my turn.

"Maven, is it possible for you to create a UV barrier shield around me?" I ask, needing to go outside, hating that I can't.

Her spell book flips to a certain page and Maven nods. Her hands swirl and her eyes spark. Lavendar smoke breathes between her palms and then she eases it against my chest. It engulfs me.

And it itches.

I don't like it. I glance at the wolves and sneer. If it weren't for them, I could walk in the sun.

"You don't have much time. I'm too new. The barrier is weak, Lex. I'm sorry." She sounds so guilty not being able to meet her expectations, but she's soared by mine.

"Don't ever apologize. This is more than enough."

"Oh, I remember there's a section somewhere that tells me how to fix your daylight problem. I can't... remember..." she flips through the pages, her tongue sticking out, and I've nearly forgotten the new threat on the property, "...The page."

"No rush. I have what I need thanks to you." I bend down, take her hand, kiss the knuckles, and scrape my fangs over her skin.

Dropping her hand, I jog down the porch steps and stand in front of my wolf guardians. I nearly choke when that phrase comes to mind, but it's true. They have been nothing but loyal since the spell broke.

I can feel the sun on my skin. It's bearable. Warm. My skin doesn't ache, but I can tell the shield won't last.

A figure stops up ahead along with a dozen others, and I forget about the sun issue.

We're outnumbered.

The wolves change into their beasts, borrowed clothes ripping, bodies growing, and their skin morphing to slate gray.

Suddenly, the dozen or so people across the field are standing in front of me. The wolves growl, threatening and Maven is at my side, the sky darkening with clouds, the temperature drops, and snow begins to fall around us.

Frigid tempers call for frigid temperatures.

Dottie and her link. Electricity bolts in Dottie's hand and Maven uses it to build her strength.

The sun isn't so hot now that it's blocked, but my thoughts come to a complete halt when I see who is standing in front of me.

"Father?" I choke, staring at him unblinking. He can't be real.

He looks the same as the day he disappeared. His clothes are new, dirty in some spots as if he fell on the ground. There's a haunted expression in his eyes, deep purple circles under his lashes, frown lines along his mouth.

Iridescent rivers fill his eyes, and they overflow, flooding his cheeks. He studies my features, but it's obvious which twin I am because of skin tone. "Alexander?" My name a bubble in his throat, and I remember the last time I heard him call for me.

In the dark.

Under attack.

Telling me to go after my brother.

"You're dead." I press the heels of my hands to my eyes and bend in half, pressing my elbows against my knees. "You're dead. You're dead. You're dead," I chant, my chest breaking all over again like it did in the year 1900. I can't believe this is happening. I am mentally unable to.

The pain will kill me.

Did the wolf bite mess with my mind after all? Am I hallucinating?

I open my eyes to see him, and he kneels, disregarding the wolves behind me. He's crying too. His hands cup my face, his eyes darting over every line as if it's the first time he has seen me.

He feels real.

He sounds real.

I place my hand on top of his and break when I feel him.

"You're real." The words are unstable and broken as the years of missing him burst free.

"My son," his voice cracks. "My son. You survived." He gathers me in his arms, squeezing me so tight my bones crack. His hand buries in my hair as he holds my head to his chest.

I'm a child all over again, just a teenage vampire needing his father and I weep, gripping his shirt as we fall into relief.

"It's you. You're here. How?" I lick my lips, the salty flavor causing me to wince. "How? Atreyu said—"

"He's alive?" he stands, looking over my shoulder to see if he sees my twin but all he sees are the two dogs, I mean people, we took in. "Wolves," he sneers and launches himself at the one I considered an enemy until recently, but Maven lifts her hand, freezing him in the air.

Gently, she sets him down on his feet. "Wolves that were put under a spell by a Brenden Hall. He came to collect a debt your father owed."

My father's face loses its color, his hair in a mess of spikes from running his fingers through it. "He came back?"

"We have a lot to talk about," I nod, wiping my face.

It's a miracle.

"Where's Atreyu," he asks again, eyeing the werewolves with crimson irises. "Who are these people?"

"We got bit by wolves. We made it to the tombs. Atreyu is still asleep."

"My son." The words are garbled with regret as he pounds his chest. "My son!" he raises his voice, knees buckling until he falls. "He'll never wake." He is full of doubt as he screams, the kind of agony that's ripped from the chest. "He'll be gone. Finally, I made it back and he's gone. I can't live in this world without both of you," he says to me, lifting his head to look at me through pearly tears.

"That's not true," I begin to explain. "There's hope. I'm here. I was bit. I fell into a coma and for 121 years, I laid in that coffin, but Maven—" I reach for her, stretching out my arm and she cradles herself at my side "—Maven is my beloved. Father, meet Maven Wildes." I put emphasis on her last name and immediately his eyes round, forcing one last tear that's been threatening to spill over to finally fall down his cheek.

Father stands on shaky legs, wiping his hands on his pants. "Wildes," he says her name in a hushed tone. "You're related to Sarah."

"I am," Maven says.

"You opened the portal again." He looks at her in awe. "I don't understand how. It took a sacrifice to close it before."

A sacrifice...

My chest begins to ache as I put the pieces together.

Mother.

In order for the portal to open and close, someone must die. There has to be a way around that. We have to see what the portal holds, where it goes, if it truly goes anywhere.

Maven's breath hitches. "My Pa sacrificed himself to end the contract Brenden had. The warlock wanted me. He knew I'd exist. He wanted a Wildes as a mate, but Pa stopped that." She glances away and stares at the space where he died. "He must have completed the spell when I tried to open the portal and failed. His blood must have soaked through the ground. It's the only thing I can think of. I tried. I heard your voices, but I wasn't strong enough."

"I've been speaking to that damn portal for 121 years, coming up empty," Father explains. "I'm thankful to be home and to you for bringing my son to life and for bringing me back. I'm so fucking happy to see you, Alexander." His forehead is against mine, his hand holding mine so tight, I think he has broken a few bones. "Forever in my blood, son. Forever."

I'll heal.

The temporary pain is worth knowing my father is alive after all this time.

He lets me go and takes a step away, a haunted expression of guilt crossing his face. "I'm sorry for what you had to lose due to my father's heartache. If you'll excuse me, I'm going to go see Atreyu." Father keeps a wide berth of the wolves, untrusting like me, but listens to what Maven said about them.

Father is forgiving, but it will take a while to forget the bloodshed they caused.

And what they took from us.

In a blur, he's gone.

"You look good, Lexy."

I whip my head around to see Uncle Luca and Greyson, flanking the sides of a tall woman with white hair and violet eyes.

Rarity.

I take a slow step forward, but the barrier breaks and the sun begins to sear me. I scream and Rarity dashes to my side. She carries me into the house, Greyson and Uncle Luca peering down at me.

"You've always found a way to get into trouble that I can't figure out." Greyson rubs his chin with a sly smile.

Maven is at my side, pushing her wrist into my mouth and I drink, the burns healing.

"How is it that you can't walk in the sun?" Uncle Luca is perplexed, watching the burns fade on my arms and neck.

"It's the side effect of waking up from the venom." Maven begins to flip through the book again. "But it also means, anyone who pledges themselves to the coven is immune to the venom."

"Rarity." I sit up and take her in. She grew up to be beautiful. Even though she has such different features, she looks just like mother. I hate I've missed her grow up. All the small moments, the long nights of her crying, teaching her everything about vampire life, it was taken from me. "I've missed you." I only got to hold her a few times, singing lullabies, reading the Monreaux history book to her in the library to get her to sleep.

I loved her so much. I had so much planned for her. I wanted to protect her, to be the brother she looked up to, but now there's a stranger in front of me. She's a woman.

And she probably doesn't need me anymore, not like I need her.

I haul her into my arms regardless and she meets the hug with the same force. "I've missed you too," she whispers. When she pulls away, her eyes shine like crystals. "I know we don't have much, but I remember what you gave me in the time you held me. I loved it when you held me and read that boring book."

I'm stunned. "That's impossible for you to remember. You were hours old."

"I remember everything I see, Lexy. And I've missed you so damn much. I love you."

I needed to hear that. I needed to know my family still needs me. "I love you too, baby sister." I push a white strand of hair behind her ear. "I guess you're no longer a baby." I frown when guilt and sorrow wrap around me.

She buries her head in my shoulder and squeezes me tight again, crying as I hold her. I stare up at the ceiling and blink the emotion away, or try to, but the happiness, the relief, it won't stop. It's all bombarding me.

Letting go of her, of father, of Luca and Greyson, it isn't an option. I refuse to live through that again.

Stretching out my arm, yet keeping Rarity tucked to my side, I offer Luca and Greyson to join in. Without question and with huge grins, they engulf me and Rarity.

"Vampire hug!" Uncle Luca shouts, always fun-loving and happy, but I hear the vibrato. He's feeling this moment too.

"I've missed all of you so much. Where have you been?" I ask, unsure if I truly want to know.

"We've been on another side of the veil I can't explain. Even after all these years. We tried so hard to come back home, but the portal was impossible to open without a Wildes, that's what a mage told us," Luca explains, leaning away to speak.

"A mage?" I gasp. "Wait, mother? Is she alive too?" I know better than to ask that. She's dead, but like the young vampire I am when it comes to mother, a small flicker of hope remains in my heart for her to live.

"No. It's her blood that closed the portal so the wolves couldn't come into the portal. She sacrificed herself." He solidifies my fear and while the affirmation hurts, it feels good to truly know.

"Introduce us, Lexy. Who are the new people?" Greyson tucks his hands in his pockets, a muscle ticking in his jaw as he stares at the wolves.

If the wolves make it a full night with vampires who want revenge, they might just survive to live a full life.

"You tell me." I look behind him to see eleven others waiting uncomfortably. Men and women combined.

"They are our friends." Uncle Luca holds out his arm. "Luna is fae. Reuel is an elf. Everyone else is a vampire from a gypsy coven that travels through portals, their witch died, leaving them stuck in the in between like us."

There are other portals? I want to know more, but later.

"The tall bulky one is Amory, then it's Finnick, Gullivere, Amberella, Zaffre, Alastair, Alaric, Tala, and Drayce is the one with the Viking haircut."

I stand and realize I'm about to be a Master to more than a few people. My coven is growing. "I'm Alexander Monreaux. Master of this coven."

They all kneel and Drayce thumps his chest. I notice a bit of wild, untamed warrior in him. He has long dark blonde hair, shaved on the side and a braid. I bet he's been around for a while.

The elf catches my eyes too. He's got dark brown skin, the color of the night with irises of snow and pointy ears with multiple rings.

"Before you pledge your allegiance, let me introduce you. This is my beloved, Maven Wildes." They all look at her as if she's not real. "She's pregnant and she's to be protected at all costs. This is her familiar, Dottie. We aren't sure what she is yet, but she's powerful and joined my coven this morning."

Drayce's eyes widen, taking in the red image of her creature around her. "Gods, I've never seen anything like her."

Dottie blushes under the assessment.

"Don't make her feel uncomfortable." I stand in front of her, so she doesn't feel attacked. I move on. "That's Whiskey, Pa's familiar. He's ours now. And then there are the werewolves."

The vampires hiss but the fae and elf remain unbothered as they stand to the side.

The wolves drop to their knees and bend their neck, a gesture of submission.

"They were bound by a spell from a warlock that's now broken. I turned Brenden Hall and forced their bite. He's in a coma now, somewhere. It broke the spell. This is Anwyll and Aziel."

A few vampires look skeptically but some have pity and sympathy on their faces.

"Now that the portal is open, we expect more will come and this new power you hold here will be challenged. A Wildes magic is rare, and people will want it," the fae, Luna, states in a hypnotized tone, her eyes clouded as if she's blind. "This won't be the last of us, but many will be enemies."

"But a sacrifice is needed to open and close it. It should be closed now, right?" Maven asks, jumping her sights from me to the fae.

Luna shakes her head and her voice is soothing, a tint of harmony in her tone, reminding me of a harp playing in the distance. "It requires sacrifice to open. The portal closes when the witch who is bound to it dies."

That's new information. All this time, the rumor was that Sarah closed it. She did, only in death.

"Oh boy," Maven mumbles, bending down to scratch Whiskey's head.

I clear my throat to change the subject. We can't worry about the portal right now. Too many good things are happening to stress about what ifs. "Well, until then, let's celebrate," I announce. "To being alive. To having my family back."

"Aye, I love a good party. Where's the fucking ale?" Drayce gets to his feet and smiles.

My father has disappeared, but I know where he is. While I'm hurt this is hitting him all at once, I'm thankful he's home. My family has returned. New hope has arrived.

It's time to start over.

We are no longer damned.

I'm going to rebuild.

A Wildes love is the power, the force of change, the hope we need.

They are the magic.

BRENDEN HALL

I crash through another dimension, my wolves gone, my army snapped from their trance.

I fucking hate the Monreauxs and I'll stop at nothing to kill them now. I've done it once; I'll do it again.

The venom staggers me from right to left and I find myself in an open cemetery. I stumble to the nearest open grave and climb in the hole, my exhaustion pulling me into the darkest corner of my mind.

Having a little magic left, I pull a casket from thin air then create a headstone to fool the stupid people.

I have no clue where I am, but stars surround me or perhaps it's the wolf's venom piercing my heart.

Lying down, I bury myself in the casket, and cast a final spell to spill the dirt on top of me causing utter oblivion.

There's a beloved for everyone. I know mine will find me.

And when she does, we'll wreak havoc in the universes and make them ours.

We will love in hate.

All while the Monreaux coven will never walk in daylight again.

I clutch the ripped paper in my hand.

It has been mine ever since my great grandfather and his wolf army burned her at the stake and ripped this page out for safe keeping.

They might have won this battle, but the war ahead will be long and bloody.

I'll burn Maven too.

History always repeats itself, after all.

Page 576 has all the answers.

And they are *mine*.

Epilogue

MAVEN

Seven months have passed since Alexander's family has returned. His father, Severide, stays away mostly, and visits with Atreyu. He stays by his side, reading books and telling stories of the days before the present. My heart hurts for him. He lost so much and he's clinging onto it for dear life.

He forgets to eat, withering away until I bring him blood. It's always from a deer since he refuses to drink from another.

His loyalty to his mate is impressive, yet sad.

Will he never know happiness again?

"I brought you something to drink," I say, pressing a hand against my belly as I knock on the tomb.

He's reading Pride and Prejudice out loud.

He slams the book closed and if I'm not mistaken, a hue of pink touches his cheeks. I figured out why Severide is still alive now that his mate has died. The bond is broken but the years remain. It's a chance of hope for him but I know all he sees is eternal doom.

"Atreyu loved this novel. When he wakes, don't let him fool you with his grumpy demeanor. He is a big softie." He takes the large pitcher from me and sips it, wincing since it's deer blood but forces it down. "Can you... do you sense anything for him? Will I lose him?" he finally asks me, a question I've been waiting for since he has arrived.

"No. I don't know when, but I feel it. It might be a while, but his future is clear to me." I place a hand on Severide's shoulder, a gentle gesture to reassure him. I hope my answer brings him solace.

"He doesn't have long."

"But enough time to hope," I retort with a lift of my brows.

"I suppose." He doesn't believe me. "I've been so caught up in my own turmoil. I haven't asked how my grandbabies are doing. Are they healthy?"

I grin, rubbing small circles over my stomach. "Yes. Very. Active too. Luna says they are doing great. I don't want to know their sex though, so I told her not to tell me."

"I can't wait to meet them. You're such a blessing for vampires, to know beloveds are real, to know my son woke from the worst curses because you found him, I owe you my life."

"You owe me nothing because he saved me too." I take his hand in mine and hope he can feel the calming flow of energy I'm sending to him.

"I can't believe the wolves are friends now. It's... another reason why I'm not around. I watch them and they seem genuine, but all I see is my wife dying in front of me." A haunted sorrow passes across his face, his heartache a constant flicker in his eyes.

"I understand. Take your time. That's the only time that matters." I begin to walk away, knowing the conversation is done.

I hear him begin to read again and the strain in my heart grows.

Lex must feel it because in a second he's in front of me in the dusty hallway of the catacombs. He sweeps me into his arms and zooms to the bedroom. He's touching me all over, cupping a protective palm over my stomach. "What is it? You're sad. Is it the babies?"

I love his concern, but I ease it quickly. "No. It's your father. I hate seeing him so devastated."

"He won't ever leave that room. Not ever. I feel like he's still lost to me all over again," Lex explains, and I hold my hand over his, one of the babies kicking against his palm. It makes him smile.

"He won't be there forever. I promise." I know it. I don't know how, I just do.

Things have changed so much around here. We're a ragtag coven of different species, but we get along. The wolves protect Rarity as she is out and about, going to school how she always wanted, so they stay near her. The brothers try so hard to prove their worth, I just hope the vampires see their efforts soon.

Greyson is head of security again.

Luca wants to be a doctor even though he isn't a natural born fae, but Luna thinks he's a natural and will do well.

The portal must have stopped their aging process. It has to be the magic. I want to learn more, but I'm wondering if the magic fused with their DNA, altering it, changing what we know of vampires. It's the only explanation as to why they are alive.

And it's the only one I have.

They live day to day not knowing if they will die and I've made it my mission to find out if they will.

Everyone is growing and learning. Times are changing. I wish Pa were here for it, but the change wouldn't have happened without him. He's the reason we have all come together.

I've searched and studied for Dottie, still coming up blank on what she is. Maybe we will never know.

And while searching, I've learned there is no page 576. The spell book lied. It isn't there. So I've been trying to strengthen the UV shield I made him so we can go outside together. I've only made one strong enough to last an hour.

It's maddening.

Lex feels my change of mood and lifts the gown from my body. I can't wear much these days, dresses are the only thing that are comfortable.

"So pretty," he praises, taking my heavy milk-filled breasts in his hands. He bends down and takes a nipple into his mouth. "Remember when you said you wanted to have your way with me?"

I'm wet immediately thinking about our bet from so many months ago. I flick my fingers and my vines and roses appear, snaking around his ankles and hands, then pinning him to the wall.

Hitting it a bit harder than I intended.

Oops.

Imagining the vines ripping his clothes from his body, they do just that, leaving him bared to me. Wetness puddles between my thighs and my clit throbs with excitement. His cock is pointed straight, hard and leaking. A vein trails over the meat, pumping it to its full mass.

Feeling frisky, I flick my fingers again and one wraps around his sturdy cock, tightening to the point the tip turns an angry shade of red.

He shouts, struggling against the vines. He could get free.

But Lex doesn't want to.

He loves to surrender.

"Beloved," he warns, flashing his fangs. He shoots forward to bite me, and I lean away. He growls in irritation.

I begin to stroke his cock, using the vine to do all the work and his eyes flutter shut. A rose drifts its soft petals down his body, his skin pebbling in goosebumps from the combination of a soft and rough touch. I tighten the vine in my mind, twisting it manically around his cock.

He shakes, his eyes promising blood and pleasure.

I let another vine drift across his balls. Since his legs are spread, he's open and vulnerable. I test the water, pressing against his taint.

"Oh, fuck. Oh, fuck," he squirms. "Maven..." he pants, pulling against the greenery.

One snaps.

"Don't make me enforce them with silver." I wrap another vine around him, and he nods, sweat building across his forehead.

I push the creeping green plant toward the back, circling it around his puckered hole he's only let me play with a few times.

He hates how much he loves it.

I slip it inside and press against his prostate and he shouts, his muscles trembling. The tendons in his neck protrude and he's seconds away from losing control.

I run my hand down my body and circle my clit, the pink petals wet from witnessing him falling apart for me.

Whimpering, I project what I want into my magic. The vines stroke his cock faster and pump gently into his ass, hitting that button every time.

"Oh god. Fuck, Maven."

I stuff his mouth with a black rose, and he screams behind it, ropes of his warm come splashing against my stomach and chest, making a huge mess.

An approving carnal sound has him leaning down, eyeing his dollops of cream. He rips from the wall, grunting as I allow the vine to slip free from between his ass and he attacks me.

He throws me on the bed and feasts.

On me, my body, and my blood.

And I will always take it all from him... for him.

Eternally.

ABOUT THE AUTHOR

I want to write anything and everything, from badass men and women to characters who want to rip each other's clothes off. I plan to 'take it all' like the good little girl I am. Feel it tomorrow, am I right?

Social Fangbangs:
Facebook: @AuthorJauaryRayne
Facebook Reader Group: @January's Raynestormers
Instagram: @author_01Rayne
Twitter: @author_01Rayne
TikTok: @author_01Rayne
Website: www.authorjanuaryrayne.com

Scan Here For Easy Fangbanging Access:

ACKNOWLEDGEMENTS

FANGBANGERS,

From the bottom of my want-to-be vampire heart, thank you for reading Eternally Damned, my first full-length novel. I hope you enjoyed Alexander and Maven as much as I did. Alexander was the reason why Shallow Cove Dimensions exists. Without him, this series would not have happened. It was meant to be a contemporary romance, just a singular place, but my vampires hit me out of nowhere and now this universe exists. I'm eternally thankful for the couple who started everything.

The biggest, most thankful, huge, shouting from the tops of the world thanks to the bloggers who took a chance on me to read it along with my team of Alpha readers and ARC team. To Give me books for the work they have done to get this book out there! :)

To my close-knit fangers, Dallas Ann Designs and Carolina, my heart could burst with how much I appreciate you. You have no idea how much your belief in me gave me the motivation to create this universe. I'm forever in your debt, forever grateful, forever thankful. I truly believe I couldn't do this without you. You do so much that I cannot do and I'm in awe of you. I love you both.

And finally, the biggest kiss to my husband, Adam. Your unwavering support, the way your rally for me, the way you love me, have faith in me, and give me energy when I'm resigned—I love you. Every day, you resuscitate the belief I need in myself. I'm so glad i get to fangbang you for the rest of my life.

ALSO BY JANUARY RAYNE

SHALLOW COVE DIMENSIONS-SALEM

PREQUEL: ETERNALLY HERS
BOOK 1: ETERNALLY DAMNED
BOOK 2: ETERNALLY CURSED– RELEASE TBD

Printed in Great Britain
by Amazon